April 7, 1881
Coroghan , Ireland

"I don't want to live here in Coroghan our Michael, and I don't want to end up in the Poor House in Dublin Road.   M'Ma says that's where we're heading if things don't change around here! Michael, do they make you work in the poorhouse, when you're only eleven?"

I was a great deal bigger than our Michael even though he was just a year younger than me. He was ten but I looked like I was two or three years older. He was short and thin like my Father, I was big and buxom, like nobody I knew, but his wiry frame didn't stop him from tackling the heavy jobs on the farm. M' Pa always said that we must all put our backs into it if we wanted food in our bellies. So we both worked on the land, hoping and praying something would grow, pulling and shoving as hard as we could, lifting and carrying as much as we could.

Our Mary Ann was lucky because she was only two and m'Pa said she would get in the way.

"Mother o' God, woman!" he would shout at my mother if Mary Ann came near him when he was working outside. "Can y' not keep the child from under m' feet?"

Mother was pregnant with our Bridget at the time, and it was hard for her to be carrying her and holding Mary Ann at the same time, so that was yet another of my jobs, to keep Mary Ann away from Pa. I didn't mind, I would rather pretend to play "mothers and babies" than lead the horse and plough.

1

But when m' Pa was inside the house, it was a different story. I loved him when he was in a good mood. This was usually on Fridays after he'd been to the market in Tuam. I wasn't sure what he did there, but it did make him sing and dance. When he left, he would ride the cart there holding the reins high in his hands, but somehow he always needed us to help him out of the cart when he came back and the reins were never in his hands. We could hear him coming down the lane singing the old Irish songs at the top of his voice, and we would all run out to meet him.

"Oh, Ellen m'girl, I love you so!" he would shout. "There's no finer in the whole of Ireland! Begorra, you're the apple of m'eye and the reason for me living. I need your bosom for me head, for my loins ache for ya, Mrs. Luby!"

I never understood what he meant, not back then. I thought he had an apple stuck in his eye that was aching him, but I never saw an apple in our house, so I knew that couldn't be right.

Once I was so hungry, and our Michael showed me a tree full of them in the Cathedral yard, and we ate and ate until we were sick – come to think of it, I was aching that day, but I never got one stuck in my eye!

When we were helping our Pa we must have looked a sorry sight -- one huge, pregnant woman, a nine-year-old girl (strong and big for her age), an eight-year-old boy giving the orders, and a toddler pushing between our legs and making us slip in the mud as we tried to carry our heavy load.

We would finally get him inside, laugh, and then fool around. Everyone was covered in mud and dirt, and our Michael would rub his dirty hands into my nose, and I would shout and scream and run around the table. Our Mary Ann would cry at the noise, and our Ma and Pa would be cuddling together, not thinking of the mud. Oh, I loved Fridays!

Then m'Ma always went with Pa to their bedroom to help him wash and change. Pa would get the hot water first, in the large bowl they had on the heavy set of drawers and we would keep Mary Ann busy pulling the mud off our clothes and making mud pies from it. Sometimes Michael would throw it at us, and it didn't half sting when it was dry and hard.

"Ow!" I would shout, but not too loud because m'Ma didn't like to hear us shouting when she was washing Pa.

I think she liked Fridays too. She always had a smile on her face that day.

After washing, Pa would have a short rest while m'Ma gave her attention to us. She would lift down the tin bath tub from the hook behind the door, our one and only door to the outside, and set it in front of the peat fire. First she would pour in the water which Pa had used and then she would top it up with water from the kettle. All three of us would get in together, and I helped Mary Ann as best I could.

For dinner, we would have fried potatoes. She always boiled the tatties before Pa came home, and after our bath would mix them with a little flour and milk, form them into potato cakes, and fry them until they were brown. Oh, I loved Fridays!

The winter of 1881, I remember, had been very cold and wet. Now, even though it was the first week in April, not much could grow in the mouldy soil. The potatoes we had stored in the barn to get us through the winter were rotting, and the cows were thin and hungry. Their milk was watery, when they gave any at all. Even the River Claire was starved of fish. Our Pa said that often happened when the river had iced over. I knew he was worried, but our Michael could not see it.

Our solid stone house was cold and stark. The windows were small to keep out the cold but they also kept out the light. The stone slab floor had only one dingy mat near the fire but we were luckier than a lot of people around our parts because we boasted two bedrooms, one for the grown-ups and one for the kids, however, our bedroom didn't have a window.

The next day m'Ma kept cleaning the black caste iron fire range over and over again with black polish even though it already shone so bright that you could almost see your face in it. Tears were running down her face. She kept wiping them away with the back of her hand or her forearm, but that left black streaks all over her face.

"Biddie my love," she kept saying to me as she cleaned, "I'm getting it ready to cook, I must have it clean for the food y' Pa has gone to buy. Don't you fret, he'll not let us down. He'll be back soon...Oh, Saint Patrick and all the saints in heaven take care of us..."

Then she continued in a voice that sounded like a whimper; "he's going to bring us some hens, some to eat and some to breed so we can eat eggs again., and maybe a pig or two and some bales of hay for Beauty...she's been such a good horse to us through this long winter...and he'll call at the corn mill for fresh corn...and we'll have such a grand feast, such a grand feast, we will, we will..."

But with each sentence her crying turned to sobbing and then to coughing and then oh, Lord above. She was yelling in pain. She fell to the floor as she tried to reach the rocking chair near the fire.

"Ma, tell me what to do," I screamed, terrified.

4

Her cries woke Mary Ann, who had been having her nap in Ma and Pa's room. "Mammy, Mammy, where's Pa?"

Michael, who had been out cleaning the stable, heard our screams and ran in to find out what was happening.

I was holding Ma's polish-streaked face with my two hands and kissing her to stop her crying. I never noticed the cut on her forehead and the blood oozing out.

"Did she fall on the fire?" Michael shouted over the noise. "Where's Pa?"

He ran to the pot jug of water we kept on the sink, but he was too small to lift it, so he ran and got a stool to stand on. I think he wanted to bathe her head.

"Michael!" I shouted over Mary Ann's cries. "She's stopped making sounds, she was gurgling and choking before but now she's closed her eyes and she won't talk to me."

With a crash, Michael slipped off the stool. The water jug hurtled down with him and smashed on the stone floor. The noise woke our Ma up, but she was making funny faces – faces I had never seen her make before. Not really funny, but ugly...faces that frightened me.

Michael picked himself up and looked over my shoulder at Ma. We were both frozen with fear. Only Mary Ann's sobbing broke the silence. Then Ma moved her head and began to speak, very softly at first, each word taking forever to make. "Go to Grandma Quarter's house and bring her here. Quickly, quickly, tell her it's time..."

My Grandma Quarter was my mother's mother and she lived with my mother's brother, John...I ran straight out of the house into the bitter wind and rain outside without even thinking of taking my coat and hat, running and saying over and over silently, "Grandma, it's time! It's time..." What did this mean? All I knew was that Ma had hurt herself badly and that her face was black from the cleaning and red with the blood from her fall and that she was crying and that all she wanted me to remember was to tell Grandma Quarter, "It's time!"

Grandma Quarter lived in Camane, the next village over. Not far by cart, but my small legs couldn't go fast enough. I cut across the fields slipping and sliding in the bogs and wishing I were bigger and stronger, and praying that Grandma would be in her cottage when I got there.

She must have seen me from her window because she ran out to meet me. "Jesus, Mary, and Joseph, whatever is the matter, child?" she shouted to me. "Is it your Mammy?"

"Oh, Grandma, she fell and she has a black and red face and she's making faces and crying and our Michael fell and the water is on the floor..." The words tumbled out of my mouth. "...and Mary Ann is crying and I don't know where m' Pa is...and she said it's time, it's time!"

Had I said it right? I must have, because she turned around and left me panting on the path while she shouted to Uncle John. "Bring Mayflower and the cart as quick as you can! It's time, our John, and our Ellen needs me, and she's ready!" As he raced to get the horse and cart, she yelled after him, "I must get clean towels and a few things from the house and then be here at the front door!"

I sat on the ground watching all this and not understanding anything, but I did know they were going to help m' Ma. Grandma Quarter knew everything because she talked to God every day. I jumped up when I heard the sound of their horse's hooves. Grandma ran out with her arms full of things and we quickly hurled ourselves and the things into the back of the cart and Uncle John whipped the horse into a gallop as soon as we were safely seated.

"Go, John, go! Ellen is ready!" Grandma urged him, and in no time at all we were at our front door. By the time she had clambered down from the back of the cart, Uncle John was already through the door. When we got inside, he had lifted our Ma in his arms and was carrying her into her bedroom. "Michael," he ordered, "you put Mary Ann in the rocking chair there, near the fire, and comfort her."

Then he went out to the water pump to fill the kettle and one of Ma's big pans. He set them on our clean cooking grate. Michael helped as best he could while I sat in the rocking chair with Mary Ann. I put my arms around her to comfort her but couldn't stop staring in wonder at all the activity.

Grandma took charge immediately. Even though she closed the bedroom door, we could hear her shouting, "God help me!" And I'm sure she knew him well because the priest always told us to speak softly to God, but m' Grandma was not doing that. I also heard her say some bad words. They were the same words our Michael had said once and he was clipped about his ears for saying them. Maybe Grandma had stubbed her toe on the bed, because it was hard to say good words when that happens to you.

Then m"Ma shouted out so loud that the walls shook. I covered my ears and Mary Ann's and rocked the chair faster and faster. Michael looked up to Uncle John for an answer.

"Your Mammy's not hurt," Uncle John said, "she's having a baby, just as our pigs did last year...Y' remember? You both were there to help me that day. Old Porgy made a lot of noise, but she was all right, now, wasn't she? Remember all them little babies coming out, one after another?"

7

"Is our Ma going to have a lot of babies?" I asked.

"No, not at all, at all."

"Well, I'm glad about that," said our Michael, "'cause we've no tatties left and the milk is weak."

"But you know nothing, our Michael," I told him. "Our Pa's gone to Tuam to fetch us some chickens and some eggs and some corn and some hay for Beauty, and we're going to have a feast like the saints in heaven."

"Now, how is Pa going to carry all that when he sold the cart last week?" snapped Michael. "And if I heard right, he was going to sell Beauty next!"

"No, he's not! He'd never do that! You're a dirty filthy liar!" I screamed. I leapt off the chair after him and nearly put our Mary Ann on the floor, but all I could think about was hitting him as hard as I could. I wanted to kill him.

"Be quiet, you two!" Uncle John shouted as he stepped between us. "Your Mammy needs quiet. You are to behave, you hear? When all is done, I'll take m' cart and go look for your Pa, all right?"

Our Michael was very lucky that time.

I felt like crying, but just at that minute m' Grandma opened the door with a bundle in her arms. She was smiling down into it and speaking softly to God. After she finished with God, she spoke to us very quietly and said, "You have a little sister, you two. She's to be called Bridget, your Mammy says. Tomorrow I'll take you to Tuam to the Grand Cathedral of the Assumption. Perhaps the Archbishop John McHale himself will be there to speak in our Irish and bless us." She looked around the room. "Now, where in God's name is Mr Patrick Luby when he's needed?"

Then she asked us to clear out a dresser drawer for the baby to lie in and told Uncle John to mash some tea, we did all those things straightaway. My Grandma had such a kind asking voice that you never wanted to disappoint her. Michael and I carried the drawer into the bedroom and put it down between two chairs as she told us to, then she laid Bridget down in the drawer.

I jumped on the bed to kiss m'Ma. She was clean and soft and I loved her so, but Grandma took charge again. "Now you be letting your Ma have her rest both of you!" she told us.

M'Ma rubbed her hand through Michael's hair and patted me on the shoulder before we left the room.

"Uncle John," I asked. "Can I go with you to look for Pa? 'Cause Michael's the only man here now, so he needs to look after the house and take care of m'Ma and Mary Ann and Bridget."

"Sure," he said. "Come on, then."

Of course, Grandma was able to take care of everything quite well herself, but our Michael always felt good being called "the man of the house," and I knew that would persuade him to stay at home to protect the family.

I ran outside and jumped up onto the cart next to Uncle John, and we trotted down the lane towards Kilkenny Road, neither of us saying a word. When we reached Duffy's Pub, Uncle John stopped the cart. We could both hear the old Irish songs being given the full treatment by a voice I recognized. Uncle John raised his eyes to heaven and shook his head.

"Now, you wait here, Caty my lovely." He jumped off the cart. "This is no place for a young girl." He said that in the same voice of authority that m' Grandma used when she means business and she wants us to obey without question. When he went through the open door of the pub, the music and singing stopped, but then I heard glass smashing and wood breaking and voices started shouting my Pa's name and Uncle John's. I listened, not daring to move, but I was frightened that Mayflower might take off. So I started talking to him using a special voice so he would obey me.

"Now there, my lovely, stay still," I told him. "We're not going to let anything happen, are we now? Whoa, horsey! There now, good boy, please keep still! Everything's dandy..."

Speaking to the horse helped me to keep calm and not think about what was happening inside the pub. Still, Mayflower didn't like all the commotion, not at all. He started to neigh and throw his head around, so I decided to grab the reins. Just in time – Mayflower took off, slowly at first and then faster and faster down the lane. I tried to hold him back but I wasn't strong enough.

"Uncle John, help me!!" I shouted. "Pa! Help me!...dear God, help me!"

But nobody heard. I decided to talk to the only thing that mattered – Mayflower. "Whoa! Whoa, you stupid horse!" I shouted. "Stop! Stop!"

But that didn't work either. The lane was rough and bumpy, but I managed to hold on even though the reins were flapping in all directions. Suddenly Mayflower reared up and made a terrible neighing noise before heading into the field. For the first time in my life, I loved that it rained in Ireland because it had turned the field into mire, and Mayflower couldn't pull the cart through it. But the cart rocked from side to side, faster and faster and then turned over, throwing me down into the bog.

I ended up lying half under Mayflower. One tired and frightened horse and one little girl who was determined not to cry. I looked around but saw nothing except a long furrow in the field, the evidence of my escapade. Who was going to find us? Was I going to die in that bog?

Then I realized that I still had the reins in my hands. I hurt all over when I tried to move, but I wriggled out from under the horse, which wasn't so hard to do because the ground was so soft.

I stood up, talking to Mayflower in my special voice while I took her out of the shafts and coaxed her to stand.

Then I looked around again, wishing for m'Ma to come for me, but I couldn't stop the tears as I realized she wasn't coming. She was with our Bridget, our Mary Ann and our Michael – she couldn't leave them and come for me.
Following the furrow we had made, I led Mayflower back through the field and along the track. We walked very, very slowly. Both of us were sore, sad and smutty (I have a different word I would use but I'm afraid God would strike me down for my bad language.)

In the distance, I could see Duffy's Pub. Now the commotion seemed to be happening outside. I hadn't the strength to shout out. I could barely put one foot in front of the other, and I was sure they wouldn't hear me because they were shouting loud enough to wake our own St. Jarlath, the patron saint of Tuam, himself. What was happening?

Uncle John seemed to be fighting with m'Pa, but the other men were taking sides, with some jumping on Pa's back while others were punching Uncle John and still others were shouting and jeering, glasses in hand.

Then suddenly Thomas O'Leary, one of m'Pa's friends, shouted over the din, "Stop! Stop! Patrick! John! Will you all look there – for the love of Mary, it's your Catherine! Look over there! She's a sorry sight, I be tellin' ya – "

Mayflower gave a loud neigh just to make the point clear and make them take notice, and they did. Uncle John left m'Pa on the ground and ran toward me. He swept me up in his strong arms, took the reins from my grip, and gave them to Mr. O'Leary.

Uncle John spoke to me softly in my ear while hugging me like a baby. "What a state you're in, child! What happened? Has your family gone mad today or something?...Never mind. Let's get you into Duffy's to wash your cuts and bruises. Your Pa can stay in the road where he belongs for now!"

I was too tired to argue I just wanted m'Ma or m'Grandma. I didn't like the smell in Duffy's, but my body hurt so much that it was easy to ignore.

It was, however, the last thing I remembered until much later, when I woke up in our house, in the bed all us children shared, but our Michael wasn't in the bed, and Mary Ann wasn't in the bed, just me, and Grandma was sitting next to me gently stroking my head. I thought I had died and gone to Heaven!

She was talking to me in that special voice she used for God, and I couldn't understand clearly what she was saying, but I just wanted to stay there forever. Then I heard voices rising above her soothing chants. My mother and father were having a humdinger of a row – something about Beauty, money, and drinking in Duffy's, but I couldn't make sense of it all.

"What did Pa do to make m'Ma so angry?" I asked Grandma.

"Doesn't matter, child," she soothed me. "It shouldn't concern your little head. Your Mammy and Pa will sort it out in time."

"But I want to know, Grandma, I'm the oldest and I should know," I insisted.

"Oh dear, just listen to you now! Is it wanting to grow up you'd be wishing for? That'll come soon enough – I can tell you that for nothing!"

I decided not to get her angry. There were enough angry people in our house for the time being. I would ask Michael later if he knew anything.

I must have gone to sleep, because later I was woken up by m'Ma putting Mary Ann into the bed and telling me to scrunch up so Michael could get in. That put a quick end to my luxury for the day!

I waited until Mary Ann went to sleep, which she always did very quickly. Then I whispered to our Michael. "Michael, do you know what happened to Beauty?"

"Pa had a plan," he whispered back, "to sell Beauty. There was a good race meeting today and he thought there'd be people around with money who loved horses and would buy her."

"Oh, no!"

"But when he was leading her down the track and on to Kilkenny Road, she faltered a little and made one weak neighing sound, and then she dropped to the ground dead!...Maybe she knew where she was heading..."

"Or maybe she was just too feeble to go any further?" I suggested. I remembered I had asked our Uncle John how old Beauty was and he had told me he was eighteen which was old for a horse that had been made to work so hard.

'What happened then?' I pushed him to go on.

"I don't know," he said, but I always knew when our Michael was lying because he would blink his eyes, and I was watching him closely as I lay beside him, and he was blinking, for sure.

I shoved him. "Now you tell me what you know, Michael Luby, or I'll kick you where it hurts."

"Well when Uncle John came back I heard him talking to m' Ma but I don't think you will like to hear. What they said?"

So, he told me, and I wished later that I hadn't asked.

"There was only one thing Pa could do," he whispered. "Sell Beauty for horsemeat. He knew that Thomas Flynn, the butcher, would be in Duffy's Pub and that he's always ready to pay money for horseflesh. Whenever people ask him why he buys horseflesh, he always says, 'Times are hard.'"

So our Michael went on to tell me that m'Pa had turned back along the road and gone into Duffy's and found Mr. Flynn, and that he had sold our lovely, lovely Beauty for someone else to eat. But then he realized the that pittance Mr. Flynn had given him wouldn't buy our family the food we were in want of, so he decided to "drown his sorrows."

Neither of us quite understood that last bit. "Maybe he put the 'sorrows' in the River Claire?" I suggested, but our Michael shook his head.

14

After a long pause, he said, "I think it was something to do with drinking a lot, because that's what Uncle John had told m'Ma, and that was why there was such a furore between our Ma and Pa."

"I don't believe you! Pa would never sell Beauty for horsemeat," I hissed in his ear. "If your story was true, I would've seen Beauty lying at the side of the road 'cause I was there!"

After he fell asleep, I lay awake trying to work out why I hadn't seen Beauty. Then I remembered Mayflower rearing up and turning into the field. Had he seen Beauty lying there in the road? Or maybe he had just been frightened by a shape lying in his path. Either way, someone must have moved Beauty before I got back to the road because she wasn't there when I led Mayflower back to the pub.

Not all my questions had answers, especially the most important one. What was going to happen to us now? We had no horse to pull the plough or take us into Tuam for supplies. We had no money because m'Pa had drowned his sorrows somewhere. Bridget would be all right – she could get milk from Ma but our cow had stopped giving milk, so we wouldn't have any.

This was a right kettle of fish. We really were in a fix.

I had to think of something to help, I was no stone jug, I had brains as m'Ma always told me .

So April 7th 1881 had not been a good day for me – no, I tell a lie. I did get a new baby sister. God does move in mysterious ways, as my Grandma always said. I fell asleep exhausted from all the sayings buzzing in my head.

Chapter Two
A Working Girl!

With the help of Grandma Quarter, my mother's mother and her brother, Uncle John, we managed to get through the next year. Then, we had another addition to our family, Margaret was born. M' Pa and Michael were not so happy it was another girl, but I guess you can't choose, can you?

I was ten now and big for my age, and Pa had heard in his usual hangout that the posh Crashworthy family, who owned the timber mill in town, were establishing a match factory and were looking for girls with nimble fingers to work in the factory.

"Now then, is this not a blessing from Heaven?" were his words.

The next day m'Pa walked with me to the factory, which was on the outskirts of Tuam. He held my hand as we walked along the road.

"You must leave the talking to me," he told me, "but remember to say that you're twelve years old if they ask."

When we reached the High Cross, the stone cross that stood in the centre of Tuam, my eyes nearly rolled out of my head with the sights and sounds. It was about mid-day, and all around the cross were musicians, flute-players, pipers, ballad singers and dancing men and women, all playing in discordant rivalry with not a care in the world, just having a good time. Although their clothes were dirty and ragged, the bright colours were startling to my eyes, and the music so lifted my spirits that I was happy to be alive and living so near Tuam.

"These be travelling folk, Catherine," said Pa. "They come here for a good friendly crowd who will laugh and cry at their antics."

I wanted to stay and watch them longer, but m'Pa pulled me away. He was eager for me to get to the factory. As we left the town centre and began climbing the hill to the factory, (well, I was actually skipping and humming the catchy tunes the musicians were playing). My fate now lay in front of my eyes, but my mind was still with the music behind me.

When we reached the factory, Pa went to speak to Thomas Murphy, the manager. I stood outside the office door on the cold slab floor waiting. There was an awful smell in that corridor, the kind of smell that stayed in your hair, on your clothes, and even on your breath. It was a smell I would later get used to.

M'Pa got me the job and I started the very next day. I got up at five and helped Ma do some things for the little ones. Michael was already outside helping Pa with the farm.

I would eat my bowl of bread with hot milk poured over it, and then start my long trek to the factory. It usually took me about an hour to get there in the winter but it was shorter, of course, in the spring and summer.

My journey to work took me past the railway station. The line came from Athenry to Claremorris and stopped at Tuam. I was always making up stories in my head about the people who rode on those trains and the places they went to and indeed, why they would want to go from place to place? Was it to see family or to watch their husbands play in cricket matches? Uncle John had once taken me to see a cricket match in Tuam. Of course, the gentry played the match. When he told me that the other team had come by train, I wondered then how those fine ladies got in and out of the doors of the train with all those skirts. They must have had a carriage to themselves.

The work was repetitive and boring. My job was to dip the match head in yellow phosphorus and later we packed them in large wooden boxes which when filled we carried away on our heads to the holding bay. I wore a piece of cloth on my head to protect my hair but many of the girls didn't bother. . I had made friends in the factory which was easy to do as we came from the same background of poverty and large families; and so our conversations were in tune. One girl became my very special friend. Maggie Marsden was her name. We were so opposite in stature you would never guess we were the same age. She was small and wiry, like my brother Michael but she had a heart as big as my backside, which was indeed big. She had scraggily long dark hair that was greasy through lack of washing and deep-set eyes that reflected her constant tiredness. She started at the factory the same day I had so we were put to work at the same bench.

We all looked forward to our mid-day break from work. A group of us would sit outside on the side of the hill to breathe the fresh air, and get out of the sulphur smell. From this vantage point, we could look down to the railway station below and Maggie and I always made for this same spot.

One beautiful day when we were all sitting out in the open, my friend Maggie pointed to the station below.
"Can you see all those people down there, Caty? There's some kind of meeting going on."

We could see a makeshift platform with posh folk standing on it talking to crowds of people. It was a really good-sized crowd for these parts, so they must have been important. There looked to be three people on the platform taking turns speaking.

When we went back into the factory, I asked Mr Flynn if he knew who they were. He told us that a very important man called Charles Parnell had come to Tuam with M.P. John Philip Nolan and Captain Willie

18

O'Shear. He said we were ignorant because we did not know that Parnell was the great man who had formed the Irish Land Purchase and Settlement Company Limited. All those big words left me cold but I was not alone, Maggie shook her head and rolled her eyes as well.

However, much later in my life I was to hear of these two men again and I remembered this day I looked at them with awe. It transpired that Mr. O Shear's wife, Kathleen had an affair with the important man Parnell, so, her husband divorced her and it resulted in them all being ruined. It taught me, never be in awe of someone because they are rich and influential.

The best part of my life was having Maggie to talk to. We would laugh because I would say, "I have two sisters called Margaret, one big one and one little one." Maggie and I understood each other. We shared the same hellhole during the day and a similar home life at night. Her house was smaller than ours and her family was larger so she always had something to grumble about. But I tried to cheer her up as much as I could. We talked about lots of things, Maggie and I. What it must be like to ride on a train, win a lot of money at the horse races, live in a cottage with lots of babies and have a rich husband who would buy you new clothes every week. We loved to talk and dream did Maggie and I.

Working in the match factory was dirty, cold, and very smelly. I couldn't grumble because it did give us extra money to buy food from the market. It was my job to shop for the basic essentials that Ma needed each Friday on my way home after I was paid. The market stayed open late on Fridays. I think it was their busiest day..

M'Pa made me a little handcart. It was just a box on two wheels with a rope to pull it along. I was embarrassed to be seen pulling it, so I found a little hideaway in the bushes on the hillside up to the factory. After work, every Friday I would hang about talking with Maggie near the factory gates until almost everyone else had left. Maggie knew what I was doing, so she didn't mind. We would walk down the hill together, pulling the cart and all the time dreaming and talking about our fantasy worlds.

"Do you think we'll work here all our lives?" Maggie would ask as I pulled out the cart from the bushes.

"'Who knows? Only the good Lord knows, so my Grandma says."

"Well, I don't want to work in that factory for another minute. I hate it! I do, Caty."

Every week, she would say the same thing. She and her family lived in a rented cottage in Carnage. Ten of them lived in the one room – her mother, father, and eight children. It was tiny and damp, and they had no land to call their own. Maggie was the eldest, so she was the one who needed to go out and work. Her Pa worked for the gentry, so they had a roof over their heads, but he was not paid much for all his toil. However, he did often produce food from some remarkable places, from under his coat or inside his hat. We always had a good laugh when Maggie explained all his magic places, but there wasn't much laughter at their house. Maggie told me she hated the smell of babies, wet bottoms, the toddlers' dirty pants, and the stink of bodies crushed together.

"Smell me, Caty. Don't I smell awful?" she would ask.

I always loved the smell of babies, but all I could smell on her and myself was the sulphur. It soaked into our skin, our hair and our clothes from the factory.

So we would go to the market together pulling the cart behind us as if it weren't there.

Sometimes the music would be playing in the center of the town, and pipers and dancers would be making their wondrous sounds, weaving in and out of the crowds. The dancers' colourful clothes and movements chased away our dreary thoughts and cheered our tired bodies.

I always put a halfpenny into the box for the musicians, but I never told m'Pa about it. "The flour cost more," I would tell him. Or, "the tripe weighed heavier than I thought it would."

I did love Fridays and our time at the market. It was our big adventure of the week.

That evening, the sun was setting fast, so we made tracks home after shopping for our usual meagre groceries. Maggie and I both knew we were helping our families live a little better, even if we hated the factory and the conditions we worked in.

"One mustn't grumble. It's all part of God's master plan," as my Grandma would say to me.

I said goodbye to Maggie at the end of the lane and pulled the cart home along the muddy track. As I reached our house, I had a very strange feeling. Where was the usual noise and commotion that I was used to hearing when I arrived? I opened the door, pulled the handcart in behind me, and shut the door quietly. It felt like church. It smelled like the church. Everyone was in m'Ma's bedroom.

What was the matter?

Without taking off my coat or hat, I opened the bedroom door and looked inside. M'Ma was in bed sobbing and rocking baby Margaret. Little Bridget was lying on top of the covers between her knees and. m'Pa was standing on one side of the bed with his head bowed, his hands on the shoulders of our little Mary Ann in front of him. On the other side of the bed, the priest and Grandma were kneeling. They had their hands together and were speaking in the Irish tongue.

Our Michael was at the foot of the bed. I stood next to him but kept looking around for a clue to these strange happenings.

M'Ma wiped her eyes. "We've lost our Margaret to the angels," she told me. "They've taken her on the long journey home."

What did grownups mean, talking such rigmarole I thought our Margaret was home, what was the long journey?

The priest began leading us in prayer, so I got down on my knees next to Michael with my hands on the foot of the bed.

"I don't understand…" I whispered to Michael through my praying hands, but he didn't answer he was crying. I had never seen our Michael do that before, and he just kept shaking his head, which made his tears shower over me. I took off my bonnet and wiped my face dry with it and listened hard to the priest and my Grandma's chant hoping I would understand what was happening. I looked over at m'Pa, but all I could see were his shoulders shaking up and down. I stretched up a little so I could see my m'Ma's face but I couldn't – it was buried in the shawl that was covering baby Margaret.

Can't she see she's smothering dear Margaret to death? I thought. Then I realized – death?. Oh, no! Not our little Margaret, She couldn't die, she was too little and I hadn't kissed her that morning…no, the angels can't take our Margaret! I won't let them take our Margaret…

I got up and ran around the bed and began hitting the priest on his back with both fists. No words came out of my mouth, but I was crying and mouthing, "No! no!" and finally I shouted, "the angels can't have our Margaret. Do you hear me?"

Grandma stretched up and pulled me to her, wrapping me in her arms and rocking me down to her side with the special voice she had been using to speak to God a few moments ago. I didn't understand why the angels needed our Margaret. She was so very little – what could she do in heaven? Who would take care of her?

M'Pa reached down and took little Margaret in his arms. He kissed her gently and wrapped her in the shawl. Then he took her out of the room with the priest at his side.

I don't remember anything very clearly from then on except that we took her in a box that the grownups called a "coffin" to the Catholic Cathedral of the Assumption, in Tuam. Was it the next day or the one after that?

The cathedral was huge, with a big square tower. Over the door was a large painting of some kind. M'Pa called it "a coat of arms." On top of that was a large Cardinal's hat. I remember looking up to see these things before and asked what the carving was, but I didn't really listen to their answer. On this day I looked up at the wall of the cathedral and the stone faces that looked down on me were forbidding; they looked scary -- a frightening sight for a bewildered child.

I grabbed Michael's hand as we walked inside. The cathedral was gigantic, dark and cold. Archbishop McHale was standing at the altar with the tiny box in front of him on a table. He was chanting in the old Irish language that only Grandma could understand. She was smiling, so I thought he must have been saying nice things. I didn't want to leave our Margaret's box, but I did wish I were home in front of the peat fire listening to Ma's sweet voice singing instead of listening to Archbishop McHale.

After the chanting, they dug a hole in the ground outside and put our little Margaret into it. They covered the box with the soil and threw holy water over it. I froze with fear watching all this.

I know that my eyes were popping out of my head because our Michael told me so later. Heaven is in the sky, I thought. Not in the ground! How would our little Margaret get out of there?

I wanted to know, but nobody was listening to me. For weeks after I would go to the cathedral and look at the grave where Margaret had been buried and hope that the ground would be disturbed. Then I would know that Margaret had escaped and gone up into the sky with the angels.

After the third week, I could stand it no longer. I went to m'Ma and asked her, "How will Margaret ever get out of that hole?"

"The angels only want Margaret's soul," she told me. "Not her body. They took her soul when we were in the cathedral, and only Margaret's body is lying in the ground now."

This answer still left me with many unanswered questions, but I wasn't going to be able to dwell on them in the next few weeks because bigger things were about to happen.

Chapter Three
The Dilemma

It started as an awful smell that woke us up in the early morning hours. I tossed and turned and was aware that Michael also was fidgeting. We both sat up almost at the same time and curiously looked at each other. Outside we could hear both our parents talking and decided to go outside to see what the commotion was all about. We had only our night-shirts on but the heat of the morning air seemed to swirl around us.

As we opened the door we could hear crackling and saw splitters of fire reaching up to the sky.

I ran to Ma for comfort and Michael headed for Pa. Together the four of us hugged together watching the lights in the sky.

I was just thankful it didn't seem to be on our property but seemed to be up on the hill. Our house was pretty isolated but over the crackling noise we could hear a resounding noise from the villagers nearby. Their shouts seemed to be in unison, everyone was looking at the hill. . The smell was unbearable.

"What's making that dreadful smell?" I asked Pa.

He pointed toward Tuam. "I think it's something on the hill over the town...something big, by the looks of it."

I tried to focus but the air was now getting very dense and foggy making the shapes disappear from the horizon.

The smell was getting worse. It filled the air with a kind of gas that made it hard to breathe, so Ma made us go back inside. The fire was obviously too far away from us to be effected but she was not sure about the fumes that permeated the air. Of course we obeyed her and went back inside.

What d'you think?' asked Michael, as we returned to bed. Our Bridget and Mary Ann were still sleeping, oblivious to the commotion

"Well, I do know one thing for sure," I said. "That smell is part of me. It's sulphur. And I think the match factory's on fire!"

Michael set off laughing, rolling off the bed and onto the floor. He shoved his hand into his mouth to keep the noise from waking the babies. Tears were rolling down his cheeks. Finally he quieted down, but he was still gasping for breath and guffawing from the floor.

"So what's so funny?" I asked.

"S-s-somebody must've asked for a light –" he chortled, "and got more than they bargained for."

Suddenly the truth of the situation hit me. The match factory was my work, my contribution to the family. If the factory burned down, my life was finished. If I had no work, we would have no money. What would I do now? I could not see the humour in the situation, but Michael wouldn't stop laughing.

"Be quiet! You'll wake the babies," I begged him, but he paid no attention. To him, the match factory catching fire was just a joke.

Outside our bedroom, I could hear m'Pa cursing. "The English bastards would be the only ones to do such a thing! I'm sure of it!"

In all my life, I had never seen an Englishman around our parts, so I wasn't so sure how Pa was so certain it was the English. I had heard that there was work to be had for everyone in England, so why would they come to Tuam to set fire to our factory? It made no sense to me.

We didn't go back to sleep but we both knew that we had to obey Ma and stay in our bedroom. When I heard my Ma noisily banging around the kitchen I decided to get up. I was uncertain as to what I should do that morning. Was I to go to work as usual? Was it really my factory that had burned? I needed to ask Ma and Pa the answers to my questions.

They seemed to be arguing about the situation from last night's goings-on so I walked passed and headed for the water pump.. They didn't stop me so I reckoned it was safe to venture outside. The air was dense with fog and the putrid smell was worse than our rotten potatoes. The cold fresh water made me jolt but at the same time sigh at the realization that I might not have a job and therefore, our family income would be diminished. I needed to go there to find out.

Pa was also curious to know if it was indeed the factory that had burned, so when I went back inside to have breakfast he suggested to me we go to find out. Ma was not happy with this she was afraid it was still too dangerous to be near a Match factory that had set on fire. She also told us to be aware the authorities would be snooping around and could pin this 'accident' on any likely bystander. My Pa, as usual, poked fun at her fears and told her half the villagers and most of Tuam would be curious to see what was left of the factory and he had to find out if anything was left of his daughters work place.

I pleaded with him to let me go with him and reluctantly he agreed. As we left our small holding and headed for the road Pa was not surprised to see a small army of people all heading in the same direction with the same curiosity on their minds. The procession headed for Tuam like a parade of jovial party goers all eager to witness the ruin of the rich factory owners, their misguided malice forgetting the real dilemma. No factory, no work for the locals, no work for me. We went in and out of the town of Tuam gathering more and more people in our wake. Their

27

excitement overpowered the nauseating smell and their enthusiasm permutated the air.

We climbed my familiar hill towards the factory like a swarm of insects aiming for a potential meal. All were smiling and making derogatory remarks. All I saw was devastation, a ruin of burnt wood were once a thriving factory making money was for its owners and also money for me and my family once stood.
Some revelers shouted insults against the British and others with remarks aimed at the Factory owners getting their just reward. I seemed to be the only person there not enjoying the scene.

I tugged Pa's coat in the hope he would take me home but he was enjoying the spectacle too much.
"You go back to your Ma luvy and tell her I will see her shortly."

In my heart I knew he would head for Duffy's bar to mull over the day's happenings with his cronies but I needed to talk with my friend Maggie.

Later that day, Maggie and I sat on the fence near her barn trying to figure out what would become of us and our families. I told her what m'Pa had said about the "English bastards" who he was sure had done it. She and I had both heard tales of killing and torture to take away our beloved country. We had heard them in church, in school, in songs, and in stories at bedtime, and we started talking about them. The troubles between the Irish and the English were embroiled in religion, money, work and land, all similar struggles that happen to invaders who venture into foreign lands.

"But, Maggie," I said, "I can't help thinking that a lot of killings were done by men on both sides, so both sides are wrong...why do men always want to fight and show how strong they are?"

28

"Our men are defending our country, so it's right for us to hide them from the authorities and take care of the wounded. The men have to protect the women and children," Maggie said.

"Why is that?" I protested. "I'm as strong as our Michael, and bigger in the bargain! I'm sure I could kill the English bastards that burned down our factory."

"We could, we could," agreed Maggie as she jumped off the fence, pushing her skirt into her pantaloons and running through the field. I did the same and followed her, but I picked up a piece of wood and brandished it, yelling, "I will kill the first Englishman I see for all the hundreds of years they've made us pay,"

"Let's get them, Caty!" Maggie shouted back as she waved her fists in the air. "They burned down our factory!"

We ran around in circles until we exhausted ourselves from all our yelling and screaming, then we fell on top of each other laughing and crying at the injustice of it all. The English bastards had burned down our factory, and now we had no jobs to go to, and they wanted our country as well. Rocking each other, we shouted that we hated the English, hated fighting, and hated men, who did it all.

"We need to promise, Caty," Maggie finally said, "we need to promise each other on this very day that we'll never marry and that we'll stay together always!"

"We'll have our own cottage, Maggie, and blow the men who want it all."

"That's fine by me, Caty..." she replied, hugging me, "but just now I'm a bit hungry and it's going dark, so shall we be going back for now?"

We strolled back in silence; confused by feelings we didn't understand. Our bodies were growing up, but our young heads were muddled and our thoughts were too full of emotion. One minute I felt as if I could fight the world, but the next I wanted to cry. To top it all off, when I got home and went to the outside privy.
I found that my bottom was bleeding.

I went to see Ma. "Ma, I cut my bottom when Maggie and I were rolling in the stubble in the fields," I told her, with fear in my voice.

"Come with me," she said, and began leading me into our children's bedroom.

"Its okay, Ma," I said. "It doesn't hurt too much," but she shut the door and sat me on the bed and took me into her arms.

"Don't be frightened," she told me. "You have the women's curse. You're bleeding from your bottom because God is telling you that you're now a woman and not a girl anymore, and he'll be reminding you of this every month when you'll bleed for a few days."

"Does it happen to boys, too?" I asked.

She shook her head, "Only to girls, not boys."

Well, didn't I just expect that would be the case – because when all was said and done, God was a man. But I didn't say any of this out loud for fear that God would put more curses on me. I didn't ask m'Ma any questions either. This was bad enough. I had to talk to Maggie the next day to find out if she knew that blood wasn't spilled only in wars, as the songs told us, but every month by every woman, whether they liked it or not! What a confusing day.

That night as I lay in bed next to my brothers and sisters, I had the most terrible stomach ache, but I tried to put it out of my mind. How could I explain to our Michael, who was never going to have it anyway, that I had a curse for being a girl?

Life was not fair.

The next morning, after I did my jobs, I asked Pa if I could go to the factory to see if anyone was there to pay us what was owed to us in back wages. Of course, he agreed, and I ran across the fields to Maggie's house. She was helping her Ma with all the children, so she wasn't happy about Maggie leaving, but when I gave her the same excuse I had used with my Pa, she was more than glad to let Maggie go to get some money.

"I would have never thought about our wages," Maggie said as we set off along the short cut through the fields, "but I suppose they do owe us something for the last few days."

"'Course they do, but I don't know if anyone is waiting around for us. We can only go and see."

It was a beautiful day. Cross-leafed heather and bog cotton brushed our boots as we made for the factory. I knew I had to ask Maggie about "the curse," but I didn't know how to start. Well, straight to the point was the only way, so I just blurted out, "Maggie, have you had the curse?"

To my surprise, she answered, yes.

"Then why didn't you tell me about it? I would've thought a good friend like you could've warned me!"

31

"Well, I thought you had it first but hadn't told me about it, so I just kept quiet. It's not the kind of news you spread around, Caty, now is it?"

I pulled a piece of grass from the field and stuck it into my mouth. I had to think. In February, m'Ma had had another baby. She called it Patrick after m'Pa, and I remembered there was a lot of blood around then, but m'Ma hadn't seemed to worry much about it. She said it was only natural for a child to come into the world that way.

"What about all the blood when babies are born?" I asked Maggie. "After all, you have a lot of brothers and sisters..."

"M'Ma says that's the way that babies are born every year, or thereabouts, and nothing but the Lord can stop them."

I understood what she meant because I knew that my Ma's stomach was growing again, and both of us knew what that meant. One good thing was that little Patrick had made our Michael happy because he had been praying for a brother. A houseful of girls was not his idea of fun.

We started up the hill in silence, picking daisies as we leaned forward, climbing toward the smell of sulphur. It filled the air everywhere since the fire, so we held the daisies to our noses as we got closer to the scene of the fire.

Smoldering embers were all that remained of the factory, and of the industry that had been responsible for feeding the people of Tuam, who otherwise could well have starved in the bad harvests of the past few years. We saw some well-dressed men picking their way through the blackened wood with the help of their fine walking sticks. They were shaking their heads and muttering in disbelief.

"They're from the Crashworthy family!" she whispered, catching at my arm to hold me back, but it was too late for us to hide ourselves, even if there had been anywhere to hide. They had seen us.

"Now what would the likes of you be doing around here, my pretties?" asked one of the eldest of the men.

"Well, begging your pardon, sir," I stammered, "but Maggie and me used to work here, sir, and we thought...well, what we did think, sir was that we might have some money due to come to us for last week, and that maybe someone would be here to give it to us?"

The men started roaring with laughter and clapping one another on the back. One even had tears running down his cheeks – not in sorrow, but in mirth.

My mouth fell open in shock. What had I said to cause so much glee?

Maggie pulled at my sleeve. "Let's get out of here quick!" she whispered, but I was not for going yet.

"Excuse me, sir," I continued, thinking about my Grandma and how insistent her voice could be. That gave me courage, and I went on, hoping they wouldn't laugh at me again. "But we are due our wages. It's only right and proper, and what's more, it's the law, sir."

I really had no idea what I was talking about, but it sounded good to me.

"The law now is it?" the old man bellowed. "You upstart! And don't you know, I am the law?"

His voice rang out through the hillsides and blew us down the hill, rolling us off our feet and sliding us away from this demon that stood on top of the world. I was scared to death, and as we ran I looked at Maggie and she was afraid too. We ran until we had no breath left to move, and then we both fell down shaking and sobbing but holding each other for comfort.

"Oh, Caty you were so brave there!" Maggie wept. "I could never have spoken to them like that! What were you expecting?"

"For him to put his hand in his pocket and pay us would have been nice."

"Oh, you're a real one, you are, Catherine Luby! Taking on the gentry, were you not? Sticking your nose in their faces and threatening them with the law. You're better than any man I know; afraid of nothing."

"Well, that might be, Maggie, but it didn't get us any money, now did it? So how do we make up for the missing wages in our houses now?"

We walked back in silence. There was nothing more to say at that moment, nothing to say and nothing to do about our dilemma. Nevertheless, tomorrow would be another day.

We parted company where the track split two ways, but first we gave each other a quick hug. We both felt the need for comfort, and that was one thing that was in short supply for both of us.

When I reached home and passed the shed, I could smell that Pa was making poteen again. "It's no use wasting the tatties that've gone soft," he had told Ma. "Better to make poteen from them." But the smell was awful.

I could hear our Michael in there with him listening to his tales, so it was better that I didn't disturb them with my bad news. I had nothing to show for my confrontation with the gentry. They didn't care one whit if the Lubys starved or not.

But we couldn't feed the babies poteen, (m'Pa's alcoholic drink made from potatoes), now could we? There just had to be some other way I could make money.

Chapter 4
An old head on young shoulders

I was sick of eating cabbage and onion and potatoes with onion with the occasional fried bread. Things were bad I had to find some work to help out. I was 13 years old now and had been without a job for too long. I walked to Grandma's house with our Mary Ann and Patrick in the box on wheels. M'Ma had not been feeling well and was getting bigger every day and her poor legs were all swollen with the weight she was carrying. It was the least I could do taking the young ones off her hands for a while.

Oh! If only the rain would let up for day or so. I had put one of m'Pa's old coats over the babies' heads but they did not like it and kept fighting each other to get it off. It was hard enough pulling them along the muddy track with the rope burning into my hands and trying not to let the whole thing topple over. I didn't need them both screaming at the same time.
My boots were slipping – the soles were real thin, but not to worry, what was a bit of rain to hurt. I was going to Grandma's and she always had a soft-boiled egg for me. I began to sing one of the songs Grandma had taught me years ago.
'One man went to mow, went to mow a meadow
One man and his dog went to mow a meadow.
Two men went to mow went to mow a meadow
Two men, one man and his dog
Went to mow a meadow...............

I sang along reaching 'ten men went to mow' just as we arrived at Grandma's. Good timing I thought.
Grandma's cottage was small but warm. Warm to the skin and warm to the heart. She made her usual big fuss of the little ones lifting one under each arm and running into the house with me following behind.

"Well, would you look at you, what a sight for sore eyes. Now be taking all those wet clothes off and let us get near the fire. Take your boots off, Catherine Luby, and don't be treading all that mud through my house."

I hung my coat on the nail behind the door by jumping to reach it. The hook was set for Uncle John's convenience, one day I will not have to do that. As I was taking my boots off, I watched Grandma tending to the babies. She took off their bonnets and their 'hand me down capes' using one hand for each of them so they didn't feel left out. She kissed them, hugged them, and then slowly lifted them on to her knee as she sat in the rocking chair near the fire. She took off their little boots and rubbed their small toes after first putting the palm of her hand in front of the fire to warm. .

Grandma's living room was more spacious than ours because m'Pa had made an extra bedroom for us kids dividing our living space. Grandma had more furnishings than us and all were made of solid wood. Rugs covered all the concrete floors and pretty floral curtains hung from the windows, which there were more of in her cottage and therefore, more light shinned through. It was warm and cozy.
I joined them sitting at Grandma's feet getting red cheeks from sitting too close to the fire. In no time at all the babies were asleep and together we put them down on Uncle John's bed that lived in the corner. Now it was my 'special time.'

"Let's be having a nice cup of mashed tea and maybe if you are lucky I could give you one of our fresh eggs from this morning. John is getting them to lay regular now; he says he has a secret method that he is sharing with no one. He's a card is our John!"

I know it was wrong but I was really hoping the babies wouldn't wake whilst I ate the whole egg myself. I am sure Grandma knew how I felt because she smiled all the time I was eating.

As we drank the tea, she asked about m'Ma and the farm and how things were doing in general and luckily, because I didn't want to tell her the absolute truth Uncle John saved me by coming in just at the right moment. He nearly went flying over my boots that I had left just on the doormat in my eagerness to get to the fire. He picked them up and looked at the bottoms.

"Well it's a good job I'm nimble on my feet Caty luv, or it's a bad fall I could have been getting. Now I think these boots are no good for anyone's feet," he said as he went to get a box from under his bed.

He pulled out the last and the tools and began to repair my boots. The box also had pieces of leather which he cut into shape with his sharp knife. He put the boots over the last, which was a solid piece of metal, shaped like an upside down boot. It held the boot in place whilst he worked on replacing the soles of my boots. When he had finished he gave me a jar of fatty looking stuff, which he told me to mix with soot on the rag he gave me and polish them good.

Next, he picked up the babies' boots and did the same to them. He seemed to have different sizes of lasts, for all sizes. What a magic box! Uncle John was the best cobbler in the world for me. When he had finished he told me to put the slimy stuff on the little boots as it was good for the leather and he would brush my boots until he could see his face in them. As he brushed, he started to tell us about the cricket match he went to the Saturday before and how he had heard that the Cathedral of the Assumption was looking for a cleaner. Old Mrs. Kelly couldn't get down between the pews these days so was going to work in the church house instead.

"Well it struck me young Catherine that maybe you would have no problem bending between the pews, how about giving it a try?"

"Now John," interrupted Grandma, "don't you think our Caty is a bit too young for that position? That's hard work for such young shoulders."

I butted in quickly to say I worked in the Match factory and they never knew my actual age so I'm sure I could hoodwink an old Archbishop who had no idea of girls and their ages. I realized as soon as I had said it that I had blasphemed my Grandmother's beloved Archbishop so I apologized quickly and hugged Grandma tightly. I was just so excited.

Then, that mind of mine motivated my tongue and I went rattling on with all sorts of nonsense. I was so sure I could clean the Cathedral and do it well. I told everyone there. I was ready to try this. Who did I need to speak to? Did Uncle John or Grandma know this Mrs. Kelly? I pleaded with Uncle John and with Grandma to help me.

Grandma told me to get the babies home and leave her to find out more about the job. She said she would talk to Mrs. Kelly and see what was possible. Pushing the handcart back home I was glad the rain had stopped because I was so pleased with my boots they were like new again. There was a fresh smell to the air. The grass glistened with dewdrops and the small stonewall that fenced the field seemed to gleam back at me and tell me it was feeling good after the great wash down it had that day. In the distance, I could hear the train, which Uncle John said was the Athenry to Claremore's line and my mind wandered again thinking of all the people going places in their beautiful clothes with money in their pockets. Slowly the sound faded into the distance and I was left with only one thought, of money – money I could get if I could convince the Archbishop I was big enough and strong enough to work in his Cathedral.

The young ones were sitting in the cart enjoying the colours of the sky they could see through the bare trees. Their little heads were moving from side to side taking in the smells of dusk in Ireland. We always grumbled about the rain which seemed to go on for months without stopping and then again, when it did cease, the freshness of the air was the very 'breathing salts' we needed to clear our bodies. God was good.

Now what made me think so spiritually all of a sudden? Maybe deep down I was preparing myself for the 'holy job'? I had to think good thoughts from now on and forgive God for giving me the 'curse'. There was always going to be three good weeks out of four so Catherine Luby, think positive and plan!
What would I wear? I had my nice shiny boots, thanks to Uncle John, but my own clothes still smelt of sulphur, m'Ma had tried all ways of washing them but the smell still lingered. I would talk to m'Ma as soon as we reached home.

I lifted the young ones out of the cart and took them inside. Ma was still lying down with Bridget beside her on the bed, Michael was still out there with Pa. I set them down on the floor to play with some spoons and put the kettle on the fire. Tea was always a good 'pick-you-up' I was sure Ma would welcome it when she woke up. The noise of the banging spoons and the spitting kettle on the fire woke m'Ma up gently and she smiled with her face and her eyes, as only she could do.

"Fancy a good cup of tea?" I said knowing she wouldn't refuse. "I need to ask you some things, Ma, but take your time I'll bring it to you there."

"No I'll get up," she said, "you die in bed. I'm coming to the table; slowly I am, but set it there for me will you?"
I poured two mugs of tea, I couldn't find any milk but I did find sugar so I put plenty in to give m'Ma energy. She looked ready to drop the baby any minute to me, I had seen her like this many times before.
I told her the news about the job and at first she came out with the same words as Grandma, about my age and my inexperience. I was not going down any negative path. I knew I could do it and told her so with

every ounce of conviction that she just laughed and shook her head. I think she knew I was not going to be talked out of it.
"I do want to look good Ma, Uncle John has mended my boots but what can I wear?"
First impressions are most important."

I don't know where I got that sentence from it just came into my head. Maybe I had heard it in church. I was getting many good thoughts all of a sudden and I was sure God was guiding me.
M'Ma told me to go fetch the big box from under the bed in her room because she thought we would find something there. Another magic box from under the bed! I dragged it from the bedroom to the table but I couldn't lift it so Ma told me to just open the big catches and we would see what we could find suitable for a growing young girl.

I didn't know that m'Ma had such colourful clothes. I had always seen her in black. She told me that Grandma had made the clothes from remnants left over from her sewing days working for the Crashworthy family. Ma had worn the clothes before she got married. They had fitted her then but as the years had gone by there had been no use for them and anyway they would not fit these days.

I was in a trance as we pulled out a beautiful blue one with a white collar, then a floral one. Next was a navy skirt complete with a white blouse with a frilly collar. The children were also looking on at the colourful scene in the kitchen. Whooping as they mimicked my own responses to each one I held up in front of me. It was a magical moment for all of us. Sharing that moment was for m'Ma, memories of the past, but for me, a fairy tale glimpse into the future as I imagined a new Catherine Luby. I imagined a young lady with nice clothes and money in her pocket, and this young lady worked for the Archbishop, no less.

I spent the next hour trying each one on in turn. As I said, I was a big girl for my age. Tall and full bosomed with big feet to match! I was thirteen years of age but going on for sixteen in my head and body and that was how it would go in years to come. Ma used to tell Grandma that I aged a year every six months! I was almost as tall as m'Ma now and the clothes would only have to be altered in length a little. We agreed I wanted the boots to be covered because they were so clumsy and my feet were so big.

This interlude of pleasure had brought colour to Ma's face and she was now as excited as I was. She thought I should wear the navy skirt and white blouse to go for the job as she could rework the skirt easy enough; it was straight and didn't need much sewing. Also, the waist could be fixed with a small tuck in the band. Oh, the excitement was breathtaking; a special bond was made at that time between m'Ma and me. My grown-up feelings were bringing us closer. I was going to wear her clothes, with her blessing. What was more she had promised to get Grandma to alter the other dresses.

When I went to sleep that night, my thoughts were in the clouds. The maroon velvet, the floral print, the beautiful frilly blouses and the sky blue dress with the full skirt; I wore them in turn as I floated through my dreams. While I sank more into my slumber I could hear my mother's voice singing as she sewed my navy skirt. The angels of heaven who were carrying me shoulder high to the Cathedral of the Assumption were joined by her voice.

Chapter 5
In God's House

It was decided that Grandma take me for the job. After all, she was the one who knew the people in the Cathedral. As we walked hand in hand along the road she coached me in the right way to talk to the Archbishop (if he was to speak to me), but if it was the Housekeeper then I was to leave it to Grandma and say nothing! You know I was very excited, not at all nervous. I began to skip as though my heart was lifting my feet in the hopes I would glide through the air. The smell of the bogs and the moors were filling my lungs with the power to achieve. My Grandma squeezed my hand and gave me her look of disapproval.

" Now my pretty, you are to act with calmness, however hard your heart beats, however frightened you are, you must never show your feelings in your body, just your pretty face. Time will come for showing your feelings with your body and that time is not now."

Grandma spoke a lot of riddles at times, but years later I was to understand these riddles as the voice of experience, the voice of good old common sense.

We reached the Cathedral and this time I looked over the large door at the Coat of Arms and the large Cardinal's hat carved above it. I even looked and nodded with a smile at the strange stone faces looking down at me from above. Nobody was going to take my great feelings away. I walked into God's House with my head held high but my hand still holding Grandma's.

Mrs. Kelly, the old cleaner, walked slowly towards us and welcomed Grandma in Irish (that bit I did know) and then she talked very fast as Grandma nodded and smiled. I was told to sit in the pew and wait; they both went through a side door together.

I stared at the vastness of this building and the rows and rows of pews that filled every space. Gold and silver shone from the altar glittering in the glow of the candles that stood proudly on crisp white cloths. Did one person clean all this? How did one person make this look so clean and shiny? I gulped with the enormous amount of work this would take but decided to kneel and pray. God would show me the way. I prayed harder than I ever had done in my life before, pleading and begging God to show me the way. I looked up when I heard voices and saw my Grandma smiling and nodding as she looked at me in approval. I knew my prayers had been answered; I knew the news was going to be good- I just knew!

I was to start training the next day with the guidance of Mrs. Kelly and the sanction of the Archbishop himself. There was just one drawback. Mrs. Kelly preferred to speak in Irish and when she spoke in English it was in a thick accent but Grandma said that shouldn't be a problem for a girl who was surrounded by Irish speaking adults. It was true that most of the time the adults spoke in Irish but the young spoke together in a sort of mixed English/Irish dialect that was neither one thing nor the other to the outside listener.

My Grandma bid a kind farewell (in Irish) to Mrs. Kelly and I followed suit with the same words hoping I had said the right thing. I must have said something to please them as they laughed and patted my head. We left the Cathedral by the side entrance, which led to the graveyard.

Grandma wanted to stop at our Margaret's graveside on our way out. I was not too happy about this as I still could not bear to think of her lying under all that soil but there was no getting out of it. Grandma was determined and pulled me along the paths between the gravestones until we reached poor Margaret's grave. Here we both knelt in silence. Grandma was mumbling in the Irish but I just closed my eyes and thought of her angel face with the chubby little cheeks. "Well, let's be going Caty you have a big day in front of you in the morning, you must get plenty of the shut-eye."

While we walked home Grandma gave me hints on how to deal with Mrs. Kelly and some of the Irish phrases she might use when asking me to do things. I listened intently and memorized the parts she told me were important. I wanted desperately to show all the family that I was a real worker and capable of working for God and my family!

The sun was going down fast in the murky sky, giving that chill in the air that makes your nose run just when you have nothing to wipe it on. . I had one hand in Grandma's and thought of using the sleeve from my other arm but I thought again, when I realized that grown-ups did not do that! I sniffed as quietly as I could and looked up to the sky above.

'Tell me, Grandma," I asked, "where do all the birds go at night?"

"Well, they need to rest like us all so they find a friendly tree or a bush with no prickly leaves. Sometimes they go to the edges of the cliffs and find themselves a little nook or cranny to hide from the outside world. We all need to do that sometime or other and the little birds are no different."

"I bet they have a good view from up there."

'There is no finer sight, little Caty, than the soft silk grass of Ireland speckled with the colours of the buttercups and daisies. If you look out there, you can see the beauty of nature. Look, the heather lies like a carpet over the bogs. We are truly blessed. When those birds go to the cliffs by the sea they have the chance to see the power of the Almighty himself pounding on the rocks to let us know that we land-lovers don't know the half of it! There is more to God's world than Tuam in Ireland."

She stopped talking and walking to take in a big breath of the air, then she looked at me and smiled before we continued down the stony path that led to our house; we arrived home just in time before the sun set. Inside everyone was waiting eagerly for my news. We hardly got through the door before the question began. When I gave them the good result they shouted with joy in unison. Michael danced me round the table and Ma and Pa clapped their hands and chanted, "Hooray for Caty, hooray for Caty, she's our girl, she's our girl!'

I felt I was flying like the birds Grandma and I had just talked about, but I certainly did not want to hide or sleep at that moment. I was too proud, too excited, too elated to be loved by everyone in my family. That moment was to stay transfixed in my mind forever, as a most wonderful moment in time; one of those still pictures that you recall to memory when you feel the world has lost its lust. So you memorize those good times, (unconsciously) so they can never be hidden from memory.

Chapter 6
Waiting for a sign

That year seemed to pass very quickly. In May, 1886 m'Ma had another boy and named him John. I grew a lot both in mind and in body. My speaking and understanding of Irish was now very good, thanks to Mrs. Kelly and her patience, but I had missed talking to my friend Maggie who I could always open my secret thoughts to.

Then one day walking home from the Cathedral I spotted Maggie sitting on the wall where the two paths divided from Tuam to my village. I waved and shouted as I approached her, but she gave me just a small wave of her hand. I knew something was wrong. I ran towards her shouting her name and mine in case she did not recognize me. As I got closer, I knew she had been crying. I sat on the wall besides her putting my arm around her but saying nothing, she would tell me in her own good time, so I hugged her shoulder and patted her hand to stop her rubbing her face.
"Do you want to talk, Maggie?" I said softly, "you can tell me."

She sniffed as the tears continued to roll down her face so I gave her my piece of cloth I always carried now to wipe my nose, (it was one of the grown-up things I did now instead of using my sleeve). She was shaking so I thought she might be ill.

"Do you need a Doctor, Maggie? Please tell me, I am your best friend. Is it your Ma, is she sick? Oh! Maggie please stop shaking I have never seen you like this, what do you want me to do?"

She started to talk so fast that I found it hard to follow, she was speaking in English and I was out of practice. She was talking about losing her job at the Manor House and having no money to give to her

Ma. She was mumbling something about getting dirty and not liking it. I was so confused I didn't know what to say.

"Hey Maggie, my job is dirty too, all that silver polishing makes your hands change color." As I spoke, I saw a faint smile come to her face.

"Caty Luby you could always find a way to make me smile but you don't know a half of it locked away in that Cathedral everyday with God watching over you. There are bad people, Caty, people who are dirty."

"Well of course I know that," I said to defend myself, "there are men who work in the mines or even the fields, even ourselves when we worked at the match factory, you said yourself that was a dirty job!"

"Not dirty like that, Caty, dirty in the other way."
I was confused and did not know what to say next, so I asked about the job and why she left.

"Was the job too hard, Maggie? Did you do something they didn't like? Oh! Please tell me so I can help you stop crying.'

"No, I didn't do something they didn't like! He did something to me I did not like, Oh! I can't tell you Caty it's so bad!"

"Did that Mr Crashworthy hit you Maggie?"

"Well not before I hit him. I kicked him too, but it didn't make any difference he was too strong for me."

"You hit Mr Crashworthy?" I stuttered in misbelieve, "the old codger who wouldn't pay us our wages after the fire?"

"No, it was young Mr Crashworthy, Charlie boy, as he's known in the family, he's worse than his Pa."

"Well, I suppose they can sack you if you hit them, Maggie, the Gentry have the last say on that score."

"I didn't get the sack, they didn't dismiss me, I ran away, but I can't go home and tell m'Ma, She needs my money from the job to make ends meet." Maggie said between sobs.

"She'll understand, if you tell her about him hitting you, I just know she will."
I was still holding her with one arm around her shoulder but she shook me off saying she didn't want anyone holding her ever again. She hated people touching her. This was not my Maggie. We had always hugged and touched each other. I shook my head and jumped off the wall.

"So if I can't help and your Ma can't help, then help yourself Margaret Marland. I have tried my best. Goodbye and good luck I say, I'll maybe see you around sometime."

I began to walk away towards home but Maggie shouted for me to stop and almost knocked me over as she ran towards me throwing her arms around me and pleading with me to sit down and listen to her .She wanted to talk and she wanted me to listen. We sat back on the wall and Maggie poured her heart out to me with the most frightening account of her time at Crashworthy Hall.

She had gone to work as a scullery maid at the Hall about the same time I had started at the Cathedral. Maggie was not as big as I was; even though was 14 years old now, lifting and carrying had been hard work for her. She told me she went to bed early, before the rest of the household staff because she was so tired at the end of the long day.

Everyone knew that Mister Charles, had a liking for the drink. He would often slap the bottoms of the parlour maids as they carried out their duties. Maggie had never seen him close because her work did not cause her to be in the same area as the family so when they warned her about him she didn't feel threatened.

There had been a big dinner party at the Hall and the work had been long and hard so Maggie went to bed as soon as she was able. The room she shared with the two parlour maids was at the top of the servants' stairs. The small steps went narrower as they went higher and were often slippery from the damp air. The only light came from a skylight in the roof at the top of the stairs. When it was dark, you had to feel your way up to the top. The night of the party Maggie had climbed up those stairs almost on her hands and knees she was so tired. She had thrown off her working apron and her dress, fell on to the floor mattress in just her slip, and went to sleep immediately.

She told me she was disturbed by the sound of what she thought were the parlour maids, Lucy and Polly, coming into the room but she was too tired to open her eyes. It was then she felt this big heavy weight fall on top of her!

At this point in her story Maggie stopped and held on to both my hands tight, so tight I thought she would break my fingers. I encouraged her to go on.

Obviously, after a big weight falling on top of her she was gasping for breath but as she opened her mouth to take in air a large thick tongue was pushed into her mouth. Groping large hands moved around her body squeezing and pulling at her flesh like an animal. Maggie said she tried to scratch his face but his big hefty body pinned her to the floor. He then snapped the elastic in her knickers and ripped them down.

Maggie paused and looked to the ground. I was spellbound in disbelief. Even the birds in the trees and the cows in the fields were silent as if they too wanted the next installment to begin.

"I don't know if I can tell you what happened next Caty. Will you always be my friend if I do? And you won't tell a sole what I say, not your Ma, your Michael or anybody, it's got to be our secret, do you promise, cross yourself and hope to die if you do."
I crossed myself and made the promise as fast as I could so she would continue, and opened my immature brain to visions unknown that were to fill it with horror.

As his thumbs hooked the top of the knickers, he lifted up slightly and Maggie tried quickly to roll away but he grabbed at her legs pulling her knickers down to her ankles and dragging her back to the mattress. She tried to hold on to the legs of the small table but this just fell over spilling the water that was in the jug and bowl all over them. Even this did not cool his ardour but seemed to fuel it more and make him worse.

He had hit her hard across the face stunning her for a moment as he unfastened the buttons of his pants. At the same time he pinned Maggie's arms over her head holding her wrists tight to the floor. After a short pause she explained that she had felt something long and hard go between her legs and almost split her in two. She struggled to move him but this made him worse. He put his mouth over hers and again forced his thick moist tongue between her lips. Then Maggie stopped her story again.

"Oh! Maggie, Maggie," I cried with her, "how horrible for you. How did you escape him?"

"I passed out," she said, "I don't remember anything more until Lucy and Polly were standing over me asking questions and trying to get me up from the floor on to the bed they shared. They advised me to run away because this was a habit of Mister Charles to try to get the maids alone to have his way with them. They told me he would try it again if I stayed."

I rocked Maggie in my arms, and she let me hold her, but as I looked close I could see the bruising on her face and neck, maybe all her body was covered in bruises, I didn't know. I told her it was all over with now and we would have to think of something to tell her Ma.

"But it might not be over with, Caty," she cried, "Lucy said I might have a baby after this. I don't want a baby, Caty, I want to die, I want to die."

"Now don't be talking like that, the good Lord looks after good Catholics." I heard myself say. Now wasn't I being the religious sanctimonious friend.

We sat and talked for about an hour until we came up with the most feasible story to put to Maggie's Ma about her leaving the Hall. She was to say she was carrying dirty water down the stairs to swill it away and she slipped falling down the stone steps and letting go of the bowl, which flew through the air and hit the Housekeeper, Mrs. Meyers on the head who happened to be passing the stairs at the time. After this big commotion, Mrs. Meyers sacked Maggie on the spot for 'clumsy bodily harm'. (I had heard this phrase somewhere and it did sound good).

I went home with Maggie for support. I watched her Ma's face as the made-up story was told, then Mrs. Marland said a strange thing.

"You're not telling me everything our Maggie, are you?" ,
Maggie began to sob and I swallowed hard and held my breath.

"Mrs. Meyers has been hitting you, I can see the bruises on your face, and you are not going near that place. No not over my dead body will you set foot in Crashworthy Hall again."

I let out a big sigh!

It was three weeks later when I met Maggie again. She was running on the road towards me shouting, "I got the sign, I got the sign." As we met, she told me the curse had come and God did love a good Catholics after all.
The good clean air of Tuam felt good.

Chapter 7
A time of discontent

Our small cottage seemed to go smaller as the years passed by. Baby John was 18 months old and toddling around and feeling as cold and hungry as the rest of us.

Shoes were a big problem; we could all pass hand–me-down clothes to each other but shoes were worn out before they could be handed down. The Society of Catholic Ladies had a monthly jumble sale where you could get, for a small amount of money, almost any article of clothing; they even had furniture, pots and pans and hand-made socks, but shoes and boots, that was another matter. They were in short supply.

They stored the goods inside the Cathedral and so I was well aware when shoes or boots did arrive for the next months 'Jumble'. Mrs. Kelly also knew that our family was in great need of shoes and boots. When I did some extra work or made a good job of something she asked me to do, I was always rewarded in the form of a pair of shoes or boots from the store. How she arranged this feat, I was never to know but it was a good exchange as far as our family was concerned.

The land around our farm was barren for months. The harsh winter had come early and very unforgiving, everywhere you looked was mire. When we woke in the morning, the hillsides were shrouded with a thick mist. The barn seemed hidden from our view, as it was covered with a film of vapour. For me there was no difference between night and day, my world was murky, dark and wet. The cold, humid weather ate into your flesh and bones and even a shiver could not get rid of the dampness in the body. The peat was wet, the wood was wet, and lighting a fire in the cottage was a major task.

It rained and snowed and the gales blew at our very spirits and left us listless to the fight. I was sure it would be better somewhere other than Tuam. I had heard Uncle John talk about his friend in England who was working making roads and making money. The man's wife was working too and they already had a small terrace house that they rented with just the two of them living in it. Mrs. Kelly's son was there too; he sent her money every month, so she said. I had to persuade my family to move. Tuam was finished; there was no food in the soil and no work to be had. I must make m'Pa see sense.

This was harder than I thought. m'Pa was finding his solace in the poteen and the boys were doing most of the outside work themselves. I tried my luck with m'Ma. She was so worn out at that time she would agree to anything I said.

"We'll see what you can find out Caty," she proffered, "nothing could be worse than the way we live now."
I went to Grandma's house to see Uncle John to find out as much as I could. He was very positive about the prospects in England.

"It's either the United States of America or England 'cause Ireland's not giving us anything that I can see," he said with gusto, "I'd be thinking about it myself if the old Dear was fit."

Grandma was getting water from the pump so did not hear Uncle John's last remark. Putting the kettle on for tea was always the custom when a visitor arrived, if you wanted it or not. As she struggled with the heavy kettle full of water, I could see what Uncle John meant. She panted and patted her chest with exhaustion as she put the kettle on the fire.

"Now my little precious what are you planning here? Is it to England I heard you say? I don't think your Pa will be too pleased with that idea, do you?"

"I don't care what m'Pa says about the English. I know he thinks they are all bastards, excuse my language Grandma, but if there is money to be made, I for one am interested."

I only went to Grandma's that day to find out more information from Uncle John but the more I heard, the more I defended myself. I felt even surer that I was going to try to persuade m'Ma and the kids to leave, even if m'Pa didn't join us.

I stayed all that Saturday afternoon learning the different possible routes out of Tuam and into England. The railway to Douglas was the quickest way over land to the ferry, but when Uncle John told me the possible cost for just one ticket I knew that way was not possible for us. I left the house miserable and angry. All my hopes to get out of this place and have a better life had been shattered by the fact that it took real money to escape, money; we did not have.

I called to see Maggie on the way home. I needed to cheer myself up before heading home. I had not seen her for weeks because usually on my Saturday off work I would help m'Ma around the house. I had gone to Grandma's that day telling Ma I had to get my boots repaired by Uncle John, so now I had time to see Maggie.

I knocked at the door and as Maggie opened it she pulled me in with a big smile filling her face.
Walking into her cramped, poky cottage, I saw her Ma feeding the babies 'pommies' (bread, milk and water) to satisfy them. The place seemed to have a strange quietness about it as I went in. The children did not seem to have the energy even to cry at their discontent. The small fire gave off very little heat; it could not even dry the moisture from the stone walls or give light to the room.

Maggie held on to my hand as she guided me through the overcrowded kitchen to sit down at the table next to her. She told me to hang on a few minutes, then we could talk. Her mother was rocking the two babies and soon all three of them were asleep. The toddlers went into the one bedroom to play together and finally I had the chance to tell Maggie of my plans to leave Tuam, but how the cost was going to stop me before I started.

"Oh, let me go with you, Caty, please. I cannot stand this existence. The children seem to get on my nerves even more since I came back home from the Hall and to think I could have had one of my own doesn't bear thinking about."

"First things, first, Margaret Marland, nobody is going anywhere until we can get some money from somewhere; have you any ideas in that quarter?"

"Not at this moment in time, but truthfully I'm going to think hard about it, Caty. My Ma always says 'where there's a will there's a way'; the women in our families had a saying for everything. It was the way they survived their hard lives.

"We both need to ask more questions to those who have family that have gone to England. It seems most of the people who have left are men and we are mere girls, but this should give us an advantage; they will think we are just asking out of curiosity not from necessity. Let's keep our eyes and ears open,
Maggie, something will turn up I can feel it".

"You always make me grin, Caty, the world is never a dull place with you around. You'd make a silk purse out of a sow's ear you would."

Another saying we had heard from the womenfolk. The sayings cut down the need for them to learn more vocabulary and so questions and answers were redundant; just a nod of the head would be enough.

"That's as maybe but I had better be off, m' Ma will be worried to death if I'm out when the sun goes down."

I left Maggie's and walked towards home thinking until my head ached, but no solution to the money matter came to me. M'Ma needed my money from my job at the Cathedral to keep us going and there was no extra left for savings.

Chapter 8
The idea!

It was one of those signs again from God; I just knew I was in the right place at the right time. I was between the pews on my hands and knees cleaning the floor when I heard a voice talking to God and the Holy Mother asking for help. It was Mrs. Raftery pleading with the good Lord to give her the answer. She was talking about her job at the timber factory and how she could not manage the job for another minute. The dust was affecting her chest something bad. She was coughing up splinters, no less, (or so she said) but she needed to work – was there no help in God's earth to give her this day? She went on at some length but I carried on backing down the pew cleaning until I reached the end. When I stood up, I think I startled her for she jumped up from her knees patting her chest.

"Holy Mother of God, child, you gave me a start then. Where did you come from?

"I was just doing my job, Mrs. Raftery, cleaning the Cathedral. It's my job."

"Well, with all the Saints in Heaven child you gave me a fright."

"Can I ask you a question Mrs. Raftery? I couldn't help hearing your prayer and I may have an idea. Do you get more than four pennies a week for your job? I'm sorry if I sound nosy but I think God might have an answer here."

"I get six, but I work every day of the week for that."

"And would you work for four pennies and have Sunday off, if you could?" I asked, trying not to sound as if I was prying.

59

"Sure, that would be heaven sent, young Catherine, I could see the little ones more and give our Kathleen a rest from them. So what have you in mind?"

"Well," I coughed and cleared my throat before I spoke.
"If I could make it right with Mrs. Kelly we could maybe swap jobs. That is if they would take me at Rishworths? What do you think?"

"Would you do that, Catherine? My job is so dirty and thankless, I just sweep-up the shavings from the floor of the factory, and I can tell you it is non-stop. The dust and the shavings get into your throat and on to your chest; it is a rotten job. Now you have this clean job here in the peace and the calm of God's House. This is Heaven on earth. My job is a hell hole compared to this. What will your Ma say Catherine; she will never let you change. I know if it was me I wouldn't."

"Well, let me deal with that," I said with authority. "You talk to the foreman and I will talk to Mrs. Kelly. I'll come by yer house Sunday night at six to find out what can be arranged. Will that be good enough with you?"

"My you're a piece of work Catherine Luby, if ever I saw one, but Sunday it will be. Now leave me for a few moments while I talk to the Good Lord in private."

I went into the side-chapel with my cleaning rags in my hands but a big question in my head. What had I just done? M'Ma would never allow it and Grandma would spin. Nevertheless, I would have two pence a week to save if I could carry it off. I would soon have enough for all of us to travel to England. I decided to tell Mrs Kelly everything, after all, she did have a son in England doing very well and sending her money in the bargain.
I needed to strike while the iron was hot (a saying I had heard my uncle say often; yes, the men also had their phrases). Maybe these sayings

enabled us to speak in English better since they would fit in to many different circumstances. Mrs. Kelly was coming from the house of the Bishop and coming towards the chapel. I had to say it now and ask her to help.

It was easier than I thought once I had her talking about her boy who worked in the coalmines just outside the city of Manchester. I told her of my plans to get my Ma and the girls to a better life; the boys could stay with m'Pa and work the farm. She shook her head at the thought of me doing such a thing. Such a manly thing, she said, not at all a thing for a young girl to do, but then she told me she thought I was able to do anything I set my heart on. She would pray for me, and say nothing for the time being to the Bishop, she said he left these sorts of things to her.

I was halfway there but I asked her for just one more favour not to say anything to Grandma, just yet. M'Ma was easy; she was so busy with the babies.

On Sunday, I went to Mrs. Raftery's house hoping for the best but fearing the worst. She smiled as she opened the door and hushed me in. Well, the foreman had agreed to let her go immediately, as long as she had a replacement. Mrs. Raftery had told him her niece would do the job. That was to be me. She told him my name was Catherine Raftery. I was sixteen years old and I was very fit. I was to start next Monday at seven sharp.

I went immediately to tell Maggie of my good fortune. I asked her not to tell anyone I was leaving the Cathedral to go to the factory.

We laughed together as only we could. We speculated on the fortunes that could be made in England. The fine clothes we would wear and the dashing young men we might meet? I would come back next Sunday to tell her all; she could not wait, and neither could I.

I left the house on Monday morning as usual, kissing the babies and saying 'cheerio' to everyone, just hoping nobody sensed my excitement. In my pocket, I had one of Pa's biggest handkerchiefs to put around my mouth to keep out the dust. I was very pleased with myself for thinking of that. In fact, I was so smug with myself as I walked into the factory that first day, I shudder to think about it now.

The match factory had been a palace compared to this factory. The noise, the dirt, and the heat inside were unbearable. It was a large brick building divided into sheds with few windows and a cold stone floor with large machines that seemed to have cutting saws attached. The foreman watched me constantly and never let me rest for even a minute to fix my 'mask'. He mocked me in front of the men at every possibility.

"Look-out here comes the bandit, be careful lads she might have a gun tucked away in that apron."

I was wishing I had, and then I could blow the man away for good. Oh! What was happening to me I had not been there a day and I was thinking of killing someone? God help me!

I had swept out four sheds and had worked non-stop for six hours. My throat was as dry as a bone and I was feeling very dizzy. I went outside at the back of the factory where the River Clare flowed. I dipped my head in the water rinsing the dirt from the inside of my mouth and nostrils. I was aching all over and I had not even finished the day. I had to speak to the foreman.

I lay back on the grass looking up to the sky and planning what I could say. The clouds rolled by above my head looking so clean and white against the blue sky. In the distance, I could hear the noise of the train puffing out its smoke to join the clouds on their journey to the sea. The Irish Sea, that carried the ferry across from Dublin to Liverpool,

England. I imagined the sea was bobbing the boat up and down and a gentle wind helped the boat in its crossing.

I woke with a jolt as I heard the voice of the foreman yelling and swearing at me to get back to work. I pulled myself up, took the brush inside but asked for a word with the ugly man towering over me. I asked him if I was possible to split my wage with someone else. If two people did the work for the same money would he be willing to accept this?

"What do you think this is young lady, a charity house of sorts? First, Mrs. Raferty gives you the job and now you want that two of you work for the price of one! Do I look stupid?"

"Begging your pardon sir, but I think you would get double the work for half of the price," I spluttered out not knowing if I could back it up or not.

"Well, I haven't got time to stand here with you, just do what you have in mind and if it doesn't suit me by the end of the week it will be the back of you for good and proper. Remember not a penny more than sixpence will I pay."
What had I done? If I were to share my wage, I would only have three pennies instead of the four I got at the Cathedral. . I had to talk to Maggie and come up with something before tomorrow or I would be out of a job altogether. What a mess, what a mess!

Chapter 9
Taking chances

I walked home with my head bursting at the seams with possible solutions. I knew the only person I could talk this over with was Maggie; she was the only person who knew about this job. I decided to cut across the fields. It had not rained for a long time so the bogs would be dry and hard. I pulled my scarf tight around my head and lifted my skirt so I could run without it catching my boots. I did not feel the sharp wind; I did not smell the heather or slip in the cow dung. My concentration was pointed like an arrow flying through the air; my eyes were only on one target, Maggie's cottage lying on the horizon in front of me. I reached there breathless as well as tired and my thoughts were so mixed up now; I asked Maggie outside to sit on the verge and talk.

I told her the full story about the job being too much for me and of my need to make money for England and to support my family. I was regretting the exchange but I thought I could do it and now it was so hopeless, so very, very hopeless. I did not have an answer, so the tears rolled down my face and I did not attempt to wipe them away and stop the flow. I just shook my head from side to side drowning poor Maggie as she tried to get near to me.

"You're not alone in this Caty Luby, I thought we were in this together. Remember, I want to go to England as well," she said forcefully holding my shoulders from going up and down with each sob.

She was right of course but my hard days work was telling on my stamina. The sun was going down fast and I just wanted to put my head down there on the grass and sleep so my problem would disappear. I lay back looking up at the dusky sky where not even one star could break through the low clouds pressing down on me from above. I ached all over and was ready to let go of that day when Maggie spoke, ever so gentle and quiet.

"Go home Caty, go home and let me think of an answer, I will meet you at the crossroad at seven in the morning, I will think of something, I promise."

I dragged myself down the lane and into our house mumbling something to my Ma about having done some extra work for Mrs. Kelly because she was not feeling too well. My Mother, as usual, was too busy with her own chores to question me and so I just passed through the kitchen and into the bedroom. I don't even remember if I undressed or not. I did not rightly care at that time if I ever woke up.

But I did, it was force of habit I think. I had a built-in clock that told me it was 6 o'clock whatever the circumstances. I hadn't washed myself the night before so I had to get by Ma to the wash-pipe outside. Pa and Michael were in the barn and Ma was dressing the little ones so she never looked-up at me as I said, "Good morning, I'll be back in a mo."

After I had washed I had some bread and dripping with a mug of hot tea, carefully pushing some more bread into my pocket for later. I told Ma I had to go early into work and I would be late back because of Mrs. Kelly being sick and all. She sent her good wishes to Mrs. Kelly and told me I was a good girl so with that bit over I left to meet Maggie. As I closed the door I told myself I would have to find time to see Mrs. Kelly and ask her to be my good friend in my story telling, which was all for the right reasons, or was it?

Maggie was waiting at the crossroads. In the pram, she had little Rosy at one end and baby Josie at the other. She was rocking the pram and looking anxious as I approached.

She didn't give me time to open my mouth but started walking immediately pushing the pram with one hand and pulling me with her other until we turned out of the lane and on to the road. The answer, she said was simple. As long as she took care of the babies, her Ma was happy, so money was not the real issue with her. The answer she came up with as we walked to the factory was not so simple.

We would have to find somewhere to hide the babies but be near enough for her to keep slipping back to see them and spend some time with them. As they were so small she insisted they did a lot of sleeping! She had brought milk, and rags to change them when they wet themselves. I just shook my head in disbelief. How could we carry this off?
The sixpence she said would be split, four pennies for me, as I would be doing the majority of work and two pennies for our English box, which she had under the mattress of the pram for our future stash.

'Simple!' she said with a smirk. I had no other answer; I said we would try it for the day. What had we to lose?

There was a tiny store shed at the back of the factory, which had a small window and seemed to be derelict, so we decided to try our luck there (at least for the time being).
The babies were sound asleep so I took Maggie inside to meet the Foreman telling him we were here to give him 'double the work for the same money'.

"Double the trouble, no doubt." He retorted as he turned away disinterested in our eagerness.

We started work sweeping and collecting the shavings from the floor and moving them out back to a collecting area where they were stored under-cover. We worked without speaking but I nodded to Maggie from time to time to convince her she was doing the job right. When I did not see her, I knew for sure where she was and I was ready with my answer to those who asked; she was at the privy shed of course.

The very dangerous escapade of ours worked more or less without a hitch for weeks to come, only because the babies were so good. During the lunchtime we took them out of the pram and played with them, changed them, fed them and rocked them to sleep. Then we went back to our chores. I don't know what Maggie told her Mother about her days away from the house, or indeed if her Mother was interested as long as the babies came to no harm but we managed the pretence for over six weeks.

Then one afternoon I noticed that Maggie had been missing for quite some time and it just did not feel right. I decided to go outside with my bag of shavings only half-filled to find Maggie. I smiled at the men in the yard as I went passed them. When the coast was clear, I made for the shed. When I got nearer, I could hear Maggie pleading with a man inside the shed to let her be.

"Well, I can hold a secret at a price, pretty girl," he was saying, "but you have got to play fair with me now."

I looked through the window and could see Maggie lying on the floor with her feet tied together and the man struggling to tie her hands behind her back. She was fighting with all her might as this had happened to her once before but she was no match for the big man.

"Look," she was saying, "I don't care how much wood you are stealing and hiding, I won't say a word if you don't."

"Oh, it will take more than your mouth to stay shut to please me my girl, I'm a bit short on the pleasure front if you know what I mean."

I was petrified by what I saw but also I was boiling-up inside at the thought that Maggie should have to go through another ordeal with a man she could not control. I looked around for something to use as a weapon and saw a hefty piece of wood lying close to the door, maybe dropped by this villainous man on his way into the shed. I didn't stop to think but charged in and flayed out at the man with all the strength I could muster. One blow sent him reeling to the ground but I took no chances and hit him again and again. I was hitting him with a fury I could not control and hatred I could not explain.

The cries of Maggie and the sobbing of the babies were only background noise against the loud thud I could feel and hear with each blow. The rage and injustice of all the big men who took advantage of young girls was my one and only battle at that moment. Men who used their strength to get their pleasures, men who expected you to work and then not pay you, men who bossed you to work like a dog for very little money and men who would kill horses for meat; well I would make meat of them. Yes, I would stop all this injustice. I do not know why I stopped but God only knows I did not want to.   Maybe, it was Maggie shouting that brought me to my senses.

I untied Maggie and she immediately went to the babies to console them as I looked down on my 'good deed' lying in a pool of blood on the ground. I could not believe what I saw. Had I done this to a man? A man I didn't know, a man who might have a wife and family of his own somewhere out there.

I was hot, sweaty and feeling quite dizzy as I looked down at my hands still holding the stick of justice. My mouth was dry and I was sick to the pits of my stomach but I could not move. God had frozen me to the spot! I was sure I was turning into stone and they would put my stone face outside the Cathedral to warn others of the wrath of God.
Then I heard Maggie's voice speaking to me in a mixture of English and Irish, words and sentences that made no sense to me. However, it

brought me back to my sanity and I tried to concentrate on what she was saying.

I threw the stick down and sank to the ground on my knees asking God to forgive me and tell me what to do. Maggie put her arms on my shoulders and her head on top of mine as we both listened and looked at the groaning fiend that lay in the corner.

"I just wanted to stop him, Maggie." I stuttered, "I didn't want it to happen to you again. Why did he come? We were doing just fine. Is he going to die? Oh! God help me, I didn't mean to hit him so hard. I thought the blow would stun him so he would leave you be. Now he isn't moving and he's covered in blood, Maggie, Oh Maggie," I cried covering my face with my hands as I dropped further to the ground.

I lay there aching with guilt but full of recrimination for the man who lay near me. Was I such a wretch that they, 'the men of justice in Tuam' would send me to prison? I started to cry and sob; I wanted my Ma, and my Grandma. I wanted them to pick me up, to cuddle me, to stroke my head, tell me they would take care of it. Make it go away and tell me it did not happen. I rolled over pulling my knees up to my face trying to make my body as small as possible, hoping the ground would swallow me up and I could sink into the ground and be lost like my sister.

"Please stop Caty; you're frightening the babies and me for that matter," I heard Maggie say. "You always know what to do, Caty, please get up, please I have to get the babies back, I don't know what to do, you always tell me Caty, you always have. I have no food left for them. The man is groaning he isn't dead; he's badly hurt I know, but we can get him help. Caty, pull yourself together, I need you. Caty I need you."

Through the haze of my self-destruction, I heard Maggie's plea. I wasn't sure if I wanted to let go and face reality by standing up, but I knew I didn't want to go through the ground and into the 'Fire of Hell'. So I slowly rose from my pit of despair and tried to face the world again knowing that I had to solve this on my own. There was no one there to help us.

I did not come up with the solution but Maggie seemed to have some ideas to try. I was to start off home with the babies and Maggie should report to the Foreman that she had heard loud noises coming from the shed as she took her shavings to the compound. She was to say it sounded like a very bad fight so she had come to tell him before she headed on home.

I did not have a better solution, I said we could try it and I would wait for her at the crossroads. I could not go back inside the factory there was blood on my hands and dirt from the shed floor all over my clothes. I pushed the pram to the edge of the River Clare and cleaned myself as best I could. I filled the babies jug with the cool water and shared it with the children. They gave me a sweet smile of innocence that somehow consoled me and I smiled back. I tucked them in and continued down the path I sat on the stone wall that divided the field from the road, and waited.

I don't remember if Maggie was a long time in coming or not, my mind was blank as I rocked the pram, but she arrived very excited.

"They believed me, Caty," she said breathlessly, "I told them to go quickly to the shed as there was a terrible raucous going on. I followed them, the Foreman and his mate Patrick O'Donnel and what do you think they said? Well I will tell you. They were ahead of me going through the door and they pushed me back saying this was not a sight for a young girl like me to see."   She was laughing and shaking her head as she continued her story.
"So, the foreman told Mr O'Donnel to help him carry the man back to the factory where they could clean him up, I waited outside and heard them talking quietly. They knew this man was stealing wood but did not know where he was storing it. It seems he would hoard it in the

shed and then go back for it at night. They speculated that if that was the case, then maybe his accomplice and the man could have got into a fight about the wood. Consequently they did not have much pity for the man. The important thing was Caty, that they said he was not going to die but have a terrible bad headache for days to come. Especially after getting the sack for stealing; that was going to be the outcome."

They told me to scoot off home and thanked me for telling them. They knew the man was stealing wood but couldn't prove it without the evidence, so now I had helped them solve a big problem and I was a brave little girl.
"There you are Caty, we are free and clear, but I tell you I was truly scared back there; I couldn't do that very often."

"'Well, I don't intend to Maggie. I am finished with sweeping up the factory. I'm never going back there; never in a month of Sundays will they get me back there."

"Well I shall go back one more time," Maggie said to my surprise, "just to collect our wages. I don't think he will refuse us our money if I tell him that the violence shocked me and we couldn't face looking at that shed ever again."
'That is the truth, that is the truth." I replied as we both put one hand on the pram and the other round each other and jointly pushed the pram along the lane back to the comfort of our homes and families.

Chapter 10
Counting the Time

I slept soundly that night, much to my surprise and decided to go to the Cathedral and ask Mrs. Kelly if she would help me with the words for a confession. I wanted to repent and get forgiveness. I wanted the episode out of my mind.

When I got there, much to my surprise Mrs. Kelly was cleaning the pews. She ran to me with open arms, said God had answered her prayers, and he had brought me back. I was confused but decided to keep quiet and smile. Apparently, Mrs. Raftery's Kathleen could not manage the children, especially when two of them became sick, so she had left the job yesterday and here I was now to fill the breach again! God had answered her like a flash (so she thought).

I decided just to nod and took the cleaning dusters from her hand; my confession would just have to wait. I got to my knees between the pews and started my cleaning in unison to my recitation of numerous 'Hail Mary's' hoping my reciprocal actions might take the place of a confession.

I continued my 'safe' job at the Cathedral for weeks to come and needless to say I did eventually make my confession after having a few coaching lessons from the knowledgeable Mrs. Kelly on the finer art of 'word choice.' She knew how to say confession in English and in Irish. She would teach me in English she told me with pride. I, however, was still shocked at the temper and rage inside of me that day. I never knew I had fury like that.

Life was calm now and I was still earning money for our 'English box'. The furrow in my brow cleared for good when I heard the 'fiend' had hopped a boat and took off abroad. He'd probably had made his money from selling wood. I was relieved and began to smile again. Even Mrs. Kelly would say I was going 'bonnier by the day'.

My smile grew even wider one particular day when Mrs. Kelly and I were having a break with tea and toast (as was our rule at mid-day). Her English had improved a lot and her vocabulary was getting greater every day, much to her delight. She was chatting on as usual about her son in England, and how proud he would be to hear her speaking English so well. I asked her about the route he had taken to get to Dublin and then to England. Very slowly she gave me the details, smiling at her new found accomplishment. He had taken the train to Dublin with money she had given him. She had been able to do this from selling the gifts that the archbishops had given her for birthdays, Christmas, and holidays. He had taken the paddle steamer 'Wicklow', a B&I Steamer from the North Wall to Holyhead, England. The crossing had taken eleven to twelve hours and was very dangerous, so she recounted. She said he was lucky to have had a safe crossing because she heard from one of the parishioners that shortly after her son had taken that journey the very same steamer had collided with another called 'Prince Ja Ja' when entering Liverpool docks, on account of the bad fog that day. She was convinced her prayers for him to have a safe journey had been heard.

I nodded my approval but I needed more information. "Do you know, Mrs Kelly, the price of travel on these steamers?"

She told me that prices varied a lot depending on what class of passage you took. Her son had taken a 'deck single' that was one way but there was a cheaper rate called steerage, which meant you travelled like cargo, and it was not very comfortable! The price she had heard was around three pence a passenger with free bread. All this information was 'food for thought' for me and I soaked in every detail.

A few days later, she had more information. An old friend of her son's had dropped by to see how she was going on and told her of another way to get to Dublin he had heard of. It was possible to get a ride on a canal barge at Athlone, if it was not full of cargo. There was no charge but you were not allowed any furniture or luggage and you had to travel alongside the horses or cattle they might be carrying. He said he thought it was about 200 miles from Athlone to Dublin. She wasn't sure how frequently they travelled through Athlone but she did know the boats were known as 'Canal Packets'. Well, she thought that was the pronunciation.

I could not wait to see Maggie and tell her all my news and to count our money. We usually did this twice a week just for fun. Maggie had been helping at one of the farms during harvesting, so she had also added to the box.
She was excited when I told her the news about the 'canal package', especially the bit about free travel. Sharing a small space with animals was not a discomfort in Maggie's book; some were cleaner than humans.

We discussed at length all the people we knew from our parts who had gone to England and each of us decided to find out as much as possible from their families about where to go when we reached there. We had a lot more planning to do before our adventure was to begin.
I wandered back to our house racking my brains for the right questions to ask and whom I would ask that would tell me the truth about England. It was a well-known fact in Tuam that some men had come back disappointed. I did not want that to happen to me. If I made the move it would be for good. I could not return with my tail between my legs and admit defeat, but I had to know what to expect and then I could prepare for it.

The sun hadn't gone down in the Autumn sky but I couldn't see Michael and Pa outside as usual. I thought they might have gone over to the far neighbour's fields to help them. I walked into the kitchen to see Michael feeding the younger ones and gesturing with his head towards the bedroom door. I moved slowly towards the door and pushed it open, just a little, enough for me to see what was going on.

M'Pa never came into the house before dark and Ma never left the babies with our Michael. Something was not right with this situation. I walked to the bed where m'Ma sat with a bowl of water and a small towel mopping m'Pa's head. I looked down at him but at once, I had to gasp and cover my mouth from making too much sound. I could not believe what I saw. I hadn't taken notice of m'Pa too much in the last few weeks but he was never so small, I was sure of that. He was coughing and spluttering as he grabbed the towel and I could see he was coughing up blood. He was breathing very unevenly and seemed to have a fever; his shirt was damp with sweat although he was telling Ma he was cold. I asked m' Ma what I should do and she told me to go for Grandma and Uncle John.

I went into the kitchen and told our Michael to go to fetch them and I would look after the children. They were not babies anymore they could play together and keep quiet if they knew what was good for them. I went back into the bedroom to take fresh water and towels to Ma. I tried to comfort her with a small hug as I could see she was crying. Tears were rolling down her face but no noise came from her, only from my Pa who was struggling to take each breath and making the most distressing noises. He was holding his chest with his thin bony fingers that held no flesh on them at all.

"Let's lift him up, Ma," I said, "maybe he could catch his breath better if we lifted him up a bit?"
Ma did not question me but together we lifted his frail, weak body further up the bed and pushed another pillow behind him. He was as light as a feather and I could feel every bone in his back jutting out into my hand like the teeth of a large comb when you pick it up the wrong way. He coughed, gurgled, and choked on his saliva forcing him to spit

out the blood filling in his mouth. He shook his head and cursed his maker for the indignities he felt.

"It's no matter Pa" I said trying to soothe him, "cough it up, it will clear your chest, it doesn't bother me, really it doesn't."

Ma had left the room for more towels and m'Pa was patting my hand and shaking his head.
"Look after them Caty, look after them for me, you're a strong one you are. I could always rely on you to come through," he gasped. He held me tight as he continued to keep my attention to listen to his words.
"I know I haven't been the best of Fathers", he struggled, "I know ....but I did try,......... God knows I tried ....but the land it wouldn't sprout. Your Ma needs you Caty; she does not have the spirit you have. Take care of her for me. I am tired of fighting. Take me God before she comes back. Let me........'

He fell back on the pillows with his mouth and his eyes still open but I knew he was gone so I quickly shut his eyes and his mouth as best I could before m'Ma and Grandma, who I could hear outside, came in.

"He's gone," was all I managed to say.

Ma rushed to the bed and fell on top of him sobbing. Grandma sat by her for comfort.

I had another picture for my memory bank, but this time it was not a happy one. Nevertheless, they still stay forever in your mind as clear and sharp as if it happened yesterday, never fading with age, never failing to bring the lump to your throat or the water to your eyes, however many years pass by. The recall of these pictures you never ask for, but when you least expect it they appear like a flash, years later, just to make you appreciate that your past stays with you. The present and past co-exist, like it or not. That is not one of my Grandma's saying either; it was one of mine. I used it regularly in the years to come.

I heard later from Grandma that Pa had died from tuberculosis; a hard word to say so folks usually called it TB. He didn't deserve to die so young; everyone said at his wake. "All this young family, what is to become of them?" I heard this remark repeatedly by the mourners, however; they did not stay around long when the food and drink had gone.

Chapter 11
Shaping the future!

A few weeks after m'Pa died, I knew we had to do something quickly. My money and the small amount Michael earned from helping the neighbours with their fields came to very little. Our land was still barren, or so we thought; we had no the money to buy the seed, or equipment to plough the land, to find out. We had to look for a better life, and England was the nearest place for us that had tales of money being made.

Good job m'Pa was not alive to hear me praise the 'slimy English' to Mrs. Kelly. She had only good words to say for them; after all didn't her son send her money every week to prove it so. The Bishop helped her read his letters so she knew a lot about his life over there.
"They're not all Protestants Caty, you will still be able to find Our Lady and a confession box," she said with conviction.

I wasn't sure if I would be looking for a confession box, if I ever got there. A few boxes of furniture and a roof over my head would be my first priority. However, I did not let Mrs. Kelly in on my thoughts I needed more information from her.

"What exactly does your son do there, Mrs. Kelly?' I asked trying to sound matter of fact.

"He works just outside the city of Manchester in the coalmines of Astley colliery, I think the name is. He has met a young girl who works at sorting coal at the pithead. She's a bonny looking girl, so I'm told.....'

Mrs. Kelly was rambling on about her son's intended, but all I was interested in was that they employed women at the pit and that must mean real money, big money. I could not get to Maggie's fast enough to tell her my latest news.

When I got there Maggie was in the bedroom, but her Ma told me, I could go in to see her. I opened the door and went in. Maggie was stripped to the waist trying on a bra that was obviously too big for her. She would have needed an apple in each cup to fill the space.

"What on earth are you doing Maggie? That's too big for you, where did you get it?'

"I borrowed it from Ma; she told me I could try it on. Oh, Maggie I want to wear a bra before we go to England. I want to look like that woman in the window of Mrs. Beatty's shop in Tuam. I am as flat as a pancake with one lump of sugar on each side; I want curves, Caty."

"Well, let me tell you it's no fun having too much in front either," I said with passion. ."My one and only bra is too tight and cuts into my shoulders something rotten!"

"Now, I'd rather have too much than too little Catherine Luby; at least you have shape."

"I have big boobs and a big backside and big hands and big feet; if you'd like me to go on." I said before laughing aloud. "He will have to be a big fellow to get his hands around me, now wouldn't he just?"

"Caty, Caty don't make me laugh so much, tell me what to do."

"Well all I can think of is to cut up a pair of your old knickers, they're soft enough, and stick them into the cups." I said it as a joke but it took Maggie no time at all to start cutting up a pair of her old knickers and pad them into the bra. She then paraded around the room sticking out her new breasts and shaking them from side to side to see the effect.

"Just a minute young woman," I said as she passed me, "I think I can see something I shouldn't." I stepped close and slowly pulled out the elastic she had left in the knickers.

I lifted it out, impressively, slowly, but the end was stuck, so I pulled again and it flipped out! The elastic made a pinging sound as it snapped back on to my hand, causing me to shout out my pain in an amusing way.

"Thank heaven I was the one to find that, Margaret my girl" I said pompously and slowly, "and not an English suitor!"

We began to giggle so much at the thought of a man finding the knicker elastic that we had to cross our legs in mirth to stop the flow of water filling our own clean knickers. When Maggie's Ma came in to see what was happening all I could do was run past her to get to the outside privy fast.

When I came back, Maggie had dressed herself, minus the padding and was sitting on the bed looking serious again. I asked her why she had a long face, all of a sudden. She bit on her bottom lip and explained that it was impossible for her to leave her Ma just now because of all the children that needed to be looked after. Maybe in a year or so when they were older it might be easier. I understood fully what she meant; I knew she loved her family too much to leave them when they needed her.

"All right Maggie," I said with a nod of my head, "but don't be too long in following me out there. I intend to start making tracks as soon as I can and I think now is the time for me to go. God knows I'm all set to get out of here and start a fresh."

Yes, I was ready. I had put into words just what I was thinking silently. Now I had to put this to my family and suggest they join me, but if not,

I had to go myself. I had saved enough for us all to go but if they did not want to join me, I would leave them some of my money to get by. My last thought was one I was not happy about, I would surely need some money when I got there to survive until I had a job.

Oh! How my head ached when I had these problems. Why wasn't life simple anymore? Would I ever find someone who would take care of me, hold me and tell me "Not to worry luv I'll take care of it."
There I was again – living in Cuckoo land!

Chapter 12
Plans, Promises and Pleasure.

For the next few weeks, I discussed my plans with everyone who would listen. Some people wished me luck; others told me I must not go without the family. Some locals gave me addresses to go to where relatives lived. As I could not read and write I didn't quite know how these would help, but I took them anyway. One bit of luck happened once again in the Cathedral. Who was it that said God looked after his own? I don't think that was Grandma.

I was working on the alter silver when Mrs. Kelly came walking down the aisle tightly holding a young man like a bride on her wedding day. She was speaking in a "posh" English voice, obviously to show off. She must have been practicing.

"Look who I have brought to see you Caty, my wonderful son all the way from England. The one I told you about who gets money from the ground in plenty. Lord save us and keep us, he does me proud now doesn't he?"

"Hallo Caty," he said. "I've heard a lot about you from m'Ma, all good I have to say. By the way, we get coal from the ground, not money, at least not until the end of the week when we pick it up from the office. I believe you are thinking of coming there, is that right?"

"Well, I have a lot to sort out before I go, but that's the general plan I have."

He hummed his approval and then with a gentle smile (an infectious smile he had from his mother) he told me how to get in touch with him in England. I was to head east when I reached Liverpool, not hang around in that city, if I could help it. He was talking so fast I just hoped it was all sinking in. It was possible he said to catch a coal barge that ran from the River Mersey into the Bridgewater canal and thus to the coalmines of East Lancashire. He rambled on telling us of fifty miles of underground canals from a place called Worsley that carried the coal. "It is a wonder to behold the feats of engineering; you couldn't imagine!"

I had no idea what he was talking about. The English words he used I had never heard before and I wondered if I would even be able to talk to the English people if I got there.
He could see I was puzzled so he used a little of the Irish and the English to explain that if I got there I was to get to Astley Green Colliery, that was where he worked and I had to go to the office and ask for him. If he was down the mine I had to wait until he came up, but he would help me find somewhere to settle as best he could. He knew the area well and he could find me a place to rent and maybe find work at the mine.

"Didn't I tell you my boy would help?" She said proudly. "You just remember the very important names he has given you, its best you follow his advice and learn them. I'll get the Bishop to write them down for me that will surely help now wouldn't it?"

"Yes, yes, of course, but just one thing more" I said with a puzzled face, "what's your name?"

They both laughed and together in unison they said, "'Jar lath, Jarlath after our patron saint of course."
I thanked them and told Jarlath I hoped to see him before he left, if he could? I wanted to make sure I had all the right information firmly in my head. It was the most important information anyone had ever given me; I had to understand it well. He seemed like a nice man and why shouldn't he be; he was Mrs. Kelly's only son.

They left me working with my heart full of joy, so much so I just had to sing and this I did, loud and clear. I marveled at the echoes and resonance of my voice, a voice I had never tried this way before, but I loved it. I hoped the good Lord did also? I polished hard, rubbing the silver with all the gusto I could. As I lifted it up in front of me, I imagined I was making an offering on the altar to the Lord for his kindness. I sang;

Holy, Holy, Holy
Lord God Almighty
Early in the morning my song shall rise to Thee
Holy, Holy, Holy, Merciful and Mighty
God in three Persons, Blessed Trinity.

All morning I worked like a beaver and sang until my voice began to crackle, so I stopped. I did not want the Lord to think I was a cock crowing inside His House! I finished all my work and left for home. I had a skip in my step and a smile on my face; the first for a long time. I knew I was on my way. I had a place to head for and a person to help me when I got there.

England here I come, on my own or not. Ma would have to make up her mind soon.
As I walked towards the farm I could see Michael working in the field with his friend Eddie O'Rourke and they both shouted and waved to me. I thought I would join them for a little chat, as I was feeling so good.

"You're looking mighty pleased with yourself," said Michael as I walked towards them.

"Well why shouldn't I after a good day's work?" I said back to him. "The night is fine and fresh so all's good in the world."

Eddie did not stop working to join our conversation, but for the first time I noticed his big strong back, his long lean arms and large hands that were pulling up the cabbages. He lifted up a handful and his face beamed and flushed to match his hair. He was a good foot bigger than Michael was, even though they were the same age. There were no girls in their family, just six boys so his Pa often sent him to our house to help us. Sensing his awkwardness, I asked them if they would like a drink to quench their thirst, and of course they agreed it was what they needed.

I glanced back before entering the kitchen and wondered why I should feel an excitement in my stomach when I looked at Eddie. Strange, I had never had a feeling like it before. I gave my Ma a squeeze around her shoulders and told her I was taking water out to the boys. She told me to take some potato bread to go with it as, they had been out a long time without a break. I wrapped the bread that was hot from the oven in a cloth and put it in a basket with the mugs. I filled the water carrier and went back out to the field.

I placed the basket down near the wall and shouted for them to join me. I could not take my eyes off Eddie, why did he look so different to me all of a sudden; I had known him all my life for heavens sake? My eyes followed his mop of red hair to his big wide shoulders, his narrow waist, and his tight breeches. With each movement of his legs my eyes became more transfixed to the bottom half of his body. His loins were covered but my imagination held no bounds.

I hadn't noticed before that our Michael's friend had transformed into a man and I hadn't had feelings between my legs before; little twinges of excitement. I would have to ask Maggie about this soon. They both sat down on the grass beside me, Michael at my side and Eddie just in front. I moved the basket between Michael and myself so I could have a better view of Eddie who sat with both his knees up, but apart.

85

"It's a warm evening," I said with a gulp, "help yourselves, I'm no servant."

They began to tuck into the bread, taking great mouthfuls that prevented further conversation for time being, so I poured the water.

"My, I didn't think I was so hungry," said Eddie when he had emptied his mouth, "but, I was ready for that, thanks Caty for thinking about us."

I was watching his mouth and not listening to his words, I was mesmerized by the fullness of his lips. I smiled shyly feeling all the time I was hot and flushed for no reason I could understand at that moment. I had to get away.
I picked up the cloth and the mugs and put them back into the basket and tried to say as casually as possible, "See you later."

After supper that night, I said I was tired so I would go to bed early. I wanted to be alone before any of my brothers and sisters joined me. I undressed to my slip and took off my knickers that felt rather damp. I wasn't sure why I felt this need between my legs, which I wanted to touch and keep there forever. I shuddered with excitement and pleasure, a pleasure I had never had before. Why did Eddie look so beautiful to me? I fell asleep exhausted and satisfied in my dreams but unsure of my contentment.

Chapter 13
The final Decisions

It was difficult for me to bring up the subject of going to England. We seemed to have one crisis after another in the weeks after Pa died. I had to be convincing. I knew that most people in our parts did not think it right and proper for a girl to go off alone. It was fine for a young man to try to find a better life but a girl should get married and settle down with her own kind.

It was no use, I had to concoct a story that would convince everyone that I had to go to England for a definite reason. I mulled about with several stories that never came to anything. Then, quite unexpectedly Mrs. Kelly began telling me about her son's wedding plans in England and how she wished she had the stamina to go on that long journey. It was to be a June wedding at a Cathedral in Manchester.
"Oh! Caty I wish I was younger and his Pa was alive, what a wonderful pair we would have made strutting down the aisle," she said this as she paraded down the middle aisle as though to accentuate the point.
I watched, all the while my brain was ticking over the possibility of my idea. So, having nothing to loose I suggested, "Maybe I could go in your place, so to speak, a kind of 'proxy' for you?"

I said it again using the Irish I knew to try to convince her and as I pulled her down to sit in a pew I smiled and nodded and looked with all my heart into her eyes. Willing her to agree to my suggestion, squeezing her hands into mine and praying in my head she would say something positive. I waited, licking my dry lips. She seemed stuck to the pew. Why did she not answer?

I tried again, very quietly and slowly using a mixture of languages to explain that I would go willingly in her place and make sure someone from his homeland was there.

"It was only right and proper he had someone there to represent his family," I said in my most comforting voice, "what do you think Mrs. Kelly; I would like to do that for you?"

At last she answered me, but as she was now crying at the same time it was hard for me to understand if it was a 'yes' or a 'no'. I decided to put my arms around her until she could compose herself. Slowly she began to explain that she was going to ask her brother to go, but the 'old sod' had never had children of his own so didn't understand love and affection of any kind, unless they had four legs and could work or feed him. She went on to say she had offered to pay his passage but using the cheapest way possible, if only he would go. He had told her he would get back to her in a few days, but she had heard nothing yet.

"Never mind Mrs. Kelly I'm sure he will go and if you like I will go too and together we will put on a show of goodwill that will knock the blocks off all those English, what do you say to that now?"

A smile began to cross her face and her head shook from side to side as she patted my cheek. My lips were dry again but I had no saliva left to moisten my satiable need for a positive answer. I wanted to shake her with the frustration of it all. Could she not see I was the answer to her problem? Not to mention she was the answer to mine.

She looked down to our clasped hands and then she turned to look at the altar. (Would this woman never understand how simple this could be?) I tried not to rush her but all the time wanting to move my hands away and stand up to make myself look more in charge of the situation. Just in time, she spoke and I knew that once more God was watching over me in the Cathedral of the Assumption. My life was beginning to look up again and probability could take over from possibility as I listened with joy to Mrs. Kelly's words.

"Well, young Catherine Luby you did get on like a house on fire with my Jarlath and if I remember rightly he asked you to visit him over there. I would like nothing better than you go with his uncle to England, and represent me at his wedding. In fact I will speak to your Mother and Grandmother myself, to get their blessings, as soon as I get an answer from Uncle Ned. I do not know how you two will get along because he cannot be doing with women and girls, so he tells me. Perhaps you will find something in common to ease the way. Now let's get back to work and talk about this another time, alright young Caty?"

I was more than all right, I was elated, and I was enthused with pleasure and excitement. My entire body wanted to sing and shout in praise and so I did as I polished. I sang and to my amazement Mrs. Kelly joined me in song, our voices full of harmony; together we praised the Lord, for he was good. After all, he had brought us together once more to solve our mutual problems. Perhaps there is a 'master plan' weaving and shaping our lives. If only we could see it. At that moment, it was enough to feel it. I was prepared for the consequences that lay ahead. Onward Christian Soldiers...I had heard this song somewhere.

Chapter 14
Preparation Time

I decided to say nothing to no one until I knew definitely that Uncle Ned was going to the wedding, and more to the point that he would take me along.

That day I had been helping Ma with the washing. It took us a full day from early in the morning until dusk to do this chore. The soaking in soda, the boiling in the brick boiler, the mangling, and the drying, all was heavy work, even with all the girls helping. That particular day was a warning of the winter days to come, and so there was no hope of pegging out the clothes to dry. The clothes were everywhere; on the maiden round the fire, across the kitchen on a string, hanging from the back of chairs; just everywhere. The air inside the cottage was clammy and humid. Even the smell of the stew cooking on the fire was overtaken by the damp smell of clothes steaming in that small space. I needed to go outside even if it was cold and icy. I put on my outdoor heavy coat and scarf and told mother I was going to fetch more peat. She nodded and continued to stir the pot of stew on the fire.

Outside I could hear voices in the barn and recognized them to be Uncle John talking to Michael, so I decided to join them. They were laughing together as they cleaned the meagre farm machinery we had. Telling jokes that were not for my ears from the way they stopped in mid-sentence when I appeared in front of them.

"Don't stop for me," I said as I made myself comfortable on a bundle of hay.

"Well, I've just finished the tale as it happens," said Uncle with a smirk on his face and a nod to our Michael. So, I decided to change the subject to something closer to my heart at that time.

"Do you know Mrs. Kelly's brother Ned O'Brian, by any chance Uncle John?"

"Now why would you be asking about him young Caty? As a matter of fact I know him well."

I didn't want to say too much at that time but I did need to know if I had anything in common to talk to Ned O'Brian about., anything I could pursue the 'old sod' (as Mrs. Kelly called him) to have me as his companion or such on the journey to England. I treaded carefully and chose my words cautiously as I asked for the right information I needed. I skirted around telling Uncle John I worked with Mrs. Kelly, as he knew, and she did not seem to have many good words to say about him.

"Now that might be because of Mrs. Kelly's religious leanings and his tendency towards a few pennies on the horse racing. There is nothing the man likes better than to go down to Ballybrit Racecourse at Galway and see them close-up. As the man does not boast a family of his own I suppose he should be able to spend his money as he wishes. Heaven only knows what he does with it 'cause he can never pay his bill in full as he leaves Duffy's after a night out."

I listened intently to all Uncle John said but then flippantly changed the subject to ask about the difference between the workhorses I knew and the racehorses of the world. I had obviously picked a good subject for Uncle John to talk about; there was just no stopping him as he described, in detail, how supreme the Irish race horses were to others.

He began in a soft voice to say, "Nowhere will one find such magnificent specimens of horseflesh as in Ireland, and nowhere will you

91

find a more horse-loving people." His voice was clear and loud as he spoke to his captive audiences who were both enjoying his favourite subject.

"Nature has supplied us with the ideal grass and water for the development of horses and then endowed us with the love and understanding of them."

He paused and rubbed his hands together before he drew in the air the shapes he was describing; "The Irish racehorse has a great bony structure, which includes its feet. It might have a smaller brain than the dog or pig, but they have the biggest hearts and are sought after the world over; you remember that." he ended with his finger pointing to us for acknowledgement.

We were enjoying his descriptions and asked him to go on. He told us we must never, under no circumstances, criticize a man's horse because an Irishman will always sing its praises loud and long and never admit that his horse has anything wrong. Every obvious fault has some explanation, and he gave us examples.

"The capped hock is 'but a bit of a bruise' he got last week and what could you expect the way he was 'lapin' the timber'. The cloudy eye is 'just because he's after staring in the sun."
The stories went on and on, now I was sure I had found something in common with Mr. O'Brian and I was determined find out more.

"Does anyone keep racehorses here in Tuam?" I asked in a matter of fact voice.

"No, not exactly in Tuam but in Ballinasloe you can see the finest of breeds. You know there is a group of us going by traps from Duffy's Pub to the Winter Fair next week, maybe you two would like to come along in my horse and cart?"

Both Michael and I spoke at once pleading him to take us with him. Our evident interest stirred him into more information.

"Well its common knowledge that buyers from all over the world come to the fair, especially from Europe. Do you realize that Napoleon's great horse Marengo, which he rode at the Battle of Waterloo, was bought at Ballinasloe Fair?"

As neither Michael nor I knew who Napoleon was, or had ever heard of a Battle of Waterloo it took Uncle John another hour as he told us about this historical event. We would have been there through the night I am sure, had not m'Ma come to find us and tell Uncle John to get back home to Grandma.

I went to bed that night with my head filled with horse stories that I was sure would enthrall Mr. O'Brian.

Chapter 15
A believable story?

The weeks before Christmas were very dim and dismal except for our visit to the horse fair. That had proven to be a real revelation for me. I had never seen so many different types of people. Old and young, rich and poor; all having one thing in common and that was the magnificent Irish ponies. I saw money changing hands in the fistfuls and all horses were bartered on the shake of a hand and a nod of the head.

The music and dancing, the laughter and singing just uplifted the spirit to a sense I could not compare, so it is hard for me to describe. I was mesmerized by the sheer pleasure the whole experience gave me.

I listened to the horse-trading jargon and tried to remember the good points they mentioned when describing the virtues of each horse. I learned to guess the height in 'hands' before it was said and found I had quite an 'eye for detail' as Uncle John put it. I realized that my whole life could change if I could only speak the language of 'Horsemanship'. Mrs. Kelly's brother would not expect me to know these facts. I would make him like me. The funny part about it was that I really liked my newfound knowledge. It seemed to come like second nature to me. I relished in every detail.

That day was a turning point for me. It was a day that horses and Catherine Luby started an affiliation that was to last a lifetime. I always had a good idea, which horse would win a race for the rest of my life. No matter what anyone else said.

Mrs. Kelly introduced me to her brother just a week after the horse fair so the 'jargon' and the excitement of it all were still with me. She made tea for us in the small kitchen in the refectory and I began to impress her brother as best I could with the tales of the fair. He was surprised, I could see it, but he made me very awkward all the same. His eyes were the roaming kind that looked at me anywhere but in my face. His mouth had a funny twitch on the right side that was neither a smile nor a smirk. He made me very uncomfortable even though there was a large wooden table between us.

Mrs. Kelly mashed the tea and sat down next to me explaining her idea for the journey to England. She was going to pay his expenses to attend the wedding on her behalf. Mr. O'Brian just stared back at us, even his mouth had stopped twitching and after looking at me and then back at Mrs. Kelly, he coughed, without covering his mouth, and then said, "Well, how much money are we talking about now? It takes a fair bit of money to get to England, you know."

"I will not see you short," said Mrs. Kelly, "and young Catherine has got her own travelling money."

"A travelling companion with her own money," he sneered, "well I never! I shall have to think about this but it's very tempting, I'm sure." He nodded his head and tapped his long dirty hands on the table.

"Well, we'll have plenty of time to talk more about this after Christmas; the wedding is not until June. Come on Caty, back to work."

All three of us walked through the vestry and into the chancel. As we were passing the alter, Mr. O'Brian remarked on the silver chalices that adorned it and what a good job his hard-working sister must do on keeping them gleaming for all to see. Mrs. Kelly said nothing but led him to the door to say goodbye and I went back to work, not as enthusiastic as before with my potential travelling companion. In fact, I was not taken with the idea at all.

As Christmas approached Mrs. Kelly and I had a vast amount of cleaning to do. Many of the relics usually kept in storage were brought out for this grand celebration. Mrs. Kelly had a good reputation for making everything shine and glitter but her poor old hands did not have the strength they used to, so she depended on me for the 'elbow grease' and I, of course, obliged.

We were a good team and before the second Sunday in Advent, we were completely ready with all our relics on view. The white altar cloths were as white as the first baby snow of winter and reflected the candle glow that flickered from the shining candlesticks. We sat in the front pew together, tired but elated. The quietness was magical; there were no need for words to each other; just a silent prayer.

I left Mrs. Kelly to blow out the candles and close up the doors, as usual, and I made my way home. It was getting late and I was hungry and cold so I almost ran the journey home. It was always pleasant to get home to the family and the warm peat fire and that night was no different.

I walked to the Cathedral the next day knowing that most of the hard work had been done for Christmas and only the final touches here and there were needed to make the Cathedral shine for all God's children. As I approached the side door I could see a policeman (brought in from Galway for sure), they were talking to Archbishop McHale. They were speaking in Irish, very fast so I could not understand all they were saying. I was about to turn around when the constable asked me to come forward and say why I was there.

I thought this very strange, but I answered him to say I was coming to work, (a thing I did most days at this time) to clean the church with Mrs. Kelly. On hearing this they both looked at each other, and back to me. Then the Archbishop spoke in English, "There's been an accident, girl," he stuttered patting my head with his soft white hand. "Mrs. Kelly has been hit on the head and has gone now to the hospital, come inside and sit down while the constable asks you some questions."

I followed them into the Cathedral and could not believe my eyes. The constable was talking, I knew, but I was not listening. All I could see was destruction. Our beautiful, magical place I had left the night before was now in shambles. The clean white altar cloths were strewn around the floor and the altar was in disarray. I was stricken with fear; I was completely horrified by the scene. Who could have done such a thing? The words were in my mind but nothing came out. My outside body was transfixed to the sight in front of me and my lips were pressed together tensely holding in my emotions. After a while I realized the constable was shaking my shoulder and speaking to me; I shook my head from side to side to answer him.

"We have some silver candlesticks missing and a precious goblet said to have come from Temple Jarlath. Unless someone is melting them down they would be very hard to exchange for money," the constable was explaining. "We will soon catch the itinerant whoever he is, I'll have him in the courthouse, and then the jail before you know it. He will not be leaving Tuam for a haven of rest, if Constable Raftery has any say in it. I will be off now to ask questions elsewhere; if you will be begging my pardon, Miss."

He spoke again to the Archbishop in a whispering voice and then I was alone sitting in the same pew as I had the night before. This time I was crying not praying, I was filled with anger and misery. I thought about the day before, of our hard work together, and of Mrs Kelly's brother. Yes, Mrs. Kelly's brother. Could that be? Would it be possible? He had remarked about the silver when I saw him last.

I took off my hat and coat and began the hard task of trying to bring back the order and beauty of the night before. All the time I was I was cleaning I was trying to answer the bewildering question of who would

97

do such a monstrous thing in the House of the Lord? Every time I asked myself, the same question, the same face would appear in my head. Mrs. Kelly's brother with his funny looking eyes. How terrible that he should hit his own sister to satisfy his own greed. He was a monster of the first degree. To think I was going to travel to England with this man. It did not bear thinking about.

I worked non-stop throughout the day. I did not feel like eating, it just didn't seem right until I began to feel dizzy and realized I was being watched by the Archbishop who was calling me to approach him at the main alter.
"I think you should stop work now, my child," he was saying in his soft spoken way, "the Lord is thankful for your dedication to hard work, so come forward for my blessing and the Holy sacrament."

I approached the altar full of trepidation and wonder why the Archbishop himself would choose to give me, Catherine Luby, his special blessing. I was still feeling dizzy through lack of food and drink that day. However, through the haze I remembered the formalities of celebrating the Eucharist. I went through the ritual feeling I was not inside my own body. It did not feel real, yet it was. I, Catherine Luby was getting the full 'treatment' by the Archbishop himself; my grandmother would never believe me.

There was a period of silence, then the Archbishop changed his voice to a louder and sterner note and told be to go home to my family and come back tomorrow to finish my good work. I nodded and backed away genuflecting with each step and questioning the apparent apparitions that seemed to glow from the scene in front of me. I grabbed my coat and went out of the side door, nearest to the altar and began to edge my way through the gravestones that marred my path. The wine had not helped my queasy stomach, but I knew I could not bring up the Holy Sacrament without bringing Hell and damnation on my soul. I rested on a tombstone trying to hold back my 'Heavenly Blessing'.

Breathing deeply and gulping strongly, I heard the most terrible noise, which stopped my next gasp for air and froze me to the spot.

The groaning noise was so close I knew it was the devil himself. The devil had come to make me sick and give up my own special sacrament. I put my hand over my mouth to stop this happening, but when I heard another moaning sound I answered it with an uncontrollable burp. This relieved my sickly feeling and gradually I could move and look around. The Holy bread and wine was now filling me with strength so a spoke out, "you don't frighten me you old devil, shut your noise and leave me be."

"Help me, please," came the garbled reply that had a familiar sound to it.

I moved cautiously from my riveted spot to peer behind the next tombstone where the sound seemed to be coming from. Sure enough, sprawled out, was a disheveled clump of clothing, which seemed to have a human form and a recognizable one at that! It was Mr. O'Brian, Mrs. Kelly's brother!

"Help me, please Caty help me," he cried as I knelt down beside him.

'What happened, for God's sake you look bad," I responded as I dug into my coat pocket for something to wipe away the blood from his face.

"I went to see my sister for a bit of a loan and we were attacked..You must have just left. The young thugs came into the church to get the silver and whatever money was around," He stuttered the words out in between his groans at my attempt to wipe his wounds.
"I chased them away after they hit Sis and then the pair set about me good and proper when I got outside. I think I must have passed out."

"Let me help you stand Mr. O Brian and then we can go back inside."

"No-way," he answered clearly, "just lend me a hand to get to Duffy's and the lads there will help me sort this mess out."

I did not like the idea, but I had no other suggestion and little strength left to argue. I was tired, hungry and perplexed with all that had happened. I needed little persuasion to pass this responsibility on to someone else. So, I lifted him up and hunched my shoulder under his arm to keep him upright. Together we made our way out of the graveyard.

We would have made a pretty picture if anyone had wanted to paint a representation of a homeless drunken couple, stumbling along the road to Duffy's Pub. We leant on each other struggling with each step to stay upright. Two bedraggled figures, having only the brightness of the stars to light their way. Groaning with each step, we scared even the rabbits from our path. With one smell of my wine soaked breath and a glance at his battered face, a sceptic could have made an obvious conclusion.

After an eternity we arrived at the door of Duffy's where I gave him a big push through the swing door and turned as quickly as I could into the field across which was the short cut to home. Agonizing with each step I took, until I reached the water pump outside our cottage where I drank my thirst away.

I tried to clean myself up so as not to frighten Ma. I would tell her only the part about the break-in and of course, of my own special blessing from Archbishop John McHale, himself; my reward for doing such a good job of cleaning. That would surely make her happy and keep her from asking some real questions? I had taken my coat off as I got through the door so she had not seen the bloodstains. Those I would deal with tomorrow. Now I was so tired I was falling to sleep in front of the family, in the middle of my 'heavenly story'.

Did I really receive a blessing from the Archbishop? Had I really found an injured man and took him to get help? Everything was so blurred, so unreal, so exhausting!

I could feel myself being lifted from the chair; maybe I was going to heaven itself for all my good deeds that day?

Chapter 16
Changes made to last.

The New Year began rather better than expected. I felt it was due to my very special blessing I had received from the Archbishop that had made God look down and notice Catherine Luby. I had grown bigger as each year had passed. l had big hands, big feet and yes, a very big bust to go with them but Grandma always told me to be proud of what God had given me and to hold my frame with head held high and shoulders back.

It was easy for her to say, but difficult for me to do with grace, luckily my backside was also big so it balanced me out overall. I walked the streets of Tuam with a confidence that grew from knowing I was strong in mind and body and happy and willing to meet any challenge with grit and determination. I would certainly need these attributes in the months to come.

It was well known by the villagers that the rich of this town always celebrated this time of the year
The Ladies from the Tuam Cricket Club social circle had a New Year celebration with a fund raising dance. I was told that the Archbishop had given a speech and told the crowd about the break-in at the Cathedral and how this 'little angel of the Lord' (his words not mine), had worked herself to the bone to get the place back to normal for the festive services.

 This very rich group of people then promised to give a reward for anyone who could give information leading to the arrest of these miserable thieves and the recovery, they hoped, of the silver. I listened to this news with awe as Mrs. Kelly told me that the Archbishop had asked her to his study and told her about the reward. However, there was more to tell and she sat me down in the pew and held my hand, patting it in her usual comforting way.

"I am to give you this envelope, Caty," she said, "The Archbishop was given it by the Ladies Circle to thank you for all you did. The ladies had a special collection which was just for you, a separate donation from the reward."

I took the envelope and opened it as carefully as I could with my big clumsy fingers and looked inside. My heart raced as I saw more money in one place than I had ever seen in my life.

"Is it really for me?" I asked, "all of it for me, but why would they give all this money to me?"

"Because you are the sweetest, most hard working girl I know Caty Luby; you alone put this church back to order for the most important day in the calendar. You deserve every penny and I told the Archbishop I did and all. It's yours, Caty, to do as you please and spend as you like, so put it away safe and lets get on with our work now."

I worked through the day in a dream-like state. I now truly had enough money for my travel to England and maybe a bit left over to help me start my new life, if I was careful. I went home that night walking on air, not a bit concerned with the bitter wet wind of January and the frosty paths we had at this time of the year.

When I opened the door I could see Uncle John talking to Ma and I took no time in pulling up my chair to join them round the warm peat fire.

"I will make you some supper Caty," Ma said "and you can hear what our John has to tell us."

I sat by the fire listening to an unbelievable story for the second time that day. Uncle John somehow knew I had helped Mr. O'Brian to Duffy's Pub that night. I think one of his friends was leaving the pub as

103

I threw Ned in? Uncle John was inside with his friends playing dominoes. He told us everyone was surprised in the Pub at the state of Ned O'Brian, but he walked past the local crowd and sat with some strangers at their table. One of them bought him a double whisky, which he drank quickly. The three men then bought several more which resulted, no doubt, in the argument that followed.

Uncle John stopped his story to sip the tea Ma had brought us and after wiping the drips away with the back of his hand, he continued. Uncle John's group of friends included Constable Raftery, off duty and in his plain clothes. They listened to these men but carried on playing their game as if they were not interested. Then they could not help but hear Ned O'Brian complain about being hit over the head by the two and left while they ran off with the loot. His voice was raised so loud and he was standing, so his voice carried every word. The two men had pulled him down and were pushing the drink down his throat so Uncle John and Constable Raftery went across to ask some obvious questions.

The two strangers had tried to run out of the Pub but the rest of the locals stopped them making their get-away. It apparently did not take long for a drunken Ned O'Brian to cry his confession to the Constable. They tied up the three conspirators and with some help took them in Uncle John's cart to the police barracks.

Uncle John told us they were eager to blame each other for the robbery, but it was obvious that Ned O'Brian had once been the ringleader. He had told these two men about the silver but the other two had got greedy and left him for dead in the graveyard where Caty had found him. Ned had told the police and Uncle John about how I found him that night and helped him get to Duffy's. Consequently, my secret was out.

The police had gone the next day to see for themselves the place where I had found Ned. They also found a grave disturbed and investigated. Ned O'Brian and the two men were going to bury the silver in the graveyard and come back the next day for it. They must have argued and hit Ned with something and fled.

"Now, to the important part of this story our Caty," said Uncle John in a very stern voice.

'I was given this reward money, six shiny shillings," he said slowly. "But I talked it over with my friend Raftery and your Ma and we all think this should be yours. You were the one who took Ned to Duffy's that led to the capture of the thieves. We just completed the arrest. What do you say about that? Do you accept?"

I was flabbergasted! Chewing the inside of my mouth I couldn't answer. I just stared at m'Ma and Uncle John thinking wildly. Do I tell them I had already received money for that night? I smiled very nervously and put my head down They took this as I sign I was embarrassed at their suggestion but I was calculating the amount I could get for my English fund in just one day! I accepted with all the grace I could muster!

Chapter 17
The way forward to my dream.

 I slept little that night as my head was swimming with the good fortune I had received. I decided to tell Ma the next day about my plans because now I had enough money for her to accompany me, if she wanted, or at least pay for someone else to go with me to England.

 I got dressed as soon as the sun began to rise, knowing that this new day would bring me the decisions I craved. I re-kindled the fire and started breakfast for the family; boiling the kettle to mash the tea and setting the table. Ma was surprised to see me up and about and seemed to anticipate that I had something on my mind.

"Well, out with it our Caty, something's gnawing at you, I can tell," she said in her motherly way.

I tried to approach the subject slowly, but then I just blurted out my wish to go to England for the wedding in June but added that I knew I had to have someone to go with me, I was aware I could not travel alone. I asked her if she would she go with me as I had the money to day for both of us?

I could tell by the way she shook her head that she was not happy about my idea and she was not going to go with me to England, all her excuses were feasible, so I had to go on with my pleadings.
"Perhaps, Uncle John could come with me? I can pay for him from the money I now have. Please Ma, can I talk to him and ask him, just let me try, please?"

I held her around her waist from the back and I laid my head on top of her head. I had grown a good deal taller than she was in the past year and I swung her around to face me and saw her face crack into a smile. "Do as you wish, my girl, 'cause I can see there is no stopping you with your crazy ideas, and if our John agrees, you have my blessing."

I could not contain my excitement and knew I had to go to see Uncle John immediately, this minute, right now, and at once! I grabbed my coat from behind the door and ran through the solid; icy fields as fast as my legs would carry me. Slipping and sliding on the white frosty grass, chasing my thoughts as they raced in front of me.
I had to gather myself at the door and get my breath back before I asked the most important question I had ever had to ask in my whole life. Uncle John was stoking the fire when I let myself in but turned around quickly to check who was there.

"Good Lord, Caty, you gave me a scare. Is your Ma and the babbies OK?"

"Yes, Uncle John," I answered quickly, "it's me who wants a word with you."

 I began by reminding him about Mrs. Kelly's son Jarlath and his wedding in June. How I had promised her to go to England to represent her on such an important day. I did not know how to put the last part (the important question) in any better way so I just hastily said that I wanted Uncle John to escort me. A word, I thought, that was very appropriate to the occasion. Then I sat down to wait for his decision. Shivering with the cold, or was it my nerves, I could not tell.

He sat down beside me and rubbed his chin. His eyebrows knitted together into a frown, but he did not speak. I sat still in the chair not daring to move for fear I would hinder his thoughts. Every ounce of my body was willing him to agree. I tried to transcend my positive thoughts

107

to him just as Mrs. Kelly had told me this was possible if one believes enough.

Yes, yes, yes. I said silently in my head. At last, Uncle John coughed to break the silence. He smiled at me and rubbed my head then gently patted my cheek. "I have known for long time young Caty of this wish of yours, and I know Jarlath well enough to know he would want his kinfolk with him on his great day."

I interrupted him in his flow, but thought it necessary to add I would pay the cost for us both with my windfall.

He smiled and nodded his head gently. Was this approval, consent? What was his decision? The suspense was killing me.

"Let me talk it over with the family, Caty," he said at last. "If they are all in agreement for us to go, then I could spare a fortnight in May or June. It would be like a holiday I have never had, an adventure for both of us, courtesy, of Ned O'Brian and friends."

I could not keep myself from hugging Uncle John and with tears in my eyes I thanked him. I knew that Uncle John had the power in my family to make things happen if he wanted them to. I knew deep down in my soul that it was now going to happen. Nothing must overturn the apple cart now. I would carry Mrs. Kelly's good wishes to her son and I would tell her today, this very day, that I was going to go to England!

Chapter 18
To be or not to be?

The next few months went at a snail's pace, but I kept busy at my work and tried to keep Ma as happy as possible. I told her ' tongue in cheek' that, I would only be away for a few weeks so she need not worry and make such a mountain out of a molehill. She laughed at my description, her thin drawn face wrinkling up so easily with the lack of fat to hold the skin taut.

I, on the other hand was filling out in massive proportions. My breasts were as heavy as they would be if I were nursing a young babby, although I did have a decent waist (if I say it myself). I was tall and straight, taller than most of the boys in the town, I often felt clumsy. Mrs. Kelly as well as my Grandma would tell me to feel proud of my body. God had given it especially to me for my care and attention. It was up to me to protect it and treasure it.
I was not certain what she meant, but I did know with a body my size I had more to take care of than most folks around.

With a smile on my face, I left work and decided to call on Maggie. Things had changed a lot in their house. Her Pa had left for England suddenly saying he was going to look for work. It was only when he did not come back that Maggie checked for her savings. He had taken the lot and left Maggie's family with nothing. Her Ma now spent her days in bed wasting away. Maggie was desperate.

The two elder brothers brought in a little money to buy food from working in the fields. Maggie had the burden of taking care of everyone; all the children and her mother. She was the 'mother' now, with no escape in sight.
I felt nothing only sorrow for Maggie's plight but relieved we had decided to split our savings long ago. It was with this guilty feeling that I

knocked on her door that was opened very slowly by one of the little ones. The stench of human waste permeated from the open door, but this was not going to deter me. I smiled at young Brian who acknowledged me by squeezing my leg. I shouted my greeting to everyone; sounding as cheerful as I could, but the sight in front of me took away my smile immediately.

All the children were lying around lethargically sucking their thumbs or twisting their clothes around their fingers. Maud, who was just five, was in the corner rocking backwards and forwards. Maggie was sat on her mother's bed wiping her down with a cloth. She looked up with a tired smile, which looked ready to break into a cry, but she bit her lip instead.

I went towards her sitting on the bed beside her and putting my arms around her frail body for comfort. She knew I cared; we had been close friends too long.

Mrs. Kelly had given me some leftovers from the Archbishops ample dinner table when she knew I was going to visit Maggie, so I stood up and began to take them out of the basket and lay them on the table. This was food, good food, but it did not seem to rouse the children from their trances. I decided to sing. I didn't know why I sang; only that I did it from instinct, or stupidity or something, but it worked. Maggie smiled first, and then, in turn, each of the children sat up to listen to my silly little ditty.

'One man went to Mow, went to mow a meadow........'
Yes, it was corny, but it had the desired effect to waken them from their trances and stand to look what was on the table.

I cut up the food and handed it out to their grubby little hands, watching as they stuffed it into their mouths as fast as they could. I wrapped some of the food and put it into the cupboard for the elder

110

boys when they got home from work. I took some to Maggie with enough for her Mother.

Maggie shook her head. "She won't eat Caty, I try all the time, but she can only swallow fluids, nothing else will stay down. I've tried, Caty, I've tried."

I nodded my approval and began to sing again to the children who were trying to mimic me with the words they knew. I sang to them and we danced in a circle around the kitchen table. I did the animal sounds and they copied me with their little bodies and their squeaky voices. Playing and laughing as only children and maybe, some adults know how. It was, and always will be, the best medicine on earth.

I stayed another hour and then left, vowing to be back soon with more food and song. As Maggie closed the door behind me I walked into the night air letting loose of my own feelings with a flood of tears. Why was the world so cruel to Maggie? Repeatedly she was the victim of circumstances. Maybe I should give Maggie my savings. I was a very selfish person if I let Maggie suffer when I could help so easily. I had to think this out. Maggie was like family to me; I loved her and could not see her in so much pain and be happy myself.

I did not sleep at all that night. How could I think of going to England and leaving my best friend in such a mess? The money was needed in Maggie's house not in my pocket fulfilling a stupid dream. I could save the money again. I was fit and healthy, and my good friend's family was not.

Next morning I pondered and wrestled with my thoughts all the way to the Cathedral, and as I walked through the enormous doors, Mrs. Kelly was already cleaning the pews.

"Well, look what the cat's brought in with a face like she's never seen the cream," shouted Mrs. Kelly from her crouched position. Her English was improving as she used phrases to fit situations, although not always with the right result, as the words were not sometimes in the right order. I apologized in a squeaky voice for being late and turned away from her.

"Did I say the words right Caty, I have just learned that one?"

I just nodded and mumbled aloud that I had a problem. Now, Mrs. Kelly just loved other peoples' problems; it was her specialty, so to speak. She took not a second to rise to her feet and sit down on the pew, as she told me to sit beside her and tell her my troubles.

I explained about Maggie and the family and how it was impossible now for me to go to Jarlath's wedding. The money I had saved and earned should go to Maggie, it was only right. I asked for her reassurance in a pitiful voice pleading her to answer me.

The jowls of Mrs. Kelly's face moved in a chewing motion as her eyes looked around the vast, empty space that towered above us. Her head was moving in circles, but her hand was holding me tight. Maybe it was keeping her down, for I had the feeling she was going to fly up to the Holy Mother's statue at any minute with all the jerking and twitching that was going on.

"Mrs. Kelly," I whispered, "are you feeling alright?"

Then she smiled and patted my hand in hers. I knew she had answers for me. Mrs. Kelly was close to God and to his Holy followers. I thought she was going to tell me I was a good girl in God's eyes for being so generous to my friend. I felt very self-righteous so I pouted my lips to stop the smirk showing.

Then my face changed to surprise when Mrs. Kelly began to tell me of all the good works the Ladies Circle does for the poor folks of the town.

The very same group who had rewarded me, also worked a number of charities.

She told me they had many volunteers who cook, sew, clean and feed families in trouble and she was sure that if she informed them of Maggie's plight they would help. They would even pay for the doctor to see to Maggie's Ma.

Now this was fine if only I could get Maggie to take charity. I told Mrs. Kelly, but she had a better idea. I was to leave it to the Ladies; they knew what to do in these situations. Mrs. Kelly said they would probably send the Doctor in first on a casual call, which always worked; everyone in Tuam obeyed the church and the doctor, in that order. I felt relieved and selfishly glad I had not to give up my dream, but I couldn't help thinking that somebody up there liked me, I felt sure of that. Once more, divine intervention had worked for Catherine Luby, and I felt smug again. Oh! God save me from my sins.

Mrs. Kelly then instructed me to carry on with the cleaning while she went to see the Ladies. They could be found, she told me, in their Club House playing a game called Bridge. It was a good time to find them together and for them to take immediate actions. She believed me about the urgency of the problem, the need was great and she knew they would help.

As she put on her hat and coat, she smiled and said, "keep your hand in your pocket, young Caty, together we will see you at Jarleth's wedding. It's not long off. Oh! by the way, your Uncle John, bless his soul, is definitely going with you; I was called to see your Ma last night and the family all agreed they could spare you both for a little while. Now, don't you slack while I'm away."

I was bewildered by all this good news. It was just too good to be true. I decided to sing in praise to the Lord as I worked as hard and as fast as I could to finish the work before mid-day mass began. Of course, I did finish in time and was just leaving to go into the kitchen behind the

113

vestry for my break when Mrs. Kelly came back. She joined me at the table and gave me the good news that everything was fixed for Maggie's family. The Ladies were astounded by the story and unanimously agreed to put right the problem for the desperate family who had been left alone to fend for themselves. Mrs. Kelly was sure things would happen quickly with the Ladies Circle in charge.

The rest of my day passed slowly for me because I could not wait to call on Uncle John to find out just when we would be leaving. When would my dream start?

Chapter 19
Breaking ties and breaking hearts.

The harsh winter passed and slowly the trees changed their colour and the ground softened to accept the ploughs. Spring was a time of renewal and more than ever before I had an open mind to accept this fact. Uncle John was true to his word. He had made the necessary arrangements to get us to Athlone for the canal barge. His cronies in the pub were more than willing to help take us in their cart after hearing all the stories, farfetched or not, that he had told them about me.

We were to leave in three weeks to give us plenty of time to travel before the wedding. Mrs. Kelly had supplied m'Ma with a plain brown suitcase, for me to use for my belongings and for the things, she wanted me to take to Jarleth. I tried to tell them over and over again that I couldn't take luggage on the 'Canal Packets', but my words fell on deaf ears. I decided to say nothing more to them and go along with their planning and packing, which they both seemed to relish.

I had decided that I would put two or three layers of clothes on and pack into my coat pockets all the extras. Uncle John was to do the same and we would think about wedding clothes when we got to England; if we ever did! He told me to let the women carry on packing and unpacking my suitcase as it kept their minds full of preparation instead of trepidation.

I tried to see everyone I cared for in those last three weeks. I know that Mrs. Kelly thought I was being ever so maudlin as I was only going away for a few weeks, so she thought. I would hug her and give her a sweet smile at every opportunity. The truth was I was grateful to her for giving me the excuse to follow my dream. She thought I was weepy because I was going to a wedding without m'Ma. I prayed to the Holy Mary to forgive me in my deception.

115

Only Maggie knew the truth and wished me well. Maggie and her family were much happier now they were getting help from the Ladies Circle and I was glad she did not know my connection to the good deeds that were coming their way. I suppose you could call that another deception by me. I would probably die in the fires of hell or even in the depths of the Irish Sea before reaching England if I carried on this way. Maybe I should just tell Ma and the family, all my friends and the whole of Tuam that I did not intend to return, but then they would not let me go! Damnation! I had no way out.

How I wished I had been born the daughter of one of the Ladies Circle and did not have all these worries. I had said this to Maggie when we last met but then she told me a horrifying secret that made my bottom jaw fall loose.

"Did you know, Caty, that some of them actually shave their top lips? I swear. They borrow their husband's cut-throat and do it to each other in private. True, true, and that is not all; do you know they wear whalebone under those great skirts to push in their stomachs and push out their breasts. I certainly wouldn't like to do that to be in their Circle."

On second thoughts, I knew I had to count my blessings. Yes, I had a big bottom and big breasts but they had the freedom to wriggle where they wanted without too much restriction. We must be thankful for big mercies; I do have something to be thankful for.

So, with my new philosophical attitude I spent my last two weeks in Ireland smiling with compassion at everyone in sight. My brothers and sisters knew I would be with them again, as soon as I had work, perhaps in the coalmines. I had heard about working on the pit face and I would send for them. Ma would bring them in style at my expense. Maggie would follow and join me in my newfound fortune. My nights were filled with beautiful anticipation. In this way the weeks flashed by and the anticipated day arrived.

Now this was not as easy as I thought. Practically the whole of Tuam had come to see us off. The Archbishop had even given a special mass for us,; praying for our safety on our long journey. I had the small brown suitcase with me, but knew I could not take it on the 'canal packet'. Ma was crying as we got on Sean Gregory's cart. Mrs. Kelly was crying and, my brothers and sisters were crying; Maggie and her family were crying, and even the men from Duffy's Pub were sniffing and rubbing their noses. If we were not quick to leave we would be floating in a water of tears before we got to the waters of Athlone.

Sean flipped the whip gently on the back of his trusted mare and we slowly left all our familiar places and faces that would always be there in Tuam.

Chapter 20
The Irish wile comes in useful

It was a long journey to Athlone but our conversation was interesting as the three of us told each other all we knew about England. The stories could have been true or full of blarney, it did not really matter. I was excited and eager to hear everything about my daydream destination. True or false, it was all the same to me. I was not going to be deterred by any bad thoughts.

Even though my mental state was good, my physical state was not. My backside was sore from the continual pounding it had taken from the wooden bench we sat on. The ample store of fat that surrounded my lower parts just made me have more parts to hurt. I was tender all over from the constant jogging of the cart. My stomach hurt from holding in my water works; I was embarrassed to ask to be relieved when there were only the open fields to go in.

"Look over there,' shouted Sean "look to your left, water, the blessed river of life for sure."

On the horizon, just to our left, as Sean said, was the River Shannon. For a fleeting moment I thought it might be the sea but my fantasy was not to be, we had a long way to go before we saw the sea, was how Uncle John put it. I had never seen such a vast river; my education had been limited to the beautiful River Claire.

"We're nearly there, young Caty, get your sea legs ready, this is where we do some fast talking to get us the ride we need," said Uncle John as he patted his layers of clothes down as far as he could. "Leave it to me and we'll be on the Canal Packet before you know it."

I looked inside the case that my m'Ma and Mrs. Kelly had so carefully packed for me. Uncle John shook his head as I opened it to see what we could discard, we both knew the rules of the Packet; 'no luggage and no furniture', if you expected to go free of charge. We also knew that we could only get a ride if they could fit us on between the cattle and horses.

Sean drove us right into the dock of the canal barge where the smell of burning peat that drove the boat through the water infused the air. It was a homely smell to me. The smell of home and the comforts I remembered. It was an intoxicating feeling that warmed my heart into a false sense of security.

Uncle John was talking to a group of men and pointing to me. Heaven only knows the tale he was telling. I took out of the case all I could stuff into my deep pockets, including the small parcel that was the wedding present to Jarlath from his mother. The rest of the things I told Sean to keep but not say a word to anyone where he got the things. The case, he was to throw away or sell before he reached Tuam. Nothing should upset my Ma and Mrs. Kelly; they would be hurt if they knew I had given away the clothes they had donated to me.

"Well, I'm sure if I told them you weren't allowed to take the case on the boat they would understand. Caty I can't take these things from your Ma she needs them for the young uns just as much as me," pleaded Sean.

"Alright, but sound convincing, they might think it a tale." I said to pacify him. Then I quickly told him I wouldn't be a minute as I dived to the nearby bushes to relieve myself. At that point I didn't care who thought ill of me. I covered my body with all the extra layers and pushed them down inside my knickers and left the shrubbery.

I heard Uncle John shouting for me to join him and I could see him waving to Sean in a gesture of luck as he walked up the ramp. Holding on to all my extra layers of clothing I clumsily followed Uncle John up the ramp onto the boat. I must have looked enormously fat with all the layers of clothes, although I did have full cheeks and my face was round, anyway so the one complimented the other, in my opinion.

My whimsical feelings of the home comforts soon disappeared as I tried to find a space to sit between the cattle dung and horse manure that littered the deck. How was I going to last for 200 miles with this stench?

We set off as the only human passengers on board besides the crew, that was made up of three men. In fact, they were as smelly and foul looking as the animals they transported; to describe them as men would be a compliment. Their hands were red and raw; their mouths were lacking in teeth and their hair, (what little there was of it), stood on end, even before the wind blew. Their clothes were stiff with dirt and grease and shiny in parts that I did not want to look at too closely, but obviously oily slimy hands had rubbed the area frequently. They talked in the Irish tongue mostly, laughing and swearing about me (as if I did not understand), but I acted with a straight face and a glum smile to play the fool they obviously thought I was. My intention was to reach Dublin with no incidence, as I was the only woman on board.

Eventually, thankfully, Uncle John appeared at my side putting his hand around my shoulders and hugging me gently. He had been familiarizing himself with the canal barge and checking on its 'sail ability', was his word. He also told me how he had secured a place on the boat, which astounded me. He had told them I was pregnant and he was taking me back to our family in Dublin which I had run away from. No wonder I was the scapegoat for dirty language from dirty old men! What would the good Bishop and Mrs. Kelly think of me now? Here I was sitting in the midst of excrement, having excruciating pains of self-pity as well as fearing the Good Lord would excommunicate me-for the sins I had not committed. I dropped to my knees to pray and landed in a cowpat.

Chapter 21
Crawling through time.

I do not remember too much of the journey from Athlone to Dublin. It now seems to have been just a big blur of nothingness, if there is such a thing. The droning noise of the peat engine and the gentle swishing of the water as it hit the boat sides blunted my senses. Through the utter boredom of it all I slept, mainly on the deck and not in the small cabin below; there the smell of squalor, deprivation, and booze made me physically sick.

After trying the cabin once and then heaving my heart up, that was enough for me. The crew nodded their heads in agreement, thinking it was my 'stage of confinement' that was causing the sickness. I let them think just what they wanted; I was feeling sick with the smell of the animals and the lack of food.

We had brought some bread and cheese with us, which Uncle John and I shared as the long journey progressed, ever so slowly. The crew gave us some fresh water from a container that was definitely in need of a good clean, but we had no choice. I decided to sleep as much as possible to blank out the sights and smells that surrounded me. At least in my sleep I could imagine all that was possible in the days to come.

After an eternity of time, we finally arrived in Dublin. The crew was very helpful to Uncle John. He had told them that after dropping me off with the family he was travelling to England, They advised him to go to the offices of the 'British and Irish Steam Packet Company' known as 'B & I' to buy a ticket. They told him the address was 3-5 North Wall, but that was all they knew. Uncle John thanked the men who told me to take care of myself and to be a 'good girl' in future and listen to my Pa.

We dusted ourselves down and made our way through the streets of Dublin. The squalor I saw in this city at that time was almost as bad as the boat we had just left. I had never before seen so many people in one place, at one time all looking as if they had never seen the inside of the tin bath or a fresh stream in which to take a bath.

"Stick by me and hold tight," said Uncle John earnestly, "these folks don't look so happy to me."

I did not intend to let go of his arm, even though I was pushed and banged from all sides as we moved through the crowd. The shops and the buildings all looked so different, but I didn't have much chance to look as the ground was uneven and I was afraid I would fall if I didn't watch my step and keep up with the fast pace Uncle John was doing.

I took a breath as he asked the way to the offices; explaining two or three times to make himself understood. Finally, an old woman with just one black tooth sticking out at the front of her mouth directed us to the place.
There was a big queue of people outside the offices; a mixture of rich and poor with none seeming to get more attention than the other. We just took our place in line and waited.

From where I was standing, I could just see the tall structure bobbing up and down on the sea. An excited young woman standing next to me told me that these ships today were built of steal and steam driven, not the old paddle steamers of yesterday that took 11 – 12 hours to cross. The man with her said that these ships went at 13 knots (which must have been an English term) it made no sense to me. They were very friendly people so I listened and remembered the information, in case it was important to know.

As we got nearer to the pier, I saw the ship in its full splendour. Three black funnels stood erect, complete with a flag. That flag was the red St

George cross with a green cross superimposed on it. This information again came from the friendly couple. They had found out a lot about the boat they were to sail on. The boat in the dock we all were hoping to travel on was called the 'Lady Wolseley' and its captain was the well-known Captain Black.

I was very impressed and registered everything they told me for future reference. Uncle John was too busy finding out the basic things like cost and availability of sailing today. He came back with the good news that there was a good chance of us sailing today-if I was up to it. I shook my head and smiled at his stupid question. Was I, Catherine Luby, up to making my dreams come true as soon as possible? What a question to ask.

We slowly progressed towards the big wooden counter where very official looking men sat on tall stools writing in big leather bound books. The man behind the desk asked Uncle John how we wished to travel. Uncle John boldly answered by asking what the options today were? He spoke in a very officious way not his usual voice.

The man behind the desk told us the possibilities without lifting his head. His voice however, did change to match the different possibilities. 'We have Saloon Class," which was said in a high pitched voice, "we have 2nd Class deck single at 2 shillings, Sir," in slightly lower pitch and then he whispered, "and we have steerage for 3 pence, what will it be?"

"Two steerage please," said Uncle John in a loud clear voice, not to be humiliated by the man.

The stern face clerk asked us our names and wrote them in the book after which he gave us each a ticket, with the comment, "free bread for steerage passengers provided. Next please."

We followed the line up the ramp and on to the ship. At last! I was going to sail to England. Uncle John said we must find a good place to sit on the deck. Not too near the middle but yet not too near the rails.

"You stay just here Caty why I look around, but do not stray; I'll be back in a few minutes."

"Can I stand near the rails and watch the people and the sights, Uncle John?" I said with excitement.

"Well if you must, but don't talk to anyone and don't lean over too far."

The rail was full of people side by side all having the same purpose as me, to watch the passengers come aboard.
All the mixtures of people boarding that day enthralled me, and to think they were going to the same place as me was amazing; the rich, the poor and the not so poor. There were important looking individuals, single men and there were families, all going up the ramp on to the 'Lady Wolseley'. All of them had a smile on their face, no one was crying for loved ones or places left behind. No one looked back but purposely looked forward and around from side to side. Why were all these people leaving Ireland for England?

Coming up the gangway were two people I recognized, so I turned keeping my hand on the rail but leaning back to wave. I saw the young couple we had spoken to earlier who had known a great deal about this ship. They obviously were as happy as I was to be aboard. My eyes followed them as they went in the opposite direction. As I turned to lean back on the rail, I was shocked to feel a person so close to me I jumped in embarrassment. The young man was wearing a uniform and as our eyes met, he laughed.

I felt my awkwardness fill my blood vessels and heat my body to boiling point. He apologized with an accent I had never heard before but his voice lilted and dropped with each phrase like a psalm being said. I was mesmerized by the sound so much that I did not listen, or understand the words he was saying. I just kept smiling and nodding hoping he would understand my gesture. He kept on talking and then slowly his words began to make sense to me. He was a member of the crew; just a junior member but he told me he was always enthralled to look at the foreign ports before he went back to cast off with the rest of the crew.

I asked him with my best English pronunciation what was the meaning of 'cast off?' To that question, I received a detailed account, which again I did not follow exactly but he rambled on and on and I just looked into his sea blue eyes and blond hair and did not care a fig.

I caught myself just before my mouth dropped open at the wonderful form I was looking at. I licked my lips and bit the bottom lip to stop it opening. I thought quickly of what to say and began. "You must be under the command of Captain Black, a very good man so I heard." I struggled to think of more information the couple had told me. "I believe we are to travel around 13 knots or so, if the weather permits." I continued trying to remember the correct words and sound convincing.

"You're dead right there!" answered this wonderful voice. "The Lady Wolseley' is one of the six 'Ladies' in this fleet. She will be carrying over 200 passengers today, 100 saloon, 50 2nd Class Passengers and a yet unknown number of steerage." He gave this information as though he was standing in front of Captain Black himself, which made me smile and congratulate him. "Well! I must get to work; the devil makes use of lazy hands, I'm told,"
He began to walk away but then turned and stood to attention, "With whom do I have the pleasure to pass this time of day? My name is Paul; Able-seaman Paul Hobson at your service."

I answered quickly before my knees gave way and said, 'I'm Catherine Luby , but my friends call me Caty."

"Well maybe, we could be friends before this voyage is over and I will get to call you Caty? Goodbye Miss Catherine Luby, see you around."

Like a flash he was lost in the crowd and I was brought quickly back down to earth by the voice of Uncle John, 'I've found us a good place to bunk down on the other side follow me Caty quickly before it gets taken. I've asked that nice couple you were talking to on shore to save it for us until I found you, come on."

As I followed him my mind raced frantically about the possibility that this couple would have more information for me to use if, or when, I met my vision of manhood again.

Chapter 22
The transition from naivety

We sailed away from Dublin slowly and carefully from the North Wall and headed for what the young couple said was the Port of Holyhead. Over the coming few hours I was to learn that these two young people were newly married and were going to seek their fortune in England. Part of their plan had been to find out as much as possible about all the things that were important and essential for their new life. I marvelled at their recall of facts. They were just simple country folk determined to make a new start with as much ammunition as possible.

The light of day was quickly turning into dusk and I asked Uncle John if I could walk around the deck to stretch my legs. He was busy playing a game of cards with the young man and the lady was asleep so he consented, but told me not to talk to strangers.

The night was turning muggy and so I left my big heavy coat with Uncle John and the heavy cardigan I took off as well. I had still two or three layers on even after discarding those, but I felt a little less uncomfortable. I walked with the sea breeze blowing in my face, smelling the salt air that tingled on my skin.

As I passed the lifeboats I heard a familiar voice and the little bit of cheese and bread I had in my stomach fought for dominance. I saw him in a flash of evening sunlight standing erect on top of one of the boats, feet ajar, holding a rope and waving his cap to me to draw my attention. I looked up to him and with my whole being I completely worshipped him on high as I had the statues in the Cathedral. Lord help, could this vision be real?

"Wait Catherine, I'm coming down," he shouted, and like a wildfire, he skimmed down the rope and was at my side. Then, as if the heavens knew I needed a good douse down, they opened and the rain started. He pushed me, ever so gently, under the tarpaulin and into the lifeboat, for shelter. He followed me so quickly, that we both fell, full length on to the floor of the boat. We laughed at the way we had both tumbled together and the feeling of safety and protection came over me as he drew the sheet down to keep out the rain.

I sat up quickly, with his help, and heard his lilting voice ask me if I was hurt. I told him it would take more than a small fall to hurt a big girl like me. He didn't speak straight away, but looked at me up and down and then he spoke, "You know, I was not sure it was you as you came around towards me. You have such a glorious figure, Catherine; I didn't realize earlier because of your heavy coat. Oh, I hope I'm not embarrassing you?"

I shook my head and smiled at his question. I looked again at his beautiful eyes. They were as blue as the sea outside. Our hideaway was as sparkling as the communion wine back home in Tuam. I was captivated by the pure symmetry of this masculine body that squatted besides me. The rain was coming down hard on the cover over our heads and we both moved together in a predestined movement to the centre of the boat. Touching and guiding each other to find the precise place to be in our camouflage from the weather or was it the people?

For a while, we talked and asked questions of each other. Questions that really were of no interest to either of us. I cannot now remember what I asked or what he asked; the real questions were the unsaid ones. Was he going to kiss me? Why was I feeling those funny sensations in my stomach again? Why was his voice like music to me?
Then he began to ask why I had my beautiful hair pinned up so tightly. He touched my head gently but purposely to take out my grips and pull down my hair. I did not find his actions precocious but tantalizingly erotic even though I had never been in this position before.

We were side by side in the hollow of the boat that was swaying with the movement of the ship. His hands moved slowly down to my face where he traced the whole profile with his finger, stopping at my lips he circled several times before passing down to my chin. He lifted it slowly upwards towards his face that was steadily meeting mine without any resistance. His finger was replaced by the soft massage of his lips on mine, his masculine body moved slowly to cover me as we locked together in my first real embrace.

Nothing was predetermined as we moved together to touch and please each other in mutual satisfaction. Then Paul began to unbutton the dress I had on and slip it down over my shoulders. His disappointment showed as he found yet another dress underneath and so he repeated his quest to find more layers of clothing. I began to giggle and squirm at the quandary we had found ourselves in.

Paul was not to be deterred and kissed me full and long to take me into another sensual moment. The peeling of my layers of clothing seemed to have aroused him in a different way to me, but I was beginning to feel this infectious sexual desire erupt inside me. I was exhilarated as he exposed my large ample breast and explored each nipple, making it protrude up in a pinnacle of excitement.

This new feeling of madness and sensuality that my body was offering now desired more and more. I was in a place that was unknown and I wanted to go on. His hand went between my legs and he twisted and pulled off my panties in one smooth movement. Then as his fingers touched my vulnerable parts .... I was transported on a voyage of incredible wonder; an extremely bizarre shivering filled my whole body. I gave a whimpering scream of joy and pulled him closer kissing Paul, (my very able seaman) full on the mouth and gasping for more of the same.

The same was not to be, but the illogical discovery of feelings, before unknown, filled my body completely. I felt his hand move towards his trousers and then I experienced a protrusion into my lower parts that jolted me upwards, first in shock and then in pleasure. Unforgettable pleasure that lifted my body from its adolescent form to rise me above the tarpaulin, above the life boat, above the Lady Wolsley, above the clouds and carried me to my chosen destiny, in my chosen land.

I was floating in a place I had never been to and never wanted to leave; however, I was jolted back to the true world by the panting and blowing of this weight above me. His face was in contortions at first but then a wicked smile came across his face that made me smile. We did not move from our positioning as we both caught our breath and then slowly he rolled from me and covered my clothes around me. It was still raining very hard so we cuddled together and slept.

When I woke up, he was gone. The only evidence of my experience was the disarray of clothes around me and that aching, throbbing feeling between my legs. I crawled to the edge of the boat and slowly lifted the curtain of truth. I was still on the ship, I was still on my way to England, but my mind was as foggy as the air outside. I was dazed and disorientated and could only crawl on my hands and knees with great difficulty out of the boat. The fresh air brought an intake of breath to me and I was surprised at my lack of common sense. Of course, I could not stand up straight I was on a ship, for heaven sake!

I sheepishly left my dark hideaway and set my mind to finding Uncle John. I planned to tell him that I had found shelter from the rain on one of the lifeboats and then unfortunately fell asleep under the tarpaulin. Paul had informed me that was the name of these small boats.

He was in the same place talking to the couple, just as if the world had stayed on hold while I was spinning round in the vast big universe of experience. He greeted me and listened to my excuse with no emotion. Why did I expect any different?

Suddenly, to my relief, from this awkward moment, people began to run towards the guardrails. Fingers were pointing to distant horizons and a gradual crescendo of excited voices filled the air. All I could see through the foggy mist were some tall dark shapes. Did this mean we were looking at England?

Chapter 23
A New Place to be.

The ship took forever to dock. In fact, I do not know how Captain Black did it so smoothly. We were into our second day of travel, but my excitement on reaching England overcame any tiredness.

As the ship was stopping, I anxiously gazed into the faces of the sailors to make out 'my man'. From my distance, they all looked the same with their uniforms and hats to match. I wondered if I was ever going to see him again.

The buildings were strange to me and I said so to Uncle John who told me they were warehouses, that is a kind of house to store things.

"What kinds of things?" I asked, not very interested in the answer, but it was a way I could gaze onto the shore to find my sailor.

The young couple and Uncle John then went into a detailed account of the Sugar Trade in Liverpool. How busy the port was becoming. On the horizon, we could see the foundations of the large buildings that were going to be the future landscape of Liverpool. The structures were the grand Liver Building, the Cunard Building, and The Pier Head Docks. This young married couple and Uncle John had all the answers.

The fog had lifted, but still I could not identify the face I so wanted to see again. Maybe when we got off the ship he would be waiting for me at the bottom of the gangplank, offering a helping hand as I put down my first cautious steps onto the soil of England. Then maybe I would introduce him to my Uncle John.

 I let my imagination roam. In my minds eye as he helped me off the gangplank. I would say, "Uncle, let me introduce you to my friend,

Able seaman Paul Hobson".   As I spoke, my sailor would take off his cap and bow his head slightly, and my Uncle would hold out his hand to shake the handsome sailor who was a friend of Caty's.

I was brought down to earth with the sound of the ship's fog horn blowing out its welcome sign that told the crew to put down the gang planks and prepare to 'disembark' a term the young couple told us was the correct word for this maneuver.

The first and second-class passengers were the first to get off, or disembark, as I told everyone who could hear. I suddenly felt quite grown-up for some reason and wanted my new- found feeling to be orally proclaimed.
Uncle John smiled at my English pronunciation but I was determined to speak in English at all times from now on and at the same time to be as clear as possible when I spoke. Maybe, if I spoke more slowly then everyone would understand me?

It was now our turn to leave the ship. The four of us made a circle holding hands and wished each other luck and health in this foreign land. It was Uncle John's idea and I think the young couple were touched with his suggestion, so a short quick prayer followed this gesture of goodwill. We all genuinely felt sad to break away from this circle of friendship, but the foghorn again called us to obey and follow the crowd of people pushing and pulling each other to the gangplank. Uncle John kept hold of my hand as we were swept on to firm ground by the swelling throngs of immigrants and visitors eager to leave the Lady Wolsey.

Once we realized we were on firm ground, it was difficult for us not to sway a little. The movement of the ship does not leave you straight away and we both smiled at each other and waved our last goodbye to the young couple.

We had talked about our onward journey from Liverpool and Uncle John knew that Jarleth was probably right about not loitering in Liverpool. The information we knew must be the honest truth coming from the groom-to be to his wedding guests. Now all we had to do was find which way was east?

There were still lots of sailors around and these people seemed to be the people to ask rather than the navies who were unloading the cargo. I desperately wanted one in this crowd of sailors to be my able-seaman but it was not to be and the direction was given to us by an older man who wanted to help us with as much information he could.
He told us in detail how to leave the dock and make for the River Mersey and the place to find a coal barge that might give us a lift to the Bridgewater Canal.

The problem was we both were very hungry and thirsty. The salt sea air had made our lips dry. Pure good luck played its part and as we walked away from the docks and through the gates we saw a small crowd of people standing around an oil barrel that seemed to be on fire. We made our way towards it and the smell of roasted potatoes filled the air. It drew us closer to the chuckling crowd of happy faces enjoying their first taste of English food.

Uncle John paid for the potatoes, one each for us and put back the change in his pocket. As I took the potato from the vender who held it on a long fork, I had to juggle it between my hands. It was roasting hot but I was determined not to drop it on the ground. I used the folds of my skirt to help me and blew on it madly between the squeals of laughter our antics had brought to the assembled on-lookers.

Each bite I took with caution, trying not to burn my mouth in the process. Uncle John was not having the same trouble as I was but still he took a long time to bite through the hard skin and reach the soft mushy centre that was slowly bringing pleasure to both our minds and bodies.

As he took his last bite he put his arm around my shoulder and wiped his mouth on the back of his sleeve whilst whispering in my ear, "Lets have another Caty, if we can't finish it we can carry it with us for the journey, what do you say?"

I nodded my acknowledgment, as my mouth was full of hot potato that I was savouring to the end. Uncle John put his hand into his pocket and paid for another two of the same. The man turned over the potatoes still on the griddle top of his makeshift cooker until he found two, which were ready to eat. My uncle took off his neckerchief to wrap them and put them in his pocket for later. Before we left the group, we asked if there was a stream or somewhere to find water to quench our thirst and complete our meal. The potato man said there was a stream further down the road that was a small tributary of the River Mersey.

We both thanked the man and took the road the sailor and the vendor had both suggested. There was a skip to our step as we both held on to each other and purposely made our way down the English country lane.

Chapter 24
The road to trouble.

It was not long before we both spotted the stream brimmed over to the ditch at the side of the lane. We went into the trees and found the clearing where large round stones helped clean and purify this water. We decided jointly, that we must use this occasion to clean ourselves as well as drink away our thirst.

For modesty sake, I went further downstream to take off some clothes. The layers I had on could surely now be carried somehow if I wrapped them together, I left Uncle John to his ablutions and went into the trees to begin my long awaited cleansing. I knew I was still sore between my legs and the water would surely help there.

Loud shouting broke my concentration and I heard fighting sounds coming from the direction of Uncle John. I peered through the trees but decided not to join in at that point. I had seen these men at the potato stand. There were at least four of five of them hitting and kicking Uncle John at the same time as yelling to him to give them his money.

They were pulling off the rest of his clothes and ransacking his pockets for all they could find and take. They muttered that the girl must have gone her own way and seemed to be disappointed with their haul. To my horror, one of the men sat on top of Uncle John and consistently punched him in the face as the other kicked him repeatedly all over his body.

I wanted to leap out and fight them off but two things spared me. One that I was halfway undressed and the other I was no match for five men. I buried my head into the tree trunk and bit into the back of my hand to stifle the noise I might be making. Finally, they left quite disappointed with their loot but exhilarated by the fight.

I waited until I saw them disappear down the lane for good and then I ran to comfort Uncle John and assess his wounds. I did not care then that I was undressed down to my underclothes. I knelt by his side and slowly lifted his head into my lap. He cringed with the movement but I gently stroked back his hair to expose his bruised eyes and blood filled nose. I pushed his jacket they had left (probably because it was lying beneath him), under his head. I tore a piece of my ample underskirt and went to the stream to wet it.

I bent down to see my reflection in the water, which revealed a face I did not, at first, think was mine. I now looked like a woman as well as felt like one. I had not time to ponder on the thought, only that I was in a strange country on my own with an injured family member to look after. It was now up to me and me alone to make some decisions. I knew Uncle John could not walk too far after that beating but first I had to make him comfortable. It was up to me, Caty Luby, to face this problem. The challenge was how to solve this predicament

 "Try not to move," I whispered, trying not to alarm him too much. The whole world seemed to have an eerie silence that enveloped us. Uncle John began to shake, which I guessed maybe due to his condition, but I was not sure. I had never been in this position before. Panic was spreading through my body; tears were swelling behind my eyes. Terrified by the circumstances I fought back with that unknown strength for survival that fortunately ran through my veins at the appropriate time.

The lump in my throat subsided as the sounds of nature surfaced back into my conscious mind giving me the willpower to think again in a positive mode. Catherine Luby, the woman, woke up that day to the realization that feeling sorry for yourself and creeping into a hole was not the answer; life was out there and I was not going down without a fight! Did men think they were the only ones who could fight? I was as strong as any man was mentally and physically; they wouldn't break my spirit.

Uncle John's persistent trembling brought me back into focus. I had to go for help. If I tried to lift him and drag him I could hurt him more and in what direction would I go for help? The unknown road was straight in front but if I went back the way the way we had come, I would at least know what to expect? My logic was not very clear, but my gut feeling was to go with it.

I told Uncle John in a clear decisive voice what I was planning to do, but he had not the strength to argue so I began to move him slowly to the tree that had been my hiding place a few minutes earlier. I dressed myself sparingly and put my surplus clothing around his injured body. As I dressed, my face began to change into a smirk with the gratitude that the robbers had been fouled. We had decided to put most of the money we were carrying in a safe place so I had sewn most of our stash in a bag inside my knickers, before we left Tuam. I tapped my leg in glee and then put my hands together and knelt by my Uncle's side. I hid my smiling face with my hands as I slid down to the ground but then I spoke to Uncle John in a voice that sounded a like Grandma's to me so I put on a stern face.
"Everything will be alright. I will go to find help so you stay here and rest. Do not try to move. I will be as fast as possible; you should be safe here for a little while."

To my dismay Uncle John was now shaking his head from side to side and mouthing, no! no! He held my arm with all his might but his strength was not there and he knew it. Tears swelled up onto his bruised face un-clotting the blood that had begun to congeal around his nose. I hated to see my childhood hero so beaten and broken in body and spirit. Life was not fair. He did not deserve to lie hurt in the woods of a strange country. I wanted to cry with him but I squeezed his arm and shook my head from side to side and at last, he succumbed to my force of will. By mouthing the words, "God be with you Caty."

Chapter 25
Unfamiliar places

 I didn't want to leave him there, but to stay with him was not the answer. I walked back to the road and tried to remember the direction we had come from. We were definitely on the side of the ditch so I must now turn around and have the ditch on my other side. The knowledge of left and right was not yet in my vocabulary so pure instincts and common sense had to take over. That was one virtue everyone said I had.

I walked at a fast pace, half running and half walking, but I encountered no-one. There wasn't even a cottage or a farm worker around. Back in the home country you would at least see someone working the fields. Maybe they were all underground in those mines I was told about? However, as I went round the next bend I saw in the distance a steeple of some sort; I headed in that direction. When I got nearer to it I was certain it was a church, but not the kind of large church I was used to in Tuam. Still there was bound to be a priest in there to help me? A small wooden gate had an archway of flowers growing over it, which framed the church in the distance, but I didn't have the time to enjoy this picture of beauty, I had to find help.

I went towards the large door and looked above it expecting to see gargoyles or the like. There was only a solid stonewall which I hoped was an omen of the better kind, so I pushed the heavy door open and went inside.
This was a church unlike I had ever seen in Tuam. There were no statues at all, not even of "Our Lady". There was a tall raised structure at one side with steps leading to the top and I could not see any confession boxes anywhere. England was a strange place.

Just then, I saw a man come from out of a side door, so I called out to him, "Father I need help desperately. My Uncle is lying hurt up the road, please can you help me, please?"

He walked towards me with his head on one side. I was not sure if he understood me so I repeated my question in a very slow precise way I had heard the Ladies of Tuam talk. As he stopped in front of me, I was surprised at the way he was dressed. I had never seen a priest dress that way before.

"Now then," he began as he took my hand and made me sit down beside him. "There is no need to call me Father; I am a vicar not a priest ...but lets not dwell on that for the time being, what's this about your Uncle?"

I told him our story of getting off the boat from Ireland, buying the potatoes and then being robbed as we washed by the stream. He listened intently shaking his head from side to side and sometimes stopping my sentences to clarify a meaning. He told me to wait for a few minutes whilst he brought someone who would go with me to help. He quickly disappeared through the same door he had appeared from earlier.

I looked around for something familiar to aim my prayers. My eyes were brought to the beautiful colours of the large window behind the alter, well I think it was the alter? There were many pictures in the coloured glass that captivated my attention until the Father, or whatever he called himself, came back with a man by his side.

George will go with you in his cart and bring back your uncle to the rectory where I am sure my wife can tend to his injuries. "So go on lass, your Uncle is waiting."

I was very confused by his words, but I just followed George out of the church. We went around to the back where his horse and cart was

142

tethered to a tree with the horse enjoying the green juicy grass in the shade. He helped me up onto the cart with a politeness I had not seen for a long time. First, he dropped a small step down at the back of the cart and then he gently held my elbow and my hand to lift me up the step. He waited until I had placed myself on the side seat before he put up the step again. As he got into the driver's seat he started to ask questions. His diction was so strange to me I pressed my lips together and shook my head.

George was a kind man. I felt the warmth of his spirit as he put me into the cart. I tried to tell him in my best English that I didn't understand his questions. I apologized so he tried again, using his best English pronunciation. We were both trying to speak the same language but it was a foreign accent to both of us. The importance of the moment meant it was necessary for both of us to make communication. Neither of us could be implicit in our choices of words but we somehow struggled together to find understanding.

By gestures and improvisation I was directing George in the right direction and soon I was able to stop him at the place on the road where Uncle and I had gone to bathe. George put a large stone on the reins to hold the horse fast but the horse was happy again to feed on the grass at the side of the road. Contentment and trust was the name of the game for George and his faithful horse.

We clambered down the slope towards the water and the hiding place of Uncle John. I shouted his name as we sped down, but I got no answer. 'God, please let him be there and alive were the words in my mind', I was beginning to panic again. Then we heard the groans and moans coming from the same spot I had left him.

"Uncle John, it's me Caty I have brought help," I shouted.

George went ahead and was at Uncle's side before me. He was talking to him softly and assuring him, I think? George decided we should leave our belongings on the grass and he would carry the top half if I would take the legs and that way we would get up the verge and into the cart easier. My clothes we could come back for later.

I do not know if I was 'tuning in' on George's accent or not, but I was gaining a better understanding of him.

So together we carried out the task as a team and safely put Uncle John in the cart. I ran back to get the clothes. I knew my uncle was safe and before long we were on the road back to the church.

I repeated my thanks to George and then I pondered on this experience. There were good and bad people in every country. Language was not the only thing that brought people together because actions spoke louder than words. Here was a stranger taking his time to help us and show kindness while doing it. I must remember not to rush into making decisions about people in the future just because they sound funny to me. I was stopped in my thoughts by George telling me that we would soon be at the Rectory where Mrs. Wrigley, the Rector's wife would be waiting.

"I am sure the Rector will have told her to prepare for us," was his remark.

I had to ask the question, it was bursting out before I could stop it, "George, how can the Father have a wife, do they live in the same house, is that what a Rectory is?"

George smiled at my words, then went on to explain that my Church in Ireland was Roman Catholic and this church was Church of England and the priests could get married, and even have children if they wanted. Reverend Wrigley, however, had no children at the present time. I wanted to ask more questions but we had reached the house where a pleasant looking young woman stood at the door waving to us and telling us to bring the injured man into her house, if it was possible? If not she would make sure her husband came to help.

Before we had time to stop the cart, the Father came out of the church. Oh! No he wasn't a Father in any sense of the word. Still the kindly churchman attempted to do something I never saw in Ireland; he physically helped George to lift my Uncle's injured body out of the cart and into his house.

I followed them inside as the kind lady put her arm around my shoulders to give me a comforting squeeze. They laid Uncle down on the sofa and the lady disappeared to the kitchen for a bowl of water and a cloth. She told us to leave her to it and go in the kitchen for the refreshments she had left out for us. Again, my understanding of every word she said was not entirely clear but I was led again out of this beautiful room to a kitchen full of the aromas that stimulated your taste buds to burst.

On the stove was a pot of steaming tea, which George brought to the table where I sat next to the churchman. On the table were plates of neatly cut bread; cut so thin you could not see what was inside. There were pies, cakes, and food I had never seen before, but after the shortest prayer I had ever heard I was told to fill my stomach and enjoy the fruits of the Lord's bounty.
England was a wonderful place to be.

Chapter 26
"Fitting-in"

I was so full after eating this delicious meal, that was the best I had ever tasted; I leant back in my chair and watched the churchman complete his eating. He took from his lap a kind of handkerchief and then wiped his mouth with it by putting his fore- finger pointing inside of it. He then crumpled it up and placed it next to his plate.

As he did this, I noticed that I had also one of these handkerchiefs next to my plate, so I decided to mimic this movement. It looked so refine and proper to me. It was much better to use this cloth than your sleeve, even if it did cause one to have more washing. George did the same with his cloth and then he got up from the table and started moving the plates into the sink. I rose from the table to help him but the churchman told me to follow him to check on Uncle John.

I looked at Uncle John and had to smile. He looked so comfortable lying on the sofa with a most refined lady mopping his brow. If his friends from Duffy's could see him now they would never believe their eyes.

"I don't think he should go very far this night, his injuries are too bad, they need time to heal," Mrs. Wrigley told he husband. "Perhaps we could put our visitors in our guest bedroom for tonight? There are two beds in there so that would be no problem. George could lift him I'm sure, with your help?"

The churchman nodded his approval but enquired if there were sheets already on the beds?
"I will go directly and see to that dear, you can see if Mister John, I'm sorry I don't know his last name Caty, could take some hot soup, he definitely needs the nourishment if he is to recover."

I followed my instructions and went to the kitchen to find the bowl and put soup into it. I was to find the bread and cut some. I went into the kitchen and was glad to see George was still there sitting at the table having more tea. I told him what had been said and what I needed.

"This all would happen on the one day Mary has taken off to see her family, but ne'er mind I will help yer," he said in that funny accent of his. He pointed to the cupboard to find the bowl and I was just very amazed at the beautiful plates, bowls, saucers, and cups that were packed into this space. All had pretty flowers on them and all were matching. I was awestruck, but I heard George telling me to bring the bowl to him at the stove and he would pour the soup.

"She makes lovely soup does Mrs. Wrigley, better than our Mary I think, now put it down on that tray. I've laid a cloth on it as Mrs. Wrigley likes but you need to put another small plate under the bowl can you get one and I'll hold the bowl?"

 I couldn't understand all this use of plates and cloths, but I asked just in case, if I should put one of the handkerchiefs on the tray.

"That's called a serviette, luv," he said with a smile "everyone here uses a serviette it's the way it's done in this house. That is not to say they put on the airs and graces, it is somewhat natural to them both coming from the gentry families. Now to the bread cutting, do you think I should do that for you, luv?"

 I didn't know why he kept calling me "luv" instead of Caty but I learnt later on in my travels that all folks in this area called each other "luv" and in time I grew to like this endearing term.

 I was a bit nervous picking up the tray, so George smiled and took it off me to carry it through. Uncle John had now woken up a little and was having a conversation with the churchman. He weakly answered that he was eternally in his debt for the kindness that we had received. The churchman in his frock coat stood up and shunned off the remarks to take the tray from George and lay it on the small table.

At this point, I decided to take over the feeding, at least I knew what to do with this serviette thing and I did not want Uncle John dropping this lovely china on to this plush colourful rug or sofa. I continued to feed my Uncle as the churchman and George planned their next move to the bedroom. I wasn't sure what to expect anymore so I gave up planning, in fact it was a welcome change as far as I was concerned to have someone else plan my next move.
"When he's had enough nourishment George and I will carry him to the bedroom, you must both stay the night Caty, your Uncle is not fit to travel. Tomorrow is another day and we will see what the good Lord brings us. Do you agree?"

I did not know if I should consent or not, but I could not think of an alternative at that point. As the churchman could see I was unsure he changed the subject and he asked Mrs. Wrigley to show me the bedroom where he assured me there were two beds. He was not to know that I was worried we would have to pay for this luxury in some way or another and that was the only worry I had. I think George read my thoughts and as we walked down the corridor to the bedroom, he whispered to me that there was no catch to this offer. The vicar often helped people in one way or another.

Mrs. Wrigley opened the door to a room that smelt as fresh as the roses on the walls. I had never seen wallpaper before, nor had I ever seen such clean sheets and soft pillows. I smiled and thanked her sincerely. She smiled back and said, "Go now and pour water from the jug into the bowl which is on top of the drawers over there, the towel you will find next to it. We will wait until you get into bed before we bring your Uncle through. Oh, and by the way I have put a shift on the bed for you to change into. I don't know what happened to all your clothes

148

maybe they are still in the cart. Come on George let the lady have some privacy!"

I smiled again at her words, me Caty Luby, a lady! Clean fresh water to wash in, with a soft clean towel to use instead of a course cloth and a bed to myself for the first time in my life. This was a living in England? I wanted to relish and savour every moment of it, for I was sure that paradise could not last. Why was there not a catch to it? These people did not know us; we did not even speak the same language or worship in the same way. I decided not to dwell on all these thoughts but to thank God in my prayers later and tell him I was glad he came over the water with us to this unpredictable place.

I wallowed in this washing and drying of myself. The smell of the water and feel of the towel were so invigorating. I did the motions over and over again. Finally, I put on the clean shift and got into the bed. I slipped carefully under the bedclothes and sat down in the middle but my legs shot up from the floor as I sank deeper and deeper into the mattress. I thought it was going to swallow me up it was so soft. I felt like I was in a big-feathered cocoon, sealed from the outside world from thieves and robbers.

I heard a knock on the door and voice asked if I was in bed. I answered in my best 'lady voice' that I was in bed. Then the door opened and in walked the churchman and George carrying Uncle John between them with Mrs. Wrigley close behind. My Uncle seemed to be wearing some strange clothes and was not in his outdoor clothes we had travelled in, but I hid my head in the soft pillow so I would not look too nosey about what was happening.

They put Uncle into the bed and then wished us both "Good Night and God Bless" in unison. The light was switched off but sleep was now pulling at my eyelids so my prayers were brief but very, very, sincere. All was well in this newfound world.

Chapter 27
Time to go before it is too late!

I awoke to a choir of angel voices. Was I dead and gone to heaven? I had never been so warm and comfortable when a new day had dawned before. Was I still in my dream world? I tried to focus my eyes to the light streaming through the window where the sounds were also coming from. Finally, I remembered the events of yesterday and how I had come to be in this wonderful position.

I looked across to Uncle John in the bed next to me. He was sound asleep so I got up from the bed gently but with a great deal of difficulty, I might add. As I stretched and moved I banged my toe on something under the bed. I looked down to see a sort of round pot, with a handle and decorated with the same beautiful roses that were on the wallpaper. What could it be? I lifted it up to my face to examine it more closely just as Mrs. Wrigley entered the room. My nose was inside the pot when she spoke in a whispered voice, "Oh! Good you are awake, but my dear I think you are holding the pot at the wrong part of your body."

I nearly dropped the thing in surprise but instead I placed it back under the bed and sat down, waiting for instructions or information about my clothes. Instead, Mrs. Wrigley said a strange thing, "If you need to use the chamber pot I am sorry, I will leave you and fetch your clothes, I have washed and dried them as best I could with the help of Mary, take your time, I'll be back."

With the noise in the room Uncle John had stirred and was smiling at me. Thank goodness, he looked better than last night.

"So, what are you smiling about Uncle John, me in this shift or because you are feeling better?"

"Well, both of those things and also your response to a chamber pot."

"So, clever clogs, what is that thing?" I retorted with my hand pointing under the bed.

"It's what the finer folks use during the night so they don't have to go out in the cold air, to relieve themselves," he told me as he struggled to sit up. I could not imagine that beautiful pot painted with roses being used for that, it was beyond thinking about, and who would empty it? I certainly was not going to find out. I would hold myself until I got a chance to go outside and find some bushes I could fertilize. My Grandmother swore it did the plant life good anyway.

I helped Uncle John sit up while I filled him in on all that had happened yesterday. He was still groggy but remembered some "kindly folk" helping him. I sat on his bed to explain that the kindly folk had a very queer religion not at all, as we were used to in Tuam. I went on to explain, "Do you know that the priest is actually married to Mrs. Wrigley and he carried you with the help of George, his handyman, inside this house and then to this bed?"

Uncle John shook his head in disbelief but then started to cough and his body went into spasm. I ran to get the fluffy towel from the drawers and put it to his mouth. He coughed into it and I watched horrified as he spat out blood. My mind remembered the last time I had dealt with this dilemma. Oh! God please do not wish this illness on Uncle John. I need him so much.

I went to put water on the corner of the towel to wipe his face, but he started again. The noise came from the lungs violently and noisily, followed by more globules of blood into the towel. Mrs. Wrigley rushed into the room followed by the churchman and another woman who they called Mary. She ran back out of the room to bring something or other they had asked for. The churchman held Uncle John up in the bed while Mrs. Wrigley brought a bowl to rest on the bed beneath Uncle John's mouth.

"Please don't let him die on me, please." I cried out not knowing my voice was crying aloud.

Mrs. Wrigley put her arm around my shoulders and once again led me to another bedroom. She had my clean clothes with her so she told me to get dressed and go down to the kitchen when I had finished. I was now sobbing and shaking with fright, so she helped me with my task. Her gentle soft hands and her warm smile were in unison to her quiet voice, reassuring me that a Doctor had been called for and my Uncle would be well soon.

I could not help mumbling repeatedly, "don't die, please don't die, Oh! God please don't let him die, I will always be good, I will try harder to be good, but please don't take him." Tears were running uncontrollably down my face.
Mrs. Wrigley tried hard to console me, but I was just so afraid. The blood coming from his mouth was not a little thing, he had not cut his mouth, nor had a nose burst. That blood came from deep down inside. It was a problem. I knew it. I had seen it before. "Father in Heaven look after him," I sobbed falling to the floor at the same time holding on to Mrs. Wrigley. My head was in her lap as she tried to hush my cries by rubbing my head and repeating to me to try to be strong.

She helped me up from my kneeling position drying my weeping eyes with her pretty lace handkerchief. I stopped crying for a minute not wishing to spoil her square piece of cotton with my flood of self-pity. I gained control as I had learned to do many times before and faced the possibility that whatever God wished for us would happen.
We left the bedroom and went downstairs to the kitchen. I apologized to Mrs Wrigley for my outburst and told her I must go outside for a

while. I had lost a lot of water with my tears but there was a great deal more left to be relieved the other way.

I walked through the garden and down the narrow pathway that led to the church and there I found a suitable place to relieve myself. I stayed a while behind the trees as I heard voices coming down the path. Six or seven young men and a few boys came chattering together down the path. They wore long white smocks that finished round their ankles and ruffles of white collars surrounding their angelic faces. If this was the religion of England, I was vastly falling in love with everything it represented.

I waited a little more and then followed them back to the house. To my amazement, we all walked towards the kitchen door at the same time. I didn't expect them to be going there. Sheepishly, I followed them but was crushed for a moment in a heavenly body jam. The boys were trying to move to one side to let me through as Mary called out to the boys to move away from the door and let me through, then everyone could eat at the table.

They were trying their best to let me through to pass them, but with each motion they made I seemed to feel a soft hand or a brush of a cheek or a hand on my shoulder. This labyrinth of turmoil was my maze of ecstasy. I do not wish to sound irreverent but I loved it!   This ecclesiastical gathering brought an ebullience of apologetic voices to the confusion. Smiles turned to laughter as we all moved into place around this ample kitchen space.

Mary introduced me to the choir (as she called them) and told me it was a tradition for them to eat breakfast in the house after 'sermons'; another new word for me. The plates were passed around to those sitting and standing without any formality or awkward silences. Everyone felt at home in that kitchen, it had a warm welcoming mood.

England was beginning to feel like 'home'. Another day could be spent enjoying this wonderland as Uncle John was still confined to his bed.

Chapter 28
More exposure without plans.

I was beginning to feel that time was running short and I must start moving if I was to get to the wedding on time. These kind folks had told us there was no rush to escape their hospitality, but even so, I had made a promise back in the old country to Mrs. Kelly that I would attend the wedding.

The problem was that Uncle John was not ready to travel and I was in a strange country not knowing if it would be safe for me to travel alone. I had to talk this over with somebody. I went inside to that cozy English kitchen and found George who was sitting at the large table talking to Mary who was kneading bread. They must have been talking about us because she remarked, Well, speak of the devil!" which was one of my Grandmother's sayings, whenever I arrived unannounced. She asked me to sit down and make myself comfortable as she used her apron to wipe the flour from her hands. She poured me some milk from the large jug on the table and I sat down next to George.

I could not help feeling how different their lives were to everything I had experienced before. They were not without food, shelter or heat. They did not fear their employers or they would not take their time chatting together. They just were so happy and contented and the feeling oozed out to me. I must have smiled and the milk stuck to my chin, although I wasn't aware it had until George passed me one of those small linen pieces and told me to hold on to it. I decided I would tell them about my dilemma hoping for some adult common sense to make it easier for me to fathom out.

George told me that the doctor who had attended to Uncle John had given strict instructions he wasn't to leave his bed and had given him some 'knock out drops' to make sure he heeded his words. No wonder he was sleeping so much.

I told a little white lie that the wedding was a family affair and that Uncle John and I were to be the Irish representatives to attend on behalf of the rest of the family left in Ireland. (God forgive me.) There I was in a religious place telling wholesome lies to gain sympathy and understanding. I just hoped that maybe this religious house did not see it has a serious mortal sin. I was still sitting down and lightning had not hit me, so I just took a big breath and related the rest of the story about how we had been advised to travel.

George seemed to know all about the coal barges travelling from the River Mersey into the Bridgewater Canal to Worsley. In fact, some of their parishioners, as they called the people who came to their church had relatives who worked on these barges.

Mary and George started to talk very fast in a 'lingo' that was hard for me to follow. I learnt later that this Lancashire dialect had words and phrases as foreign as the language spoke back home. They were smiling and nodding their heads and repeating the words 'yes luv' a whole lot. This endearing word was to be a password for me later to be accepted in this part of the world. I memorized the lilt in the tone of the voices as they acknowledged each other and waited for them to include me in their conversation.

At last they both looked at me, but continued nodding their heads and smiling and I just knew they were going to give me good news, so I smiled back at them. George and Mary had lived in this part of the world all their lives and it seemed that everyone was related in some way to them. They told me about the various friends and relatives who could give me help, but finally they had concluded that as a woman travelling, alone I must be safe and they would never forgive themselves if they sent me into danger.

One of Mary's nephews was married to George's cousin's daughter and he worked on the barges. They both knew him to be a dependable godly person who could be trusted. The problem was they did not know if he owned the barge or if he just worked it. If he could have passengers on the barge was also something they did not know about or even if he travelled in the direction, I wanted to go.

I wanted to push them into answering these questions straight away but I was told to be patient and George would visit the family as soon as he got word of him being at home and not travelling on his barge. They were both being so helpful and I was so relieved and happy that a way could be found for me to move on, that tears rolled down my cheeks, but just in time I stopped myself from wiping them on my sleeve and remembered the linen in my pocket. I dabbed them dry gently without blowing my nose.

I thanked them both and made an excuse to go and check on Uncle John. There was a skip in my step as I left them talking about their hopes and concerns about the promise they had made me. I was thanking God and making promises to Him that really I did not know if I could complete but I wanted a new life so much and hadn't he just followed me to England from Ireland? I looked up to the sky, and then fell head over heels into the vegetable patch that was outside the kitchen door. George came out to see what the commotion was and lifted me up from the messy ground.

"I don't know if you are prepared for this journey on your own?" he said. "The world is full of cabbage patches waiting for you to fall into."

We both laughed because he knew I was excited and was not looking where I was going. I promised him that in future I would keep my eyes open for dangerous situations and not let my big clumsy feet go in the wrong direction. I walked away from him understanding that if I was to succeed on my own I had to be more careful. I had to be more 'grown

157

up' and think seriously about my next move, instead of skipping through life like a child.

I went back to the room where Uncle John was still fast asleep and was happy to see fresh water in the jug with soap on the side of the bowl so I could wash and clean myself up. As I took off my skirt and blouse I looked down to my knickers and was reminded that I was in fact a woman. The curse had come and I knew that my little encounter on the ship with Mr. Paul Hobson had been a lucky escape – this time, just another lesson for me to think with my head and not with my heart.

Chapter 29
Making Headway

Two full days went by and George did not even mention his promise. The Wrigley's were so kind to Uncle John and me that I tried to help around the place as much as I could to compensate. Mrs. Wrigley was very worried about my uncle when the pillowcase she was changing had bloodstains on it. She sent for the Doctor who came very quickly and stayed in our room for a long time examining Uncle John.

I sat with Mary in the kitchen who consoled me with tea and tales of other people she knew who had similar problems and who had recovered. I was worried about Uncle John having the same as my father and dying here in a strange place. Mary was sure it had to do with the blows to the stomach he had when we had been attacked. Either way it was serious. The Doctor was spending so much time with Uncle John it made me so frightened.

I walked back towards the room but stopped as I saw Mrs. Wrigley handing the Doctor money and taking the small bottle from him in return. Up until then I had not thought about the expense of the Doctor. The Doctor passed me in the corridor, touching his cap as he passed. I ran to Mrs. Wrigley to ask about the Doctor's decisions.

She told me that the Doctor thought the blows had caused internal bleeding, but that rest, good food and no worries would heal him soon. The bottle contained more "sleep medicine" to make sure the Doctor's orders were carried out.

I thanked Mrs. Wrigley sincerely, but she would hear none of it. She told me that God had blessed them and she was to pass his blessings on and I was not to feel I owed her anything. All she asked was for me to go into the church and thank God for his blessings. I didn't know if I had the 'know how' to go into their Church and pray. Did they pray the same as Catholics? What rituals were asked for in this Church?

I was glad no one was about when I went inside the small building, so I acted as though I was in Tuam in the Cathedral. I knelt down to give thanks, but found to my dismay I was asking for more. I wanted Uncle John to get better. I wanted to reach the wedding. I wanted to find the coalmine and ask for work. I wanted to make lots of money. Oh! I wanted so much. I stopped just in time as the vicar put his hand on my shoulder and patted my back. A loving gesture I appreciated. I left the building with my head reeling with possibilities.

As I crossed the cemetery I saw George standing at the door of the kitchen smoking his pipe. He saw me and beckoned me over; I waved back and hurried towards him full of hope and trepidation. He was smiling between his puffs, so I quickened my step and stopped right in front of him, waiting for him to speak. He puffed a few more times and then docked his pipe out on the stone wall.

"Let's go into the kitchen to talk, its warmer inside," he said putting his arm around my shoulders and pushing me through the door. There was no one in the kitchen but the fire was blazing and there was the usual jug of water and glasses and kitchen utensils spread out on the table.

George furrowed his brow and shook his head. I gulped at his actions sensing my dreams were fading away. Not daring to ask the inevitable questions, I asked instead if he would like a glass of water, because I certainly needed one myself at that moment. He nodded but as I poured the water into the glasses, I just knew that his worried face was not a good sign. He did not speak but drank the water down then banged the glass on the table and looked towards me. He seemed tormented, harassed, uncomfortable, not at all the composed George I had become to know well.

I did not want to be the first to break the silence in case I said the wrong thing, so I looked into his eyes in a pleading way at the same time trying to keep my trembling lips from showing my true anxiety.
I sat beside him with my hands holding the glass of water I had poured for myself and slowly he took hold of my hand with both of his. He spoke in a soft voice, very slowly so I could understand him clearly. I did not look up from my glass, fearing the worse.

"This is a hard decision for me to make," he began, "you are just a young lass in a strange land wanting to do the best for your family and very determined to reach your goal."

He went on to say that he understood that time was not on my side to wait for Uncle John to go with me to the wedding. He wished that could be changed. He spoke for another few minutes about all the dangerous situations I could get myself into before I got to 'my family'. He told me he would never forgive himself if anything happened to me and he had to live with that fear.

I wanted to answer him and tell him that I wouldn't hold him responsible and that none of my relatives would either but somehow I knew that at that moment it was better for me to remain silent and not interrupt his flow of negative decisions. My vision for a better life was still holding on with a thin thread of optimism. My mother always told me that I was a child who never took 'no' for an answer. I waited for him to clear his throat and take another sip of the water.

Finally, his tone of voice changed and he made me look him in the face as he sternly made me promise I would not let him down. I must follow instructions exactly and he would help me because he believed I would do as he asked.

"Yes, yes, "I answered him, "whatever you say I will take orders; I have to do this for the family", I said again using the same excuse as before. In

my own justification, I was on this journey to help my family. If I reached the
coalmines and got work, then I would send for the family and give them a better life. The end would justify the means, I was sure of that.

George then described how Mary had first approached her nephew. She had not been very clear so they had asked George to go to their cottage and fill them in with the details. George explained still using his stern voice, "I was trying to convince young Robert, he's the one who works on the coal barge, to give you a lift along the canal, but I also wanted him to assure me if it was possible; then was it safe?"

This Robert person had some fears of his own which George told me were understandable concerns. He did own the barge, he could take a passenger if he wished, but he was a married man and there could be talk if he carried a young woman as a passenger. His wife then took pity on the part of the story George had explained about Uncle John and me having been robbed, as we were on the way to a family wedding. She was the one who convinced her husband to do the 'right thing' and help a young woman. She would go along for the ride herself and make sure the wagging tongues had nothing to talk about.

I could not believe there was so much help and understanding here in this small village. These strangers were willing to help me and I wanted to jump with joy, but George was still holding my hand tightly. Was there a catch? How much would it cost? Were they helping me for some reason I could not make out? Why would these people want to give me a ride?

I did not ask George these questions but waited for him to tell me what had been decided by his relatives.
I was to travel on the barge with Robert and his wife Elizabeth. This arrangement had apparently suited George and for this reason he had pushed the plan forward for me to travel with them.

We were to leave in two days, but George then asked me if I had any money to pay these people. I did not know quite how to answer this. I did have a some money left in my knickers but it wasn't a lot and I did need to have some money to survive when I arrived at my destination. Was this the catch?

"How much are they talking about?' I asked nervously.

"Well, they haven't really asked for anything," answered George, "but there are expenses when you go down the canal and of course, there is food for the journey and for the horse".

"A horse?"

"Well, yes the horse pulls the barge down the canal from the towing path at the side of the canal, apparently, he doesn't always like the grass on the verges, he's quite old but very reliable so they carry food for the horse too."
"Now let's just leave that little problem for the moment" he went on, "the bigger problem is getting permission from your Uncle".
I had not thought about that and did not know how to, but George came to the rescue again. "Leave that to me. Your Uncle is in no fit state to accompany you and once I tell him our plan I am sure he will trust us and stay here until you come back for him?"

"Yes, yes", I stammered, "wait here until I come back, that's best"

I decided to let things go along as fate or maybe my destiny for this life was leading. I had not done too badly up to now. It seemed I was meant to have a better life than my mother did if only I kept listening to that little voice inside of me that told me it was possible. All was possible in this new land – England.

Chapter 30
To the water

 Two days later the arrangements had been made, mostly by my new friends. The vicar had convinced Uncle John that I would be safe with Robert and his wife who would make sure I got to Worsley for the wedding. Mary had baked food for the journey with Mrs. Wrigley's blessing. George had provided food for the horse and to my dismay, Uncle John had given Robert a little money for his trouble; the robbers must have left him something.

We were all set. However, I needed to tell Uncle John myself that I would be careful and return for him as soon as possible. It was a difficult fifteen minutes, but as I was leaving the room, Uncle John smiled and said,

"You always were a strong woman, young Caty, you were never a child. You obviously have things to do in this life that others may want to do but never take the challenge. You are a survivor and I know in my heart you will make things happen. Just watch your back and trust no one. Do you hear? You are as good and as strong as any man is but do not let them know that. Always play the woman it confuses us men, take it from me."

I went to his bed and hugged him.

"Be off with you," he said, "you're going to hurt me squeezing so hard."

I left the room without looking back. When I got to the kitchen everyone was there to wish us 'God speed'. I helped to carry the baskets, and muslin wrapped food to the cart outside. Elizabeth the wife of Robert was sitting up front with a beaming smile.

George was to drive us to the barge and help Robert get the barge moving, which was, I learnt later, not an easy task for one person to do.

We filled the back of the cart but left a space for Robert and myself and then we were off. We jogged down the road, waving our goodbyes and holding tight to the rickety cart's sides. Robert laughed and remarked,

"Are we going to get to the water in one piece, George?"

"Listen here young lad; it is safer on my cart than in your barge, I am sure of that."

"Well, we will let the young lass here be the judge of that, shall we?"

I was so happy at that moment; I felt safe just being with these good folks. I was ready for anything, ready for adventure, ready to see the life outside Tuam. Before I had chance to capture this wonderful countryside we arrived at what Robert said was our starting place. Here was a "roving bridge" where we would cross to get on the right side of the canal for the direction we were going. There was a 'strapping post' with a horse grazing and the canal flowed under this small stone bridge.

We all got off the cart and George loosened the reigns of his horse and then tied him to the strapping post alongside the other horse. We unloaded the packages and each carried a bungle across the bridge to the barge. Then I saw it. Every surface was painted. Every moulding picked out in a strong colour. There was a landscape on the side of the barge and around each window there were roses painted in many colours.

"There she is," said Robert in a proud voice, "she can carry as much as 25 tons, isn't she a beauty?"

We all nodded and made sounds of astonishment, which was enough to convince him we all approved. Even Elizabeth who had never seen her husband's barge had to say she did not expect the barge to be so beautiful. Then I knew, for sure, that she too was seeing the barge for the first time.

165

There was a boy waiting on the pathway at the side of the barge. He looked like the shepherds in the fields back home. He wore full front corduroy trousers, a jacket of the same material and a rather large cap set at a cocky angle on his head.

We were introduced to him as Billie boy, Robert's mate. We learnt that it was practically impossible to manage the barges single-handed but many of the bargees were husband and wife teams, often with children too. The two people who worked the horse boats were needed (one to steer it and the other to make sure the horse keeps going).
I looked at Elizabeth's face as she was introduced to Billie boy, but she hid her true feelings in a smile. I sensed she was covering her jealousy towards the boy. I was sure she would like to have been a lady bargee but it was some time before I learnt the true story behind this team.

"I've filled her up Mr. Robert as you said and we are standing by to go whenever you are. I didn't fill to capacity as we are carrying extra passengers, just as you said."

"Right" was all Robert said, then followed it with, "mind your heads as you go down the steps to the cabin, there isn't all that much space as you will see."

The cabin was about nine or ten foot long and about six foot wide but ever so clean, not at all like the last canal boat I had travelled on. The woodwork was scrubbed to snowy whiteness and the brass work gleamed and reflected through the small windows that were adorned with lace edged curtains. Every tin utensil was smothered in the same colourful rose design I had seen outside. It didn't seem to me to have a manly atmosphere at all, so I wondered who had been responsible for all this beauty.

I was stopped from my dreaming by the voice of Robert giving us directions to the hidden cupboards. I was very impressed by the very clever uses of space to put our belongings away and the nooks and crannies for the food storage. This tiny cabin was full of hidden treasures.

Robert assured George that he did not need his help,
"We have done this many times Billie boy and me, so we will be fine, and don't worry little Caty will meet her folks the other end and get to the wedding".

George gave me a hug and told me to be good and help. He tugged his cap, nodded his head towards Elizabeth, and wished her a safe journey and then he went up the stairs. We all followed and stood together on deck of the barge watching him cross back over the bridge to his horse and cart. Robert told Billie boy to go fetch the old nag then we could get started.

I waved to George who waved back as he trotted away down the path we had come by. My stomach and my head were very wheezy and we had not started to move. It was surely excitement and anticipation; I was not afraid. Kind artistic folks surrounded me and I had new challenges ahead.
I was looking forward to whatever was waiting for me down the Bridgewater Canal.

Chapter 31
On the water

Starting the barge off did need a lot of effort. To overcome the resistance to motion that a barge weighing 30 to 50 tons of boat and cargo has, does need plenty of heavy pulling. The speed is built up by an accumulation of manpower and horse power that Robert and Billie boy had mastered. It was important, he told us, that once they had momentum they had to keep moving. Barges do not have brakes. Once the weight of the boat and cargo were moving, the barge had to keep going and I guessed it would take the same amount of effort to stop it again. The stretchy cotton towline was taut, but the horse led by Billie boy was moving at a steady pace. Robert assured me that he knew this route well; he was familiar with the problem areas and when he would meet obstacles or other boats.

I went to the back of the barge where Elizabeth was sitting and she welcomed me with that beautiful smile and took hold of my hand. We both looked out over the rippling water towards the towpath. The cotton tow line was fixed to a sort of collar that went around the horse's hind quarter and this was held in place with a harness like the one my Father used when he put Beauty into our cart.

Billie boy was walking alongside the horse whistling a tune and occasionally patting the horse on for encouragement. The movement of the barge was in harmony with the walking pace of the horse. We felt no jolting movements; there was only a steady glide through the water. It was a very peaceful and tranquil feeling, but as usual my mind was racing forward and questions were nagging me about Elizabeth. I broke the silence.

"Is this the first time you have been with Robert on the Bridgewater?"

"It is, yes," she answered, "and it is all thanks to you thatI have had this opportunity to do this. I have waited so long but Robert had his reasons."

Her story was fascinating. She told me that Robert was born on that very same barge. He was the youngest of four children (two girls and two boys). He told her he was born three feet under water because at the time the boat was loaded. We both laughed and she went on. All the Boat people lived in closed communities and most seemed to marry boat people. The barges were their homes so they each tried to put their own individual mark in their decorative art. They were proud of their results and this kind of art was unique. The paintings were vivid in colour and in detail. Because the space was packed, they had to keep it spotlessly clean to keep away disease. Even though the family grew up on the canals, the other children could not wait to get away. The girls left first and got married to 'land boys' and then soon after Robert's brother went to work on the farm that Elizabeth's family owned because her Father had died and her Mother needed the help. Robert also became restless to leave and joined his brother.

"That is how I met Robert," she gloated.

I listened to her stories as we sat together at the back of the barge swishing through the water at a jaunty pace. The wonderful smell of the wild bank flowers scented the air. I watched the English world go by at a pace that was just right to appreciate its beauty. All my senses were absorbing the different pleasures at once but they were strangely in tune and so I was lulled into an oblivious sleep.

I woke with a jerk as I heard my name being called. It was Robert who was calling and pointing to the water... I do not know how long I had been sleeping but the colour of the water had now changed. It was now a distinctive orange colour. I carefully walked towards him as he explained. He told me that the colour was caused by iron salts in the

169

local rock, which leached out from the network of underwater canals that linked the collieries to the canal.

My ears pricked up, "Do you mean collieries as in coal mines?" I asked.

"Yes of course, that's what I am talking about."

He went on to explain the history of the canal. It was built for the Duke of Bridgwater by a self-taught engineer called James Brindley. I was only half listening to this part (I thought I had heard this before) and I wanted to know if we were near the mines, but he continued.

"The underwater canals, of course, were built by another great man called John Gilbert, and this was the way the coal was transported from the mine to the canal."

This was my chance to ask if we were near the mine as my anticipation of nearing my destination was too much to hold back.

"Are we there? Are we near the mine? What does it look like? Can I see it from here?" I spluttered all my questions out to him as he smiled and held up his hand to stop me speaking. He told me to sit back down with Elizabeth and watch the bank to our right, which I obediently did.

Suddenly into view came large buildings, the like I had never seen before. They were black and white with some black crosses determining the next level. These were the tallest buildings I had seen since leaving Liverpool but they were so beautiful. Robert told me this building was called the "Packet House". I could see people departing from this building down steps to passenger boats. We were going to stop our boat here. Robert told us, we could depart as soon as the boat was safe enough to alight.

I went to get my belongings and as I passed Elizabeth I couldn't help giving her a huge hug as my excitement couldn't be contained. Robert, Elizabeth, and I, left the boat behind with careful steps. Robert told us we would feel a little dizzy when we touched the land and maybe we would behave like drunken sailors. As Elizabeth and I held on to each other we laughed until we cried as we swayed from side to side just as Robert had predicted. Robert left the securing of the barge to Billie Boy and told him to take care of everything and then he could take a rest.

We strolled along the towpath and then we walked into a large square yard. It was an enclosed complex full of activity. There were people working outside making things. There were wheelwrights, nail makers, and even boat makers. The square was surrounded by warehouses. I was told these buildings stored goods and timber. The noise was deafening and the sights bewildering. We dodged out of the way of carts clattering on flat stones, bumping and shaking their way through the crowds. I held on to my two friends frightened of getting in the way of someone or something.

This hive of industry I had never before even imagined existed. I looked curiously at every stall, workshop, or door that was open. There were not many women around so Elizabeth and I were the victims of cat calls and whistles that Robert said were all to be taken lightly as it was just 'Lancashire humour', so we hurried on with our heads down. As I pulled my shawl further over my head I heard the familiar sound of a church clock striking the hour and asked Robert if I was hearing right? I could not write but I could count. He told me that workers were often late returning from their lunch, claiming they could not hear the clock strike one above the noise coming from the yard. The Duke of Bridgewater had the mechanism of the clock altered so that it struck thirteen instead.

This reminded Robert that we had not eaten, so we went to find the 'hot potato stand'. We juggled the hot potato from hand to hand and bit into it as far as we could before blowing again to cool it down. We walked out of the yard into a nearby street where I was met with another strange site and sound. A horse drawn cart, painted in wonderful bright colours. Inside stood a man with a white coat and flat cap shouting something I did not understand. Elizabeth turned to Robert and pleaded for an ice cream. Robert walked forward towards the cart and we followed to watch the man filling a small glass (I later learned was called a 'licker glass') full of a cold solid, milky looking substance. Robert passed one to me and, of course, I licked it. They both had one and as we stood there the man asked in a funny accent if it was the first time I had tried "icy creamy?" Robert told him I was from Ireland not from England.

"Mi a too I from Italy" he said in his funny voice. I had no idea where that was but it was obviously a nice place if they made food as good as we tasted then.

We finished and handed the glasses back to the jolly man. I had forgotten for a short time the reason for me being in England but Robert brought me down to earth telling me we must find a way to get to Astley Green colliery, the pit where he could unite me with Mrs. Kelly's son.

He decided to go back into the yard to see if any of the wagons were going that way. We waved Goodbye to the man from Italy and followed Robert into the yard.

Elizabeth and I sat on a small wall outside one of the buildings and left Robert to find transport for this important last part of my long journey. Under my shawl I had my finger crossed and was silently praying. Elizabeth touched my hand and squeezed it gently. She told me not to worry that Robert would find someone. We saw him coming towards us, not giving anything away with his eyes, when the mayhem started. A barking dog had broken its leash and was chasing a cat, just as a horse and cart came around the bend.

We watched horrified as the frightened horse bolted upright and the cart toppled over with its entire load falling on top of Robert. At first I felt I was stuck to the wall, my feet would not lift me; I was stationary in time, not able to move with the shock and horror of the scene in front of me. Then I realized that Elizabeth had moved and was bending down over Robert and holding his head. In the middle of the turmoil people came running out of everywhere towards the accident. Some men were reaching for the reigns of the horse to calm it down. Others were helping the driver get from under the cart and yet more were moving the planks of wood and barrels of nails away from Robert. I felt helpless and hopeless in this deafening situation but I willed my legs to move to be with my good friends and offer my help.

The scene gradually turned silent as men stopped work. The barking dog had disappeared. There were a lot of the men now working quietly to rescue Robert and the driver from the heavy load. I tried now to console Elizabeth and tell her not to worry. I lifted her up and took her to one side. Leaving the men room to get the rubble off Robert and lift the cart upright.

The horse was taken from its harness and led away. Two injured men, one who had become as close as a brother to me, were now clear of the debris but still not moving. Out of the crowd suddenly came a man dressed like a gentleman in a suit carrying a small black leather bag. I heard the men shout, "Here is the Doctor, give him room, move aside give him room for heaven's sake".

I hugged Elizabeth and told her all would be well now the Doctor was here,but she tried to get to Robert. This was not possible as the men held us back to give space to the Doctor. She was shaking uncontrollably so one of the men led us to his workshop to sit down with a glass of water. He told us the good Doctor was on the payroll of the Duke and was the best in the country.

The men in the crowd started to shout, "They are breathing, they are alive!"
I repeated the information to Elizabeth who started to sob and shake again.

A horse drawn vehicle with a peculiar shape drew into the yard which I was told was called 'an ambulance' and this would take the men to the Infirmary, the place where injured people went to be 'fixed'. I shook my head in wonderment of this new world that had places to fix people after they were hurt. I had never heard of it before.

Robert and the driver were put inside the ambulance, but then the Doctor turned around and came towards us.
He touched his hat as he greeted us and asked, "Which of you young ladies are with the young man?"
I answered that we were both with him but that Elizabeth was his wife.

"Unfortunately there is only room for one more passenger, so follow me please to the ambulance" then he added to me as he walked away, "we are going to the Infirmary my dear where he can get treatment, don't you worry."

I watched as he held Elizabeth's arm and guided her into the vehicle, then it was gone out of site. I took a big sigh and sat back down with my head in my hands. I couldn't cry, I was too frightened; what was I to do now? I did not know where I was. My closest friends had gone away to an Infirmary. I had no idea what that meant and I did not know a soul who could help me. I did what came naturally, and silently. I prayed.

Chapter 32
There's always a way

I felt a pat on my back from someone in the crowd around me. He was offering me a cup of tea. "Drink this up luv it always makes the world a better place."

I knew they were trying to help and I thanked them the best way I could and took the tea that was offered.
"You don't seem to be from this neck of the woods. Where do you come from?" he asked.

"I 'm from Ireland but I'm travelling to meet a friend who works at Astley Green Colliery." I proffered, "but now I'm stuck in a strange place by myself and ..."

I tried to go on but the full impact of all that had happened just hit me and the tears just flowed down my face. I did not feel I was crying but I was beginning to shake and the men were confused as what to do next. I heard a woman's voice speak above me.

"Now luv don't get yuself in a state, it won't do you any good, tha'l mak thaself ill and you'll end up at th' Infirmary"

This remark seemed to go well with one of the men, "perhaps if I took her down there, maybe Doctor can give her something to calm her down?"

The words were all jumbling in my head, some of the words I did not even understand but if I could get to the Infirmary then I could see Robert and Elizabeth.
"Could someone get me there?" I pleaded, "is it a long way?"

"No luv", said the woman "my Jack can tak thee in his cart, can't thi Jack?"

"Always does as the missus says now don't I?" the man spoke to the crowd who seemed to find it funny.
Then in a matter of minutes I was being pushed into a cart and was being waved off by all who were still standing around since the accident.

The cart was rolling over the stones out of the yard past the Italian ice cream man into the streets beyond. Unusual sights surrounded me. These streets had strange houses all in line with doors every few yards. Women stood in the doorways of some, while other women were grouped together talking, no doubt chatting about the accident, Jack said to me, as he whipped the horse on to go faster.

"It's not far luv. Nearly there," he said to my satisfaction.

The bouncing around in the cart was something far different to the slow pace we had driven Beauty back home in Ireland. Jack told me the hard surface on the road was called "cobblestones", and that they caused havoc to cart wheels, but that was good for his trade and the money he could make on repairs kept his wife and family well fed. I stopped myself thinking about home or I would have started to cry again and that would come to nothing. I had to show how grateful I was to Jack.

We went through some large iron gates and into a huge yard where I noticed were more 'ambulances'. Jack stopped the cart in front of the enormous building, which he told me was the Infirmary. He tied up his horse then helped me down as if I was injured. We walked through some enormous doors into a large, green tiled room with a desk at one end.

Behind the desk was a woman writing with her head down, but on her head was the weirdest looking hat, very stiff and white. Her clothes were the cleanest clothes I had ever seen but they also looked very stiff and uncomfortable. Her voice was different, soft, and caring as she asked us if she could help.

Jack told her about the accident and whom we were as she nodded, obviously aware of what had happened. She asked us to sit down while she went for the Doctor. I gripped my hands on my knees and gulped at the circumstance I was in. Jack patted my back as he had before and told me again everything would be fine.
I looked up as I heard a sharp clicking sound on the tile floor. The woman, Jack called a nurse, had shoes on her feet I had never seen before that tapped the floor like a soldier marching to a tune. She told us the Doctor would be with us shortly and sat down again at her desk. We heard another door open and the Doctor I recognized from earlier came through with another nurse at his side. He smiled at me and told me he believed he had seen me earlier in the day with the wife of the accident victim.

Everyone there seemed to talk like the ladies of Tuam, very slow and precise, so I felt I understood them clearly. He told me that Robert had no broken bones but was very sore and bruised. He had a bad cut on his head that he wanted to look at again in the morning. If I wanted, I could go to see him. He also told Jack that the driver was not badly hurt, thank God, he added, and if he wanted to go in to cheer him up, he could. We were told to follow the nurse through the door, which we did at a marching pace.

We entered another green room, which had a line of beds on each side. It had a funny smell that was strange to me, but I rubbed my nose and tried not to look at the people in the beds as I passed them. Then at the end of the room I spotted Elizabeth waving to me and beckoning me forward. Jack had stopped at a bed halfway along which obviously was the driver's bed. Something told me not to run but I hastened my step to see my friends again.

177

Robert was sat up in bed, a good sign, but he had bandages around his head. These bandages were not made from bed sheets as we used in Ireland but were more like the muslin we wrapped the butter in. He smiled and told me he had been lucky and not to worry he was in good hands. Elizabeth nodded but told me she would sit in the chair next to his bed until he could leave. I noticed there was only one chair, so a flash of realization hit me, I would not be staying there with them. I stopped the flow of self-pity coming over me again as I felt a hand patting my shoulder. Jack was happy to have seen his friend and wanted to get back to his workmates to tell them the news. He told Robert and Elizabeth he would take me back and they asked him to drop me off at their boat, which was moored in the basin, also to tell Billie Boy to wait for them to return.

The Doctor joined us at the bedside and asked if I was feeling better now I had seen my friends. I told him I was feeling better and I did not need any of his special 'treatment' at this time. He laughed at my Irish humour, which he said he was accustomed to, whatever that meant?

Reluctantly I walked away from my friends following the nurse and Jack down the middle of the beds. Suddenly I remembered, I had not asked Robert if he had been successful in finding someone to give me a lift to the colliery. I turned to walk back but I was stopped by a strong arm holding me. The nurse was facing me with a finger over her lips and her other hand releasing me to point at the bed of Robert; I could see he had fallen to sleep.

"You should leave him now to rest," she said in a whisper.
It was no use; my question would have to wait.

Chapter 33
Placing a bet

We left the Infirmary the way we had come in and went through the giant gates into the cobbled streets. There were houses on both sides of the street, bare of trees or grass. We left behind the strange smell of the Infirmary, but this was replaced by a stench of something I couldn't name. Very much, like the sulphur smell of the match works back home.

Jack started to ask me why I had left Ireland. Was I alone? Where Robert and Elizabeth family? A lot more questions I really did not want to answer. Therefore, I decided to get straight to the point. I told him I was going to a wedding in Astley and was bringing greetings from all the family in Ireland. I said I was the only one who could be spared from the farm as all the men were needed to bring in the "harvest." (Jesus, Mary and Joseph what a white lie.) I looked up to the sky waiting for the thunderbolt. Luckily, I only received a jolt from the cart as it went over some broken stones.

Jack drove the cart back to the yard where I thanked him for everything as he helped me alight, something I was not accustomed to experiencing. His wife and their friends all gathered to hear our news. He quickly gave them the good news about Robert and the driver and told them that they were safe at the Infirmary. They all looked towards the statue of the Grand Duke of Bridgwater and doffed their caps.

His wife asked me where I was going to stay but I did not get chance to answer as Jack told my half-invented story to all who were listening. and added that now I needed a lift to Astley to complete my long journey and to be reunited with my family (as he put it). I smiled as best I could through my teeth. They told me to go back to the boat and they all would ask around and let me know if any carts were going that way. I added that all I needed was to get to Astley Green Pit, to the office, where Jarlath, my relative would be. (Another nail in my coffin)

"Well, that will be much easier lass," he said, "the carts do deliver wood and nails to the pits. I'm sure someone will be going that way. Just leave it to us and don't you worry now."

They pointed out the way to the boat and I was yet again left to wonder if my grandmother's words were true after all. 'Somebody up there likes you Caty'. I had to say I was being helped by so many people that didn't know me. Yes, England was a wonderful place to be.

I saw Billie boy working on the boat, but he did not see me. I walked towards him trying to think how to give him the news gently. He saw me and waved. As I went towards him he asked where Robert and Elizabeth where, so I slowly told him about the accident adding quickly that Robert was not badly hurt but was staying in the Infirmary for at least another day. He was obviously relieved, but needed to be reassured as to his duties as his boss was not there to instruct him

"We will stay here tonight," I said in a very firm voice, "that's what Robert told me to do," I added "so, why don't you go into the yard up there and find something to eat and maybe have a drink in the ale house there?"
I patted my skirt to feel for my savings, but told Billie Boy to wait why I used the privvy and I would be back in a flash.

I went in the privy and took off my knickers to get to the money; it was still all there in tact. I took two half pennies to give to Billie and was going to put back on my knickers but the smell from them was awful. I had not washed in ages so I decided to go up top without them and give Billie the money so he could disappear and give me chance to wash. He gladly took the money, thanked me, and ran off in the direction of the yard.

180

I went below and closed the curtains on the little windows for privacy. There was a large colourful bowl with painted roses, of course, on the outside. Next to it was a large jug. I went up to fill it from the canal water. If the water had iron salts in it, so what, it may give me some strength, I surely needed it.

I took time washing myself, even washing my hair and the knickers that needed a wash so badly but as they were the only ones I had with a pocket inside I had to get them to dry quickly before Billie came back. I dressed and then let my hair fall loose to dry. I stuffed my money into the pocket of my skirt but then decided to separate it and put most of the florins in my bundle I didn't want to take any chances carrying all the money in my pocket.

The sun was still out so I hung my knickers over the bench up top hoping they would dry quickly. I sat at the side of them feeling embarrassed but I could see there were no other people around. It was a beautiful evening and the position of the boat just made it sway with the water as it rippled passed. I wondered where the horse was but I knew Billie would have put her safe somewhere.

From a distance, I could hear music and voices so I stood up to look. It seemed to be coming from the yard but it was hard to see anything; it was too far away. I decided to leave the boat and go to look. No one would know I had no knickers on under my long heavy skirt. The gentle breeze blew up my skirt as I walked, but it was a wonderful feeling, so I took my shawl off my head and tied it around my waist. My hair was blowing around and drying fast so I tucked it behind my ears. I felt so clean, so fresh, and so free. I put a little skip in my step to the music ahead but wondered who was making these strange sounds.

I made my way back into the yard and I saw it was now transformed from its daytime use. The workshops had their shutters up and the large doors of the warehouses were closed, but there were plenty of people

181

around. The alehouse I had noticed earlier had benches and tables outside with lots of customers around
.

Then I saw where the music came from. There was a man who had earrings and a big moustache with an even bigger smile. He was turning a handle attached to a kind of box on two wheels. It looked like a sort of hand cart we used back home... The music that came out of the box was so good that people were dancing together in tune to it.

Then I saw a strange looking animal on top of the box like a little baby but with fur and it was also dressed in a colourful hat and coat. I was mystified. While I watched this strange scene I heard a familiar voice shouting in the background – the translation I had been given by the man himself, 'Ecco un poco' (Have a little). It was the Italian ice cream man. I went across to speak with him and of course he asked me where my friends were, so I explained the full horrible story to him.

"Havva creama it is gooda for a lady" he said with his singing voice.

 I took it willingly with thanks but I had to ask him about the music and the animal. He smiled and nodded his head. "You like our music lady?"

I nodded back to him as I licked the glass full of the delicious ice cream. He told me the man was also from Italy, his own dear country across the sea. I felt suddenly close to the man who had travelled across the water, like me, to come to England.

He called it a 'hurdy-gurdy' or a 'barrel organ', but I did not care what he called the box. I wanted to know about the animal on the cart. He told me the animal was called a monkey and that many organ grinders had monkeys on their carts to attract the crowds and to make them laugh. Well, all I could say was that the people from Italy really did know how to make good 'lickers' and good music and I was glad they came to England.

We talked more between his customers coming and going and he told me there was plenty of work here in England for men and women who did not mind hard work. He told me that in this area woman did all kinds of work; in textile mills, shops and even at the pithead washing the coal. If I wanted work there was plenty around..
He was now getting very busy so I thanked him once more and left with a full stomach and a mind full of good information. I loitered around listening to the music and watching the people and then I saw Billie boy sitting on a bench outside the alehouse. He shouted me to join him and so I did. After the tune had finished he asked me if I wanted a drink. I remembered what drink had done to my father so at first I said no but he insisted. I tasted a bit from his glass, and I have to say that what the beginning of a long partnership between a glass of beer and myself.
I put my hand in my pocket and pulled out a coin, which Billie took and went inside to get me a 'glass of the finest'. He returned with the beer and some interesting news. Inside the 'public house' as Billie called it, there was a lot of talk going on about the upcoming races.

Every spring in a place called Aintree, which was not too far away there was held a steeplechase with over 60 horses taking part. The man at the bar inside had told Billie all about it. Just then, this same man, as Billie had mentioned, came out to collect the empty glasses from the tables. I encouraged Billie to call the man over so we could ask him more; he told us he would be back shortly.

As I waited, my thoughts went back to my visit to Ballinasloe Fair. I tried to remember my horse-trading jargon, and as I remembered the tickling sensation came back to my stomach. The excitement of race horses gave me this feeling. I talked to Billie about his horse but his answers were without the same passion that I felt when I was near horses.

The bar man came to our table and asked us if we wanted to make a 'bet' on the Grand National. I asked him to explain, if he would, what that meant. He was curious about my accent; I told him I was from Ireland but visiting family over here. So, he sat down with us to inform us about this great race that even those people who didn't follow the 'ponies' (as he put it) did have a 'flutter' (a bet) on this day.

Apparently, the race was run over four and half miles and the horses had to go over 30 fences with imposing names like 'Beechers Brook', 'The chair', 'Valentine's' and the 'Canal Turn'; very high and very dangerous. He said that many a horse fails to jump those fences and if the horse throws its rider, then the riders could be trampled under, if they did not roll away to safety quick enough.

I urged him to tell me more. I actually wanted more information and then maybe I would have a 'flutter'. He told me that in the previous two years the same horse had won. A horse named 'Manifesto', but then, an Irish horse won last year. My ears pricked up as he told me it was a Irish horse, owned by His Royal Highness the Prince of Wales. It was called Ambush 11

The same horse was running again and that meant it was the favourite. Therefore, you did not win as much for your bet if it won again. I asked if there was a list of horses and if he knew of another Irish horse in the race. He did know that the second favourite was from Ireland, so that maybe a good bet.

Now, the race was the next day and so I had to 'lay my bet' today, as he put it. I had never done this before but I had seen Uncle John do this at Ballinasloe Fair when we were there.

"Right," I said, "I will bet on the second favourite to beat His Majesty's horse. Tell me what I must do next, I just have a feeling, but tell me its name?"

I had to go back into the public house with him to find the 'bookie'.and place my bet. This man could write down names and record the bets so I had to see him.

On the way inside, I asked if I could go to the privy. I did not want anyone to know I had money in my pocket. I needed to increase my stash if I was to stay here in England. I sat on the privy wondering if I was to chance only one shilling, but then I took out two more. They were burning in my palm. That is all I needed. It was a sign of good luck as far as I knew. I would bet three shillings. Most of my money was safe in the boat and people had been so kind to me I had not spent much so far. This thought made me feel I could bet big and take a chance.
I walked towards the table where I was told the man taking the bets was sitting. There was a number of men pushing and elbowing their way to the front.

The bar man shouted above the crowd, "now let the lady through lads; she knows her horse and will be just a minute to place her bet. Be the gentlemen you are now." They parted and let me through and I asked in a whispered voice to place three shillings to win on the horse from Ireland that was the second favourite.
"Its name is 'Drumcree' lady. Now how much did you say you would you like to bet I understand you want a straight win?"

I nodded then slowly and a little hesitantly put down my big bet on the table. He took it and then gave me a slip of paper which he said was the proof I had placed my bet. I was to bring it back to him, "if a miracle was to happen and my horse beat the Prince's horse," he laughed as he passed me the paper.
I went back to the table but Billie Boy was not there so I sat for a while contemplating my stupidity at wasting my hard earned money on a flimsy whim; what had I done?

185

Chapter 34
Facing the consequences

I slowly pulled my heavy body from off the seat when I finished another beer given to me by the pub man 'on the house for Good Luck', so he had said. I made my way towards the boat hating myself for being so gullible and foolish with the hard-earned cash. The money had been given to me for my good deeds back in Ireland and was to help my family join me here. Everyone back home was counting on me and I had thrown it away on a bet. Tears fell down my face and wet the ground I walked on. With my head down and my shawl over my head, I began to comprehend the tremendous mistake I had made and knew no way to make it right. I would never be able to hold my head up again with the same spirit and confidence I once had. I was a traitor to my family, the family who had trusted me. Caty Luby was not the girl who had left Ireland to make money for her family; this person who was walking on the canal bank was a selfish good for nothing bad young woman, why she even drank beer with men at an alehouse! How low could that be I asked myself?

I heard voices ahead and looked up to see where they came from. There were three young men laughing as they relieved themselves from the bank wall and into the canal water below. They seemed to be having a competition as to which of them could make their pee travel the farthest into the water. I panicked and ran to hide in the bushes.

I was both disgusted and frightened. Perhaps the water was this funny orange colour for another reason than iron salts filtering from the mines. To think I had washed myself in that water earlier made me shiver, but I consoled myself with the thought that maybe the water I washed in had made me an evil person tonight. I vowed never to wash myself with canal water ever again.

The young men turned towards me as they tucked away their large appendages into their pants. I gazed with wonderment and curiosity at the sight in front of me, but at the same time my stomach rumbled with the beer and I released a loud bodily function that could not be held back. I dreaded the consequences of this act. Fortunately, for me at the same time I man came by and shouted to the youths, "come on lads. Lets be having you home, there is work to be done tomorrow. No use dilly dallying around here and wasting good sleep time".

He must have been a boss of some kind because they nodded and then ran ahead down the canal bank and out of sight. I waited until the man was also a long way from me before I left the bushes and made my way once again towards the barge. I tentatively and carefully went along the gang blank. In the silence, I looked around for signs of Billie Boy, but I was alone. I sniggered at the sight of my knickers still drying on the bench and went hastily to get them. I needed to go below and find a place to sleep and finish this awful day I had experienced.

I climbed down the steps and into the galley where I lit the oil lamp to help me locate everything. On the floor in front of me was my bundle of clothes. Strewed around the floor and scattered on the sofa bench under the window. I started to pick them up and then remembered with a jolt that I had left money in that bundle. Frantically I searched each piece of clothing not remembering clearly, where I had put it.

There was no money to be found. The florins, the shiny sixpence, the three-penny bit and the few pennies I had hidden were gone. Thankfully, the small bundle, which was Mrs. Kelly's wedding present, was still there. I sat down in total disbelief. Then I raised my voice to a scream shouting for Billie Boy to come out of hiding and give me my money back. I opened every cupboard, every nook and cranny of the barge, shouting for the world to hear that I would kill him, for sure, if I found him. I went back on deck and looked there. I focused my eyes to look around on and off the boat. He had obviously left, with my money and I didn't know where he had gone.

I was too angry to cry this time. I was angry with myself, with Billie Boy and the whole bad world. I hated this place called England. I went down below, collected my things together, and tied up my bundle. I counted the money left in my pocket which came to four pennies, two half pennies and one sixpence. I put on my knickers and deposited my remaining money into the secret pocket, vowing never to take it out again unless my life depended on it. I lay down on the bench under the window and I tossed and turned for a long time. Exhaustion from a heavy day of unexpected happenings, plus the beer I was not used to helped the course of action. But, finally my restlessness subsided and I fell into a deep sleep, the unfair world left my conscious for a time and allowed me to forget and rest.

The sun shining through the stained glass windows sparkled into my eyes and woke me up. I was stiff and soar given that I had clutched my bundle underneath me through the night. My head hurt, my throat was raw and my tongue felt rough. When I pulled myself up, I remembered the previous day's events with horror. I decided to do as I had been taught and mash a pot of tea so I could think through my next move.

Chapter 35
The road forward

I took my mug of tea on deck and sat on the bench to look at the canal. There were people leaving the Packet House and walking on to the waiting boats. The movement on the canal was bustling with activity as other barges passed me, with the barge people on board waving and wishing me 'Good day'.

I felt much better after the tea and so I decided to clean myself up, not with the water from the canal but with a cloth and the water left in the kettle. I brushed my hair and tied it up on top of my head with braid and pins.
I tidied up below and then returned on deck. Looking back along the canal bank I heard someone shouting my name. It was Elizabeth holding Robert's arm as he slowly and hesitantly walked towards the boat. When they got nearer I could see Billie Boy behind them carrying things in his arms. I wanted to run off the boat and grab him by the throat but I thought better of it. Instead, I ran to help Elizabeth bring Robert on deck and place him on the bench.

"How good to see you again" I said with sincerity, "how's your head?"

He still had the bandages on, but not as many. He told me the Doctor had said he had to take it easy for a few days and then the bruises would heal. I went to get some tea for them, as it wasn't yet cold in the pot.

"Put the food down Billie Boy, and go and lie down you scoundrel , you deserve to have a bad head mixing with such a terrible crowd, how you got them to buy so many drinks for you I'll never know?" Elizabeth said not noticing my glaring eyes piercing in the direction of Billie Boy.

"We found him lying on a table outside the alehouse as we crossed the yard", said Robert. "We were told by the Landlord of the public house that he had been drinking with a crowd of men visiting the area. They had been betting on the Grand National and drinking strong liquor until the early hours when he passed out on the table. The publican said he was glad we turned up to take him away as his friends had left him and caught the boat to Manchester."

I just nodded as the story was told and the knot in my stomach twisted and turned. I could not tell my good friends the truth. They needed Billie Boy to work for them with the barge, especially now as Robert was not as fit as he would like to be. I had been careless showing I had money; I had given Billie money for beer, and he watched me place a large bet. It had been too much temptation for him. I must have looked like I had plenty of spare money. I had been stupid in my actions and probably was to blame for Billie returning to the barge to look for more money. The enticement was too much for this poor boy.

I decided to let the whole episode drop. It was perhaps better not to say anything about my problems but to eat and thank God I had good friends to stay with. I was not homeless and hungry as I might have been. After we had finished eating I knew I had to start taking things into my own hands again and stop feeling sorry for myself. I told Robert and Elizabeth I wanted to go into the yard to look for the man who gave me a lift to the Infirmary.

"His name was Jack and he told me he was going to find out if any of the carts were going to Astley pit with supplies." I informed them, "I know it's early but maybe he has forgotten about me and I want to jog his memory".

Both Elizabeth and Robert thought it was a good idea, so encouraged me to go straight away, which I did.

I entered the yard and saw it was just as busy as before. As this was Saturday I thought the businesses would be closed, but they were not. I walked in a circle away from the alehouse not wanting to be reminded of my folly. I found Jack outside his shop working on a broken wheel rim for a customer.

I greeted him and he stood up to say, "always good to see you again good lady, so what brings you here again, surely not to see an old man like me?"

My spirits dropped as I thought he had forgotten my request to ask for a lift to Astley, but as I began to remind him he immediately gave me a toothy grin, told me he was kidding and had some good news. There was a chap going straight to Astley pit this weekend in fact. The pit had an urgent request for supplies and Jack had asked the man to give me a lift, as a favour for fixing a wheel in a hurry him.

"That's how it's done around these parts", he added. "So get here at 2 o clock this afternoon if you want to go so soon."
I wanted to hug Jack but instead I shook his hand so vigorously he laughed aloud at my enthusiasm. I turned to run to the barge to get my belongings but I shouted back. "I'll be back at this spot at two this afternoon and thanks again."

I ran so fast back to the barge I had no breathe left to give my news to Elizabeth who was hanging washing out to dry between two trees. I stopped in front of her bending down, panting and trying to speak. She just gave me her wonderful smile, put her arm around my shoulders, and told me to take my time. I looked up to her and nodded.

"You have your lift, I suppose?" she questioned and I nodded again.

She walked back with me onto the barge telling me that both Robert and Billie were sleeping below, but we should sit on the bench and talk.

When I got my breathe back I related the exciting news; that I had, at last, secured a lift to reach my destination, maybe as soon as this very day! She was as thrilled as I was and asked me if I would be O.K. going with a stranger. I admitted I had not thought of that but I was sure Jack would not put me in any danger. He did know the man.

I sat day dreaming of at last meeting up with Jarleth again while Elizabeth went to make some tea and came back with a tray with food and a pot of tea for us to share. We ate and drank together for the last time and I told her about my journey so far and about my hopes and fears for my future in England. Time flew by as she hung on every word with her eyes wide and the occasional shake of her head in disbelief at some of my escapades. I ,left some big gaps in my story. The personal bits that were intimate details I didn't feel I could share with a person like Elizabeth.
I knew the time had come to say farewell and thanks to my good friends so I asked her to tell Robert I was going but to leave Billie sleeping and tell him later that I had left. She went to wake Robert who came at once to hug me and wish me well. I stifled the tears, went to get my bundle from below, and gave them yet another squeeze of affection before leaving the barge and its memories behind for good.

I did not want to look back, but I knew they both were watching me. I kept my eyes on the road in front. I had to bring back the old determination and canny wit I seemed to have lost the last few days. I was on my own now and could not afford any more costly mistakes. I turned the corner into the yard and made my way to Jack's shop. On the way, I passed the Ice cream cart and waved to the Italian who shouted me over, "Commi here lady, what is the hurry for you? I wanta tell you something, commi here."

I went over to see why he wanted me and perhaps to say a last goodbye to him.
"Do you want me?" I asked him. "What is it?"

192

"Today is the big race and I am taking my cart to the races at Aintree I thinka you might like to commi with me for the excitement?"

"There's nothing I would like more," I said, "but I am leaving here today and not planning to return."

I watched his face grimace with disappointment. So I changed the subject and I told him about my love for horses and the fact I had put a bet on with the man in the Public House but I didn't have much hope of winning as the Prince's horse was running again, and that was the favourite to win.

"I will watch and pray for you my lovely, us foreigners must stick together to survive in this land, what do you say?"

I told him I wished I could be there to shout and scream for my horse to win, for me that would be exciting. I remembered the excitement I had felt in Ireland at the races and I shared this feeling with him. I asked him to shout for me and urge it on to the winning post.

"My horse is called 'Drumcree' remember that name, and wish me luck," I said with expectation in my voice.

"I think I will have a bet myself on the horse you have chosen, and then I can shout for both of us. I will do it with the man in the Public House before I leave".

'Do that, and let the luck be with us both," I said, "I have to go. I have a lift."
We shook hands and I left the cart, without a licker this time, but happy I had said farewell to such a special man.
I went to Jack's shop and was thankful when I saw him there rolling a wheel outside and laying it against the wall.

"Well, are you ready to go?" He shouted knowing the answer, "he should be here any minute now, he's always on time is Matt."

Before he had finished his sentence a cart full of wood veered around the corner at a slow speed stopping in front of us. "Watch it Lad, " Jack sternly said, "nearly frightened the living daylights out of us, you did, but I suppose that's your idea of a joke which I don't share, thank you very much. The lady needs to feel she is in safe hands so no more of the playing about y'ere."

"Come on Jack, tha knows I'm best in Worsley fer driving, lighten up."

"Now I'm telling yer and tha better listen, drive this young lady to Astley slow and careful like, or tha'll answer to me." he said taking the smile off Matt's face.

"Righty o, I heard thee. Now young lady have you enough room for yerself and yer bundle up there next to me? I am a very trustworthy lad as well he knows, with a wife and kids to show for it." He said helping me up on the cart.

"To Astley Green colliery we go," he shouted as he whipped his horse forward. "See you this evening old man." His last words were drowned by the noise of the cart and the horse neighing, but he let off a bellow of a noise as we rode out of the yard.

At first I sat quietly not knowing how to take the humour of this man, but then after a long silence he told me about his wife, who was sick, and the children he had to care for with his mother's help. I understood then the explanation for his peculiar form of mischief, it was to keep his spirits up, and so he did not get depressed at his situation.
We talked and I began to feel I was lucky not to have someone wholly depending on me. I was free to go as I pleased and make decisions rightly or wrongly, that only affected me, Caty Luby. I listened well

and said very little on the journey to Astley. Matt seemed to want that from me and the least I could do was give him the chance to speak out to a stranger who was sympathetic to listen as he talked about his problems.

In the distance, I could see a large structure. A tower like building with a large wheel inside a metal frame, Matt told me that was the pit and we would be there in a tick. . He drove the cart into the cobblestone pit yard. It had large buildings surrounding it and mounds of coal or dirt like mixtures in the middle of the yard. We passed a group of women working at doing something I was very curious about, so I asked Matt if he could explain. He stopped the cart near to them.

"They are known as 'Pit brow lasses' in these parts", he said, "its not so much hard work as dirty and monotonous. They rake the stones and rubbish from the coal as it passes them, you can see the endless iron belt over there. They also have to push the wagons from the shaft to the stack heaps over there." He pointed to the mounds.

I watched these 'lasses' work for a while as Matt unloaded. They were dressed in rough skirts over a sort of leggings although some did seem to be in men's trousers. They all had handkerchiefs or pieces of cloth around their heads; I suppose to keep some of the dirt out of their hair. They carried a kind of large round mesh tray in their hands.
I was eager to know more.

"How much do these women earn?" I asked.

Well, I think between 6 and 9 shillings a week, so I've been told" he replied, "not bad for young lasses of their age."

"And what age would that be?" I said cautiously.

"They'll be between fifteen and twenty four, I suppose 'cause most of these lassies get married and have babies around that time."

I had to get my mind back on track, I was here to find Jarleth and he had given me instructions to ask in the pit office for him when I got to Astley. I left Matt to continue his unloading and went in the direction of the offices. Matt told me he would join me there later as that was where he was paid.
I walked into the building where I was told the 'office' was located. Inside there were people at desks all busy writing or doing something with pen and paper. I was not able to read or write so I hoped they would not ask me to do any of those things. At the back of the office was a wall of glass with steps going up to a kind of platform, which seemed to have another office behind this glass.

 At the same time as I was gazing around a man carrying papers almost bumped into me but then asked in a very peculiar accent if he could help me. I tried to answer him in my best English voice, like the Ladies of Tuam hoping he would understand me better. I told him who I was looking for.

"The name Jarleth Kelly," he said, "is a very unusual one so I do think someone here would know of this man. Go to the desk there and ask the man in glasses if he knows a Jarleth Kelly. He will know if he works here. He does all the hiring and firings."

I didn't know exactly what he was talking about but I followed his directions to the desk he pointed out. I spoke in a jittery voice to the man,
 "I am looking for a man named Jarleth Kelly, who I think works here at this pit?"

He looked up from his work and peered over his glasses at me.

"And who are you young lady; who wishes to know?" he said in a very surly voice
.

"My name is Catherine Luby" I stuttered, "my aunt Mrs Kelly is Jarleth Kelly's mother," I lied, "I am here representing the family back in Ireland for his wedding, but I need to find him as I have lost his address"(another slip of the tongue I would rather say than a downright lie) I had to rub my nose with the back of my hand to hide my embarrassment at being so able to lie and still look at the man face to face.

"That name rings a bell with me but let me look at my files. Just sit over there on that form while I look". With that I turned away quickly to find the seat on the wooden form under the window.
Within minutes the man with the glasses came towards me with a paper in his hand. I also noted he was shaking his head as he looked at the papers.

"Well, I'm sorry to say Jarleth is not here, but I do know what happened to his betrothed. Her name was Margaret Plat, she was a screener here, but sadly she is deceased." I wrinkled my nose at this big word.

"She died, my dear." He went on, "an inspection was made, and it seems she was on top of a loaded wagon and was told to get off as the wagon had to be moved. She neglected to do so and when the other wagons bumped up against it she was knocked off and fell under the wheels."
He put the paper down on the bench and sat next to me.
"I remember the case now and how it affected your cousin. He was in total despair and desolation; he was a danger to himself and his work mates. His condition was likely to cause recklessness in his work and finally his despondency caused us to ask him to leave his mining position."

I was not sure I understood all his big words so I asked, "He's not here, and he doesn't work here in the colliery? Do you know where he is?"

"I believe, he told his mates he was going back to Ireland, but I can't be sure of that. Can I help you my dear? Do you have somewhere to go? Just sit there a while and catch your breath."

I sat there in utter disbelief. I was completely dumb. I lacked the power to move any part of my body. I had travelled so far to reach this place with the hope of Jarleth being here to tell me what to do and now he was back in Ireland and I was here in England, alone and almost penniless. I was tired of travelling. I was weary of making decisions. I had no home, no family, and no friends. No place to go. I wanted to hear my Grandmother's soothing voice and feel my mother's wide arms around me, for comfort. I did not want to be alone. Why was this happening to me? I was screaming for help but no noise left my body. I wanted to be back in Ireland where I was safe and I could laugh with Maggie again.

"Please God, forgive me I will be good, just lift me up, and take me back to Ireland," I prayed silently.

 This was how it was going to end? My hopes for a better future were just a frivolous escape from reality for this young girl from the bogs of Ireland. Why did I think I could manage this task alone? It was not right to think I could change my destiny; only God could do that – so my Grandmother had told me so long ago. I managed to move myself and stretch out on the bench where delirium resulted in my mind to shut out the truth. I was a failure.
Why could I not make a better life for myself, my family, or anyone else? Big Caty Luby was as strong as a man was but she was led by her heart and not her brain. I could see the strange stone faces of the Cathedral in Tuam looking down on me.
 I blacked out into oblivion. A lost soul!

Chapter 36
Awaking to a new life

I awoke hearing strange voices talking in words I just could not understand at that moment, but I opened my eyes to see who was making these sounds. They were softly spoken words of concern, I could feel that, but why were all these men surrounding me?

I could sense I was lying down on some kind of form or bench and it was very hard to my back, but the men would not let me sit up. One man held my head and dabbed a cold cloth around my forehead. A very tall thin man with a moustache and round eyeglasses seemed to be in charge, giving orders to a boy about our Michael's age who had a glass of water he was holding waiting for instructions. I struggled to sit up but my face met, head on, with an ethereal face of a young man smiling down at me encouraging me to take it easy and wait a few more minutes.

I leaned back but kept my eyes fixed on the image in front of me. He was young man with a mop of sandy coloured hair which seemed to be unruly when he bent over me, so he was forced to brush it back with one hand while touching my hand to hold me down with his other. He didn't listen to the tall man giving orders but looked into my eyes smiling. I noticed the freckles on his nose and the brown spots on his hands, but most of all his green eyes looking straight into mine. My stomach was having those funny feelings again. I had to sit up, I was not happy in this strange place full of men. The tall man came back into focus and I steadily recalled he was the man who had told me the bad news. I listened again to his words.

"The information I had to tell this young lassie was too much for her to handle, that's why she fainted. Give her the water Tom and she will come round, I'm sure?"

I gladly took the water from the young boy. I was very thirsty and it also gave me something to do to avert the stirring eyes and my embarrassing situation.

"Get the man who drove her here, Ginger, is he still unloading? Go to see, she needs to get to her folks where she can rest." He was speaking to my friendly faced young man who to my surprise winked at me before heading for the door.

My mind was racing, I needed to think ahead and make decisions. I had only planned to reach Astley Colliery and find Jarleth and then he would have taken care of things from there. So what now? Where do I go? I must behave like an adult and make decisions here and now.

I decided to talk to the official looking gentleman who had all the answers, and in my Ladies of Tuam best voice so he would understand me. I began.

"I was told you are the man who hires people to work here. Do I have that right, Sir?" I added the end bit because it sounded right, but I wasn't sure? "I am in need of a job Sir," I said with all the sincerity I could muster. "I have seen the Pit Lassies outside and I was wondering if you had a spare place for me there?"
He smiled down at me so I decided to stand and face him. I straightened my skirt and stretched my body to my full big stature, showing him the full maturity of my body. I watched as he stepped back and stroked his chin. He took off his eye glasses, and cleaned them with his handkerchief, and then he looked me up and down as my Uncle would look at the horses at the races. I didn't move, there was more at stake than my modesty. At last he gave me an answer.

200

"Come by next week to see me, I think one of the Lassies is leaving to get married. That's what they usually do, but you never know until it happens around here. Some men let their wives carry on working, some don't. Do you have any experience sorting coal?"

I didn't know what to admit to so I said what I had always been told, "I am big, and strong and willing to learn anything to earn money – Sir – Just give me a chance – Sir – I won't let you down."

"Well then we will see what happens next week. For now you just get back to your family and get over your shock. See, there is Ginger back with your driver. I have to get some paperwork done with him and then he can leave, sit you down there and wait Lass and don't fret."

I had no idea what those words meant; my mind was busy planning my next move. I sat down. I had nowhere else to go, so it was an easy solution. To my surprise Ginger came to sit beside me. His boss, the tall man in spectacles had left the area and gone into an office space with Matt. This man called Ginger took a pencil from behind his ear and placed it on a bunch of papers he had on his knee. I sat besides him wondering what he would say.

"I need to get some details from you if you want a job here Lass. Do you want to fill the form in yourself so I don't see all your personal stuff?"

Now I was in trouble. I couldn't read or write, I had no place to live, no family, or friends. Holy Mother of God I was in a strange country with a strange way of talking and this man at my side with his big smiling face was starting to annoy me.

"Would it be better if I filled it in for you Lass?"

He was really getting on my nerves and what was all this Lass business?

"You can put down just the basic – name and address and perhaps age if you like?"

I took a big deep breath and tried to stop the swear words from pouring out. Not that I was one for using bad language in Irish or English but I was familiar with them. I kept them under my breath and held my stomach so I could keep them in. Trying to keep my temper in control I said,

"It might be quicker for you to write them down?"

"Well I do this all the time so I am able to do this fast."

God help me. He was driving me mad. Who was he anyway to ask me personal questions? He wasn't the man who could give me a job. He was a nosey young man who thought his good looks and big smile could fool 'Lassies' to give their personal details to him. Well not Caty Luby. I was so annoyed at that moment I could have punched him in the nose. The working men in England were not much different to the working men in Ireland, so why did I expect this to change? Wake up Miss Catherine Luby (I said to myself) there is no-one here to come and help you.
Then, just as I was going to say something I might have regretted, Matt came towards us.

"I'm ready to leave now, Luv. Do you feel up to the drive back? I 'll tak it steady 'cause I have no load, so it won't be as bouncy.' Then he went on, "Mr. Jones, the boss in there tawd me your bad news, but not to worry – when one door shuts another opens."

I smiled at his accent, which I was now beginning to understand. He spoke slowly and nodded his head with each phrase he spoke to watch my reaction. It was easy to nod back my approval.

The tall man who Matt called Mr. Jones came out of the office and walked towards me.

"What was your name again Lass?"

"Caty Luby, Sir." I answered quickly.

"Oki Doki, Miss Caty Luby, see you next week," he said with a cheeky smile. Perhaps there was still some good men left around?

Chapter 37
Tackling the Problems

Matt helped me up onto the cart as though I was an invalid, but I knew he was only being his kind considerate-self. He was a man who knew what sickness and pain was all about and could deal with it without the other person feeling any guilt, and therefore I was able to accept his kindness willingly.

We walked slowly to his cart past the Lassies who waved at me with big smiles on their dirty sooty faces, which contrasted with their teeth which seemed to be whiter than the women I knew in Ireland. I said as much to Matt who gave me some information I was to use later in my life.

He told me that they cleaned their teeth with soot and salt mixed into a paste with water and this kept them white. He also said that the older women who were not married would put soot on their hair to disguise the grey.
These proud young women were known as 'Pit Brow Lassies' in Lancashire and were a special group of women. Then he went on to say that there were other proud Lassies who worked just as hard; their work was not as dirty and heavy but was inside a factory in a place called a Cotton Mill.

"Do you know anybody who works in a cotton mill, Matt?" I asked hoping for additional important information.

"Nay Lass. I guz about mi job minding my own business, not asking too many questions of folks. I knows about the Pit Lassies 'cause I sees them each week."

We trotted out of the yard at a slow pace and then he turned to me with his eyes looking up to the sky as though looking for an answer.

"Maybe someone at the pub would know, thas all sorts of folks frequent that place. I durn't have time wi wife being as she is."

"Well thanks Matt I'll maybe ask around if I don't get the job at the pit."

We both fell into a mutual silence; Matt maybe thinking of the better times he had known with his wife and me thinking of what I should do when we got back to Worsley and he dropped me off.

As though he was reading my thoughts he said, "Wher dus want dropping Lass, will back at Jack's place suit thi ?"

It was a start, so I nodded my approval and smiled my thanks, I felt comfortable with Mat but yet I couldn't tell him my full story; he had enough worries of his own. I would think of something. We jolted softly over the cobblestones back towards familiar landmarks a plan started to form in my head. I would go down to the canal and tell Robert and Elizabeth that the wedding had been delayed until next week because Jarlath was sick; something catching. That would solve the problem of why I wasn't staying with family and it would give me time to think further into my next plan– if there was any? I sighed with relief having some kind of arrangement in my head.

"At cowd Lass ? Tha seems to be shivering a bit."

I frowned and tilted my head to one side not understanding him completely.
He tried again with his patient voice, "Is -the – cowd – air –makin thee shak?" He followed these words with the action of shaking which made

205

me laugh aloud. I grabbed his loose arm and let my tears of laughter roll down onto his sleeve.

We entered the familiar busy yard still laughing. The horse reigns were pulled and the jolting of the cart came to an abrupt halt which made us both laugh even more as Jack came outside to see what all the noise was about.

"My my what a commotion is going on here," Tom said shaking his head in wonderment "and why is the young Lass back here with you, young Matt. Have yer adopted her into yer brood or what?"

"No, it's just mi lingo that maks her laugh, unless I hav a new vocation wi mi voice?"

I laughed again and shook my wholesome frame with uncontrollable glee.

"Nay then Lass," pleaded Matt "thas goin to brak mi cart then I'll hav nay job at all."

He helped me down to the firm ground and my mind was back to the reality of my situation.

"I'll be off then," I said with confidence I didn't feel, "my plans have been delayed a little but nothing I can't do something about." I began to walk away to hide my humiliation and sadness, but then remembered, "thanks for everything you two, I will no doubt see you tomorrow, all being well?"

As I left I overheard Matt telling Jack my problem and then I caught the end of Jack's reply.

"She's a feisty Lass that Caty. She'll find her way".

Chapter 38
A safe place

I walked slowly along the canal bank ignoring the beautiful surroundings that enclosed me. The smells of the late spring flowers only brought tears to my eyes and this time they were not tears of laughter. The water reminded me I needed to use the toilet. I hurried forward looking for the beautiful canal barge I longed to see. I was sure it wasn't so far along the bank.

I went behind the bushes to relieve myself and the water flooded from both ends. I felt damp and cold all over. My blouse was wet with my flood of tears so I sniffled and tried to control myself. I came from the bushes and looked up and down the canal but saw no sign of Robert's barge. I sat down on a bed of bluebells which squashed them into my skirt making ugly stains of blue and green into the material. This was my one and only skirt. My so called white blouse was wet and grey. The few coins I had left in my knickers pocket dug into my flesh. What could I do?
'Well you can stop feeling sorry for yourself" (my inner voice was talking to me again) was I going mad? I was just going to continue the conversation with myself when I heard a voice on the path in front of me.

"Caty, is that you over there?"

I acknowledged the figure in front, it was Billie Boy.
I answered him hastily before he left, "Yes, Yes, Billie it's me Caty" I waved and hurriedly got up from the ground in a lumbering fashion trying my best not to slip. I reached him on the path and briefly explained to him my story. It was no use wasting energy on Billie so I asked the obvious.

"Where's the barge Billie?" and then with foreboding, "they haven't left, have they?" I stopped him and made him look at me.

"We have moved from where we were moored to pick up our cargo to take back. We are near the Packet House. If you look the other way you can just make it out near the steps."

I looked and to my relief I saw the colours, patterns, and shapes of Robert's canal barge.
"Oh! Yes, yes I can see it Billie," I said reassured. I could see it.

'Well, let's go to them Caty, they'll be glad to see you I know."

We headed for the Packet House together. I held Billie's hand forgetting for that moment he was the person who had robbed me of my hard earned money. What was the point anyway? I was as much to blame as he was when I really thought about it. I would never have found the entrance to the large building called the Packet House without Billie but I followed him through and out to the familiar steps I had seen from the water. We went down them and onto the jetty that led us to my refuge.

I saw Robert first and shouted to him. Startled he turned around to face me and in a shocked voice said, "Caty is that truly you? What happened? Never mind, for now come aboard and I'll get Elizabeth."

I must have looked a mess and I felt very hesitant to move until I saw Elizabeth beckoning to me to come to her and when I did she just hugged me tightly which brought about another tearful reunion. My highs and lows of this day had left me exhausted and she felt it through her closeness.

"We can talk later, Caty, you need to rest. Tomorrow is another day. Come down to the cabin and I'll get you something to eat and drink."

She led me down the small narrow steps where she filled a bowl of water to wash and found a towel. She brought me a large shirt, which obviously belonged to Robert.

"Clean yourself Caty and put on this dry shirt. I will have some cheese and bread with a warm drink ready for you when you have finished."

I didn't argue. I had no strength left. I performed like a small child doing what her mother told her to do and liking the comfort and relief it gave me. She returned with a tray just as I had finished and without speaking she took my clothes away and left me alone with my thoughts. I ate speedily, gulping the warm tea down after every bite. I was very hungry, but the food was so nourishing and the tea so soothing that I just had to lie down as soon as I had finished. I managed to place the tray on the floor before heavy sleep took over my body. Yes, tomorrow will be another day.

Chapter 39
Where to now?

"Come on Caty wake up, its noon already. You should feel better now after such a long sleep?" I heard Elizabeth's voice calling me with an edge of humour not sarcastic in anyway.

I stretched and yawned as I looked around to get my bearings, but was happy to see I was in a safe place. I sat up but realized I was wearing a man's shirt and not my own clothes, but I could feel the coins still in my secret pocket. I was afraid to look and check the amount. I had to find a way of increasing it, however much there was left. I knew there was not enough to pay my way back to my Uncle and I couldn't expect these kind folks to continue giving me charity. I needed to go for a walk and sort my thoughts out.

At that moment Elizabeth appeared with my clothes, which she had washed and dried while I was sleeping.
"Couldn't let you walk about in that shirt now could I? I managed to get the stains out and they are fresh from the line so they do smell much better. I'll leave you to change and then come up for a nice cool drink and some fresh bread I got this morning."

They were so good these people I wanted to give them what little money I had left, but if I did then how would I survive?
I dressed and then went up the narrow steps to the bright midday sun, which made it hard to focus. Elizabeth beckoned me to the bench at the back and as I meandered towards her I noticed the barge was full with all sorts of cargo. Every spare space was taken.

"Mind your step, Caty, can you get to me?"

I reached Elizabeth and sat beside her to drink and eat what she had prepared for me. At the same time I was taking in the heavy cargo and obviously I had a look of astonishment on my face. Elizabeth laughed aloud and answered my facial expressions.

"Robert doesn't half load it up, but that's how we make our money to live on the land. So he tells me. We will be leaving tomorrow at first light so today will be a busy one for us. Now Caty, tell me, what happened, did you not find your relatives?"

I bit my bottom lip before I recounted my story I had planned. Trying to make it believable I continued, "It's only a small setback. Jarleth is on the mend and he is making arrangements for me to stay with other family members in the meantime."

Just as I had finished my sentence the barge rocked up and down and side to side throwing us off balance. I crossed myself and made my apology silently for my misrepresentation.

"It's only a passing boat Caty don't worry. There is a lot more traffic at this spot because of the loading and unloading."

Even so I was nervous and in a squeaky voice said," perhaps I will go for a walk on firm land, that's if it is alright with you?"

"Of course it is. You need the fresh air and it will give me chance to organize things for the journey back."

I left the barge, went up the steps and through the big doors to the yard. It was full of the same jostle and bustle as before and in a trance state I made my way to Jack's workshop, mainly because it was a place to head for; a positive decision for my melancholy, I had to shake off this depression. Jack was working outside on a wheel and looked up as I approached him.

"Have you come to collect your bundle, Lass? Matt left it with me, it was in his cart."

"Oh, yes thanks" I responded.

He went inside and I felt a bit better to know I had a few belongings left in this world.
I sat on the small wall waiting and looked around at all the activity.
Then I heard a voice I recognized. My friend the Italian was shouting to me. Jack gave me my bundle and I thanked him.

"Tarra luvs, tak care of thaself, come back if tha needs anything." I knew he was using his Lancashire accent on purpose so I gave him a quick hug on his arm as he gave me the parcel. I walked across the yard and headed towards the ice cream cart, but to my amazement the Italian was getting out of the cart and heading towards me.

"We did it, you arra fine ladie, my bootiful girl – we did it – we won – we beata the Prince we did. We did."

He was dancing round in circles waving his colorful neckerchief in the air as he performed an intricate dance in front of me. Finally in flair of movement he stopped and bowed in front of me. Falling to his knees and grabbing my hand that was not carrying the bundle and kissing it gently he continued.

"You arra marvel, you are the best. Comma, comma my cart I tell you e v e r y th inga."

He ran ahead and got into the ice cream cart and I followed him obediently; all the time trying to take in what he was saying. As I reached him I spoke very slowly and asked, "are you telling me that Drumcree my Irish horse beat Ambush 11, the Prince's horse in the Grand National?"

"Yessa yessa yessa" he said with much animation. "Oh! My luvvy it was a sight to see. Lots of horses falling down notta clearing the fences."

I didn't quite like to imagine this part but I egged him on to continue.

"Ther werra three horsy now racing at the front. Then our horsy he a gotta mad and catcha the Prince's" He took a breath to help his English. 'They were necka necka rounda the last bend but our horsy went ahead – so, a ringa my bell and jumped up and down – I forgetta my English at this time, but it no matter our Drum-a –cree he win."

I just shook my head from side to side, not able to take his whole story in my confused mind all at once but I did remember I had put a bet on in the Public House and the bet was on this horse Drumcree to win. I had put down 3 shilling for this bet but I wasn't quite sure how it all worked.

"Havva you the ticket luv ? You needa the ticket. Then we'll go together to collect."

I couldn't remember what I had done with the ticket. That night was now a blur. I know I found my belongings ransacked and my savings gone. Had Billie Boy taken my ticket? No, that wasn't possible I had the ticket when I left the Public House, but what did I do with it?

If I didn't have the ticket I couldn't claim my winnings. My Italian friend was jabbering away, planning his future and asking my approval but I couldn't answer him I was racking my brains as to where I last had the ticket.
He kept himself busy for the next ten minutes closing his cart up ready for us to go to the Public House, I presumed? I decided to think logically from the time I got the ticket. Did I leave it on the alehouse table? Where did I put it? I remember I went in the bushes to relieve

myself –did I put it on the ground while I removed my knickers? Caty Luby you are stupid, you had no knickers on.

Well what did I do when I reached the boat? I talked to myself and tried to think clearly. I continued my recollection. I got my knickers and I went down in the cabin. Did I put the ticket in my secret pocket for safety? Did I put it in a safe place in the cabin? What did I do with that ticket?

"I'll leava my cart here locked while we go to getta the winnings. Comma Lass let's find out how rich we are."
I followed him into the alehouse with my head down.
"You sita there and I'll get us a drinka beera and find out what happens next."

"I need to go to the privy; I'll only be a minute."

I ran into the privy with my bundle in my hand only to sit and think. I looked in my secret pocket but only the few coins were there. I opened my bundle not remembering its contents. My few spare clothes, the present from Mrs. Kelly were all there. I was forcing back my sadness and now I was angry at my foolhardiness. I lifted the wrapped wedding present that was tied with string and looked closely. Much to my astonishment, I saw a piece of paper that was tucked inside the wrapping string of the wedding present. Was it a letter from Mrs. Kelly to her son I hadn't noticed. Could Mrs. Kelly even write? The paper had writing on it but as I couldn't read – I had no clue to its contents. I folded the present back with my few clothes and made a bundle again, and then I put the paper in my pocket and went back into the alehouse. My Italian friend was sat at the table with two glasses.

" I havva bit of bad news Lass"

"Oh! no what next?" I said to myself.

214

"Thisa man will tell us. Do you remember he is the one who tooka our bets?"

I did recognize him so I listened. to what the pub man had to say.
"Just before the race started your horse Drumcree became the favorite so your odds are not so good. You had put down 3 shillings for him to win I believe? And you Sir put down one shilling to win. Do you have your tickets?
He sat down at the table with his ledger and my Italian took out his ticket and placed it on the table. I was shocked. It looked remarkably similar, well almost identical to the one I had in my pocket so I took it out and placed it on the table next to his

"The odds were 13-2 my friends."

I had no idea what that was at the time, but I did sense we had some money coming. He took out of his bag a locked tin box and on top of each ticket he slowly proceeded to put down our winnings.
He counted six shillings and six pence on my friend's ticket and then said he also got back his 'stake' which was one shilling. My friend immediately took my face in both hands and kissed me on both cheeks.
"A fortune for nothing my luv, seven shillings and six pence!"

I pulled away in anticipation of what would happen next. The man took the ticket and asked for my Italian to sign his name to say he had received his money. I saw him scribble something and hand the ticket over. Panic attack. I could feel it coming on. Would the man not pay me if I didn't sign? I couldn't write. I waited and watched. He counted out loud as he put the money down on my ticket.

"A tidy sum for such a young lass."

I tried to get the words to come out of my mouth, but they came out in gasps of air until finally I quickly said "Back in the old country Sir I never learnt to sign my name."

"Well what is your name Lass?"

"Caty Luby"

"So Caty Luby, I will print your name and you put a cross in you own hand at the side of it; that will do it. Now be very careful with that money a lot of folks will be glad to relieve you of it.

"Yes Sir, Thank you."

I told the two men I had to go to relieve myself (so to speak) and darted out through the door to the privy and closed the rickety wooden door. Now to my main task; I had to make sure this time. I carefully put the money in my secret pocket where it was going to stay 'come rain or shine.', as my Grandmother use to say.

After my mission was comfortably finished I went back into the alehouse to join my friend. He was also putting his money away safely in his inside waistcoat pocket,but nodded and smiled at me as I came to the table.

"Well mi Lady I thinka we shoulda go now if you are ready?"

" Yes I'm ready to go." I said not knowing where I was going to go, but I followed him out just the same.
I walked by his side and instinctively we held hands. Not in a romantic way, but in a friendly way, a protective gesture between us both.

"We arra good teama – yes?"

"Well if we are to be a team, then please tell me your name?"

"My name is Angelo Monteverdi," he said in a lilting voice lifting his spare arm into the air as though it was part of a song.

"That's a hard name for me to remember," I said, stopping him with an inquiring look.

"No no no" he continued in his singing voice, "thnka of an Angel then add the o, mi Mama always said I look -ed lika an angel" he laughed. "and what special name does your Mama call you mi lady?"

I thought back to Ireland, to Tuam , to my home, my family, my hard working Mother, my lost Father and my wonderful Grandmother and then my Uncle John who I had left behind. For a moment I couldn't express myself in this English language I had come to use.

"You do havva name – yes?" he said holding me back.
"Yes." I began despondently, "Ma called me Catherine but this name was my 'Sunday name' and mostly I was called Caty for short."

"Then Caty it will be. Come on Caty lets open the hand cart and havva ica creama before it melts away. A celebration, so letta me see what we can toppa the licka lick glasses with?'

We made for the cart which stood in the yard where he had left it opposite Jack's workshop, but now the yard had less activity it was quieter and the sun was going down fast. I had no idea what time it was but I knew it must be late afternoon. I needed to get back to the boat.

Angelo opened the cart and with his personal flair he began to fill the licking glass with the tasty stuff he called ice cream and then topped it with what I think was fruit. He gave me the first glass and then quickly

217

he made his own. I turned to find a place to sit on the small wall behind the cart where Angelo joined me.

"Nowa my Caty tella me your story, how did you find your way here to beautiful Englanda ?"
I noticed he had finished his ice ream and was swirling his finger around the licking glass to get the remains, so I said, "no you first I have some left."

He told me his Father had come to England first with his uncle and his sons. They came from a place called Chiavari, well that was their nearest big town. In fact as I listened to his story it was very similar to mine; people from another country looking to make money in England. His family was employed by wealthy landowners to work their land and in return they were given a tiny piece of land to cultivate their own food but if their crop failed then they starved. A story I had known so well back in the old country.

His story brought tears to both our eyes when he recounted the day their family and the entire village waved farewell to the young men leaving on their long journey to find a better life. With hard work and plenty of help from the growing Italian community in these parts, his family was able to send for their wives and children. I nodded my approval to this part of the story, for after all, isn't this what I was planning to do?
"Shalla stop my boring story, Caty?"

"Oh! no please go on."

His family seemed to have such a positive attitude to life but yet the humor and love of their culture and ways overcame their failures. If they didn't make money with one kind of business then they would try something else, always helping each other. He told me the Italians all shared their houses and their work with the new immigrants; family bonds were important. Even the children chopped up firewood and sold bundles to the local people.

Then his Father heard about the money to be made in ice cream and with the help of friends he set about making and selling ice cream. His story came to an abrupt end with his arms again reaching for the sky for the full

overture, "We now live in a bigga house with a bitta land; we don't havva to grow crops on, but use it to store our carts and havva a barn for the wood and things. Do you know Caty we are thinking of getting horses to pulla the carts, now you woulda be a good help there in finding the right horsy – I am thinking."

I laughed at his suggestion but it brought me back to the present position I was now in.

"I givva my story now you givva yours my Caty."

I was not about to tell him all my facts, especially the early ones, but I did give him the full story about Jarleth, keeping the lie intact about him being family, family lost, which he understood.

"Do ya havva any family here Caty, besides your sick Uncle back in Liverpool?"

I shook my head and looked down at the licking glass on my knee. Twirling it around in my hands, but gripping it tight as a baby might hold on to his pacifier. I told him about Elizabeth and Robert who would be leaving tomorrow. He put his arm around my shoulders and with a very sincere low voice said,

"Caty, we are a team, so we are family, and in my community we all help family, especially when they need it."

His slow clear non-singing voice seemed to show a different side to my Italian friend. Did he use this singing voice just to sell ice cream? He somehow was sounding different or was I interpreting it into the sound that I wanted to hear? I have to be careful. I don't want to land in trouble again following my heart instead of my head. I asked him why his voice had now changed. He told me he had two voices – one to sell Italian ice cream and another to talk to friends. I had to learn this lesson in language. There were certain 'voices' to be used when you wanted certain results. My thoughts were wandering as I digested his story along with this delicious food.

If young men can make it in this strange country then so can Caty Luby. 'If you have money you are not alone', now that's something Uncle John used to say. I did have my winnings and I did have a chance, a small chance, but it was likely I would also have a job soon. Maybe if I saw Jack tomorrow he might give me some ideas of a room to rent? Jack had helped me before and I must only trust people who have come through for me and do what they promise. Now I was more confident to answer Angelo.

"Thank you, thank you Angelo but at the moment I have other plans. I think I might have a job offer and maybe a room to rent and I thank you also for your kind words about family, we will talk again I am sure."

He returned to his singing voice, "Oke, I willa be here tomorrow selling the ici creama. We willa talka then."

I felt he was a good friend, but I couldn't let my guard down. Who was he anyway? I didn't know anything about him only his story and like me he could be hiding some truth. Even so I hugged him gently and told him I would see him around tomorrow and walked away.

The sun hadn't gone down completely but there was a chill in the air so I hurriedly went through the Packet House and out to the jetty. I stopped to catch my breath and looked around. Instinctively I feared tomorrow. I wondered where I would find shelter. It was too cold to sleep outside even if I did find a shed or a nook or cranny in this area. I didn't think it was safe or even possible. Hesitantly I strolled towards the barge and my spirits rose as I heard Robert's voice calling me on board. I decided to say very little about myself but just to listen to their stories about their day. They seemed to have such a simple life, with simple expectations but then they were English, and this was their homeland.

Chapter 40
New places – New friends

I waved goodbye to Robert and Elizabeth the next morning, carrying my small bundle of belongings tightly. I reflected back at all the farewells I had made in the last few months, but then decided I must have more positive fortitude if I was to survive and not think back – but forward.

I didn't look back again but kept my eyes on the Packet House in front that was full of goings-on. I was fascinated with each chore the men performed, (I saw no women working) and dodged to keep out of their way as they carried on their shoulders quite heavy looking loads. I didn't want to cause an accident or get hurt. My thoughts at this point went to Uncle John at the church house waiting for news. He knew I couldn't write, so I sent a message back with Robert to tell him that I was well but that the wedding had been postponed because of an accident to Jarleth's new bride so I was staying in these parts for a little longer and not to worry. Not too much information, but it was enough for the time being – what more could I do?

I reached the large exit out to the Yard and stopped. Where to now? I had made the decision yesterday. I had no alternatives; I had to carry it out. Go to Jack and ask him if he knew of a place to rent. I walked towards Jack's place and saw him talking to Matt over the top of a broken wheel, which they looked to be inspecting. They met me with open arms.

"Hiya luv," said Matt in his Lancashire accent, "tha looks full of the worries of the world, what's matter, tha can tell us."

I told him in a matter of fact voice that the canal barge I had been staying on had to leave, so I was looking for somewhere to rent, nothing much, just a room would do.

"Let me think; Caty, that is what you're called?" I nodded to Jack and waited. Then Matt spoke out.

"I'm thinkin maybe mi wife could do with a bit more help and give the owd grandma some relief. Trouble is I can't pay thee but tha could sleep ont couch for nowt."

"I suppose that's a start Lass" said Jack "at least you won't be sleeping under stars. Now I'm just thinking..."

"Watch out Lass, man's thinkin," joked Matt.

"Shut up Matt. This is serious business fur Lass. Inside of Packet House there's an office and chap in there may know of a place to rent; he places them workers in them all the time."

"Nay Lad she can't go wi working Lads; she wouldn't be saf"

I stopped their argument before it started and told them I would maybe go to ask. There was no harm in that.
 Matt hunched up his shoulders and gestured openly with his hands in tentative agreement and I turned to leave, but added "I'll be back soon, don't let me stop you working!" I joked and they nodded and smiled.
I heard the bell ringing from the ice cream cart and the singing chants from Angelo calling to his customers and I was drawn to his cart.
"Mornin Angelo," I said in my best English voice.

"Well, a good morning to you "replied Angelo in his best English voice. "Have your friends left?"

"Yes they had a full load to take back." I continued the polite chat.

"Have you found lodging yet Caty?" he said in a matter of fact retort.

"Well, I do have one offer so far this morning." I answered quickly.

"And are you taking the offer? Where is it? I know the good and the bad places around here, wouldn't like to see you in a bad area."

"That I don't know for sure, it's with a friend of Jack's, so it should be alright."

"You shoulda not taka the first place you see thara cudda be better places."

"Why are you talking in that singing voice to me when you don't need to" I asked angry at his impolite suggestion. "I am going to ask at the office in the Packet House for further places – if you want to know." I was using my Ladies Circle in Tuam best snobbish voice. He was talking to me just like Ginger, like able seaman Paul Hobson, like I was a girl to be flattered by the false smooth talk of men.

"I just wanted to offer you another choice," he persisted.

"Well keep your choices to your ice cream." I snapped back "I have places to go. Bye."

He jumped from behind his cart and grabbed my arm, "Don't stick you nose in the air to me young lady. I am trying to be a good friend and that's all, so at least listen to what I have to say."

His voice was the voice he used the night before, but this time it was calmly angry and not serenely heartfelt but it wasn't his working voice so I turned to listen after shaking his grip from my arm.

"So?"

"I was telling my family last night about our win on the horses and they were interested in where you got your knowledge of horses from. I didn't know the answer but my Father said we were always looking for extra help in the family shop. We sell ice cream and foods from a little shop, so maybe you would be interested? He also tells me that there are two rooms above the shop, one where my Aunt sleeps and one is used as a store but he thinks that can be re-arranged to fit a bed and some drawers for your things. What do you say?"

I was shocked, I was flabbergasted, stunned at his offer, unable to answer. Could I trust this Italian man, I didn't know anything about? Did I have a choice at this moment? Well, I had an offer to sleep on Matt's couch and help with his family but I didn't know them either and would their grandmother like me interfering with her situation. I had never met her so I didn't have a clue. Matt seemed a jolly chap, but he would be out all day and that would leave the grandmother in charge.

I needed time to think about my options so I told Angelo I would let him know later in the day, but I didn't withdraw my vigilance; I knew now I had to be aware of my easy trusting nature. Nobody was looking out for Caty Luby – only Caty Luby. The young girl from Tuam had learnt a lot about 'trust' in the last few months and now I had to progress and learn from my good and bad experiences with men. I had met both types since arriving in England and now I had to recognize who I could rely on and who I couldn't. I never had a problem figuring out the women in my life, but men were quite different. Maybe if I could just meet Matt's wife and her mother I would know?

Go with your gut feeling was an expression my Grandmother would say when a difficult unknown problem arose. That is what I will do. I walked across to Jack's place and was happy to see Matt was still there helping with the wheel.

"Hiya Lass. Hasta come to shine a bit of sunshine on our miserable chores?"

Once more I had no idea what Matt was talking about, but I was learning to sense friendly sounds of the English language; if only I could distinguish if they were sincere? My gut told me Matt was being sincere so I smiled and asked the important question.

"When you have finished fixing your wheel, Matt, do you think I could meet your family and then we can see if they think it's a good idea for me to stay with them?"

"Dust know Lass, I was thinkin that mysel after tha walked away."

Jack butted into our conversation to say he would continue working on Matt's spare wheel if he wanted to go now with me. I waited earnestly for Matt's decision. The day was going fast and I had nowhere to stay.

"Wife will be shocked to see me hom, but nay mind, come on Lass it's not far."

I clutched my bundle tight with one hand and climbed on the cart steadying myself with the other. I wanted to show I was capable of managing any task that confronted me.

"Nay then Luv, tha got up ther fast, that very nimble for such a big lass. Terah Jack, see thi tomorrow."

He took the reins of the cart and made his own kind sound to ask the horse to "trot on" and the horse gladly moved forward at an even speed over the cobblestones and out to the street beyond the Yard. We immediately came to the terraced houses closely built in rows with only a small space which Matt told me was called a 'ginnel' every ten or so houses. After about ten minutes Matt pulled the horse to a stop in front of one of these terraced row houses. A small boy with scruffy looking clothes and even scruffier looking hair came towards us.

"Pa Pa can I hold the horsy fo yu?"

"Course tha can lad but howd tight now."

 I stood up ready to move down the step of the cart to get off but I couldn't help to notice that this poor boy's ample curly hair was full of lice jumping around for all to see. His face was dirty and his hands were worse. Matt noticed my stunned face and guessed what I was thinking.

"He's our eldest and a real terror, loves to be outside and hates to be washed. Wife tha knows can't cope wi him what wi being ill. Cum on Caty th'al like wife."

I walked in through a heavy front door into a very small room and instantly thought of my friend Maggie back home. There seemed to be children everywhere crawling on the thread bare carpet, playing under the large wooden table and another two babies sleeping with a woman on the couch. It was the stench of urine and odors of stale food left on the table that had brought this memory back.
Matt walked towards the couch and shook the woman lying there; surely that wasn't his sick wife lying with the babies?

"Cumon Ma. hasta bin drinking again. Tha didn't know I would catch tha but I cam hom early like. Is wife alreet upstairs, hasta looked?"

I stood mesmerized at what I saw. Poor Matt was all that I could think. The woman on the couch got up after wriggling free of the young babies and faced me.

227

"So who is thee then? Has our Matt got a bit of stuff on the side?"

She laughed close to my face showing her big black teeth and covering me with the smell of drink. One I recognized as the odor from my Father in my past life. I wanted to leave quickly before I was sick. My stomach was empty and was rumbling – I needed fresh air. I went outside and leant on the wall wheezing for air.
My Father would get drunk but he was always 'happy drunk' and I never remember the smell being in our house. He went to Duffy's to drink. My Grandmother helped look after all my brothers and sisters and me but she watched over us and fed us with eggs, bread and milk and potatoes whenever she could. I remember her fresh smell and her loving squeezes of affection she always gave us children.

Oh Grandma I miss you. I want to go home. I said out loud without shame. Then I noticed the young boy looking at me and I wiped my tears on my sleeve, something I had never done recently. I was slipping down a slope of despair that I couldn't afford to do, poor Matt, poor man. I knew instinctively he was one of the good men I had met, but I couldn't help him. I couldn't live there in his house.

I could hear him inside shouting at the old woman and threatening to throw her out and replace her with me. She was yelling and swearing back at him that I was his fancy woman and she was going to stay there with her poor daughter whatever he said. Matt left the house banging the door hard. He stopped with his hand still on the door knob and glanced up and down before speaking to me.

"Cum on Lass, back t'yard it wasn't to be, I'm sorry Lass, I must hav bin dreamin."

We rode back at a quicker pace, but in silence. We both seemed to be in agreement that silence was the best thing at that time. However, just to let him know that I was sympathetic to his predicament I squeezed his arm in the same way I had done to him before and he smiled at me in recognition of my action.

"Thank you for trying to help Matt, you will always be a true friend. You are a kind man, one of the best I know."

He bit his lip at my words, so I went on, "Don't worry; your secret is safe with me. I will just say to everyone that I had a better offer."

I got down from the cart and waved acknowledgment to Jack, but walked away before the questions started. Matt would think of something to say to his friend. So Caty Luby where is that better offer?

As though in answer to my thought I heard the ice cream bell ringing, it was a big copper bell, but in the hands of Angelo it rang a melodious tune that accompanied his sing song voice he used to call his customers. Why did I feel happy inside when I heard his bell? Was my gut-feeling trying to tell me something? I had inspected my first offer – why not inspect what Angelo was offering?

"Hello Angelo can I have one of your licking glasses full of your delicious ice cream? I will pay you. Of course you know I have money to pay you. I need nothing free."

"Well, Miss Haughty Taughty Madam the price has gone up today – it is one English pound per glass for my special ice cream; do you want me to serve it to you now?"

There he goes again twisting my intentions. This man is so maddening.

"Don't be stupid Angelo, what is the proper price?"

"That is the proper price; Madam does not know how much work it takes to make a gallon of ice cream with our special ingredients."

He was beginning to gall me.

"Now is Madam ready to see how it is made and then she can decide if it is worth her money?"

"See how it is made, what are you talking about Angelo?"

He laughed out loud and this provoked me more, "stick your ice cream up your nose you Italian immigrant. I can go somewhere else to eat; places where ladies are treated well not like a toy to be messed around with by men like you." I turned around with my nose in the air.

He came in front of me to block my path.

"Now it's the Irish temper showing is it? I hope you don't think you will be treated well in the alehouse now they know you have winnings from the National?"

I didn't know where I was going, but I wanted to escape this exasperating Italian.

"Irish temper showing is it now? You haven't heard a half of it yet." I could hear my Irish accent coming out which I hadn't used for a long time. I even added a few choice Irish swear words which I muttered under my breath.
"If the two of us immigrants are to get along then I think we should try using the English Language to express ourselves ....thena we canna understanda one another, Oke?"

His singing Italian voice brought a smile to my face and then I felt the need to laugh, which I did and then he joined me in a instantaneous guffaw which I found even funnier and had to hold my stomach and sit on the wall for fear of wetting my precious knickers with my secret pocket. He went to the cart and brought me a licking glass full of ice cream which he presented to me with outstretched arms,

"My peace offering, will you come with me to meet my family Caty Luby?"

I took the ice cream which   I eagerly ate, I was very hungry, but through the bites I managed to say,
"Yes, I will," with a compromising smile.

Chapter 41
Life changes

I waited for Angelo to put his things away and to lock up his cart. With an easy movement that he seemed very used to; he soon had the cart rolling along the cobblestones with me following behind at a fast rate. We went out of the Yard gate and into the street outside, but then he took a sharp left turn down an alley way which led to an open space of land with a dirt path going through it. On one side was a big black mound about twenty feet high, which seemed to have children playing on it.

Angelo stopped to let me catch him up so I asked him about the mound of black dirt and stones. He told me it was a slag-heap where kids and sometimes adults would collect the waste coal and dirt to use on their fires. It was free fuel and the local folks took advantage of it. I remembered back home collecting peat for the same purpose. Facing the slag heap was a continuous brick wall screening the terrace row houses, but each house had a small back gate of their own. Then we stopped at a large double gate where Angelo opened first one side and then the other for us to go through with the cart.

"Come on Caty this is our place. My Father and my Uncles knocked two houses into one, plenty of room for us all and the carts. These houses even have a cellar, which I'll show you later."

I didn't know the meaning of this word, but I would find out later that it was a room under the house which was very cool and so served a function for this family. There were three other carts in this small yard and two sheds. One I presumed was a privy and the larger one I thought maybe storage of some sort. Angelo put down his cart neatly at the side of the others, then took my arm and led me through the back door.

Inside was a large wooden kitchen table with maybe four or five men sat around all eating and talking very fast in a language I thought must be Italian? They all stopped talking and looked up as we walked in.

"Everyone, this is Caty, the girl I told you about last night," said Angelo and then he repeated (I think) in Italian, the same introduction.

To my amazement they all stood up and outstretched their hands in turn to greet me. Then out of another room came an older woman carrying a large bowl in her arms and ordering the men to sit down. In a singing voice, but with an accent I had learnt to understand, she ordered the men to sit down, stop fussing and finish their meal.

"Takka the younga lady through to Anna and the girls and tell them to speaka the English with our visitor."

I looked at this rotund happy woman. She was plump but not stout and thick set like me. She was smaller in stature than everyone in the room but she was obviously in charge. She put down her bowl and then to my surprise she grabbed both my hands and kissed me on both cheeks and whispered in perfect English, "welcome to my home and family Missy Caty."

I gave her a big smile, at the same time shaking her hands and replied,

"Thank you, but what do I call you?"

"I am Mama Monteverdi to all in this a house dear, Okay?"

"Okay, Mama Monteverdi and thank you again"

I followed Angelo from the room into another room, equally large, with another large wooden table in the middle. However, around this table was a group of young women and two young girls who seemed to be preparing some type of food similar to pastry. One was rolling the dough like mixture out; another was cutting it into strips while the other was placing it on a wooden structure that had two pulleys with ropes on each end. The wooden structure was about six foot long but narrow, with maybe four or five thin wooden slats. The mixture was laid over these slats and it hung down in strips. The ropes at each end went up to the ceiling on pulleys where they were fastened; with the ropes the girls could pull the structure up above their heads. One of the women explained to me (in good English) that the neighbors used this structure they called a 'clothes rack' to dry their washing but they had found it worked just as good drying pasta. The two young girls ran to Angelo immediately they saw him and wrapped themselves around his legs.

"Are you helping to make the spaghetti my little treasures?" he said with fondness, "well hurry now help your sister to pull the pulleys, the clothes rack will not go up to the ceiling itself you know?"

I had never heard of spaghetti but I was to find out later that evening how delicious it tasted. Apparently to them 'pasta' was a stable food, just as potatoes were to my family before the potato famine made them in short supply for most people in Tuam.

We all watched the raising of the 'clothes rack' like some ritual ceremony similar to the raising of a national flag. Indeed, they saw it as their national emblem. I was to understand later that their recipe for pasta was a symbol of national pride in each Italian immigrant family as to who had the best recipe. The mixture was to be -not too heavy, not too light and cooked 'al dente'. Tossed in olive oil or butter and served and eaten immediately to prevent overcooking.

I don't remember such a formal procedure before we ate our potatoes. At my house we cooked them until they looked soft, drained off the water and then mashed them into pulp; if they weren't so soft then we left a little of the water in the pan to help the mixture. Although, I do remember Mrs. Kelly telling me that the Archbishop liked his potatoes mashed with an egg and a little milk which she sometimes put in the oven afterwards to crisp the top but I had never tasted such a mixture.

The raising of the 'clothes rack' had raised everyone's eyes upwards, but after the securing of the rope and making the knot at the end secure the completion brought on an activity of congratulations to each other. They wiped their hands on their aprons before turning their full attention to me still standing in the doorway. One by one Angelo introduced me to the women in his family. As they hugged and kissed me on both cheeks, just like Mama Monteverdi had done earlier I hardly had time to take in their names but they each repeated my name to get the pronunciation correct and their warm, cosseting natures were all I needed to confirm this was the place I wanted to be.

I do recall that it was Anna who had obviously been told to take care of me because as soon as the greetings were over she whisked me out of this room and led me up some narrow stairs telling me, in plain English that I was to sleep with her in her room because as she was the eldest, she had a room of her own. Even Angelo shared with two of the younger boys; she laughed as she imparted this information.

 Her room was very small and held just a single bed, a wardrobe and a set of drawers. Over her bed was a picture of the Virgin Mary with a wooden cross underneath. Still, the room was clean and fresh and had bright floral curtains on the constricted window. She looked at my puzzled face and told me that a mattress would be placed on the floor for tonight and then a more permanent decision on sleeping arrangements could be made later.

"We are used to having unexpected visitors in our houses, Caty, we always welcome newcomers from Italy here until they find their own place." She went on to give me more details of her family.

"After knocking these two houses together into one we all lived here jointly, but now my Uncle has done the same thing again just round the corner, but one half of the ground floor is a shop. His family lives on one side and my Aunt, his sister, who is not married, by the way, runs the shop and lives above. I know she is wanting some help, she tells us her old legs can't move her around so quickly, but that's not always true. If she catches some cheeky boy trying to pinch sweets from the counter when he thinks she is distracted she catches him with her walking stick around his neck and then before he knows it she moves around the counter preventing him leaving."

We both laughed thinking of this scene and she sat on the bed pulling me down beside her. I felt like I was back home talking and laughing with my friend Maggie. Anna made me feel relaxed, safe and comfortable in her company and I knew I had met a true friend. As though making this thought of mine a true realization, Anna grabbed my hands, looked me straight in the face and said, "my house is your house, my family is your family and we truly mean that."

"You know Anna I really feel that to be true."

"That said, lets go down and join the family. I think dinner will be on the table by now. The men always eat first because they have much more work to do in the cellar."
I followed Anna down into the kitchen and joined the family, still wondering about that basement room.
This day had begun in confusion, for me. I had nowhere to live, my friends had left on their canal barge, not knowing my problem, but incredibly everything had turned out fine. Tonight I had somewhere to sleep and a family to sit down with. I even enjoyed my new-fangled food, which, I found very hard to eat. However, I knew I would have lots of practice because it was delicious – their recipe was the best!

Chapter 42
Watching a family at work.

After we had finished dinner Mama Monteverdi told Anna to take me down to the cellar to see if the men were actually working and not taking it easy. She laughed in her unique way and then grabbed my arm and pulled me towards a door that was out in the corridor.

The steps were narrow and steep, so we had to be careful because the light was not good in this space. . We were met with a hum of activity. The room was whitewashed, like Uncle John had done to the kitchen back home. This gave it a fresh clean look. I noticed two enormous pans boiling (what I found out later to be milk). The men all had big white aprons on and were adding ingredients from the sacks, which stood on wooden slats on the floor. I recognized Angelo as one of the helpers, but I don't think he noticed me?

They seemed to take it in turns to stir these pans and so I took the opportunity to ask Anna about these goings-on.

"Caty they are making ice-cream, didn't Angelo tell you where we made it? The various ingredients are another of our families' secrets, but I know we make the besta icee creama around here," she said in her singing voice waving her hands in the air.

The flames of the cooker were turned off by Angelo's Father who noticed my perplexed look. I had never seen a fire turned off before. I wondered how they did it. He sent Angelo across to explain to me that it was called 'gas' and it was this gas (when it was lit) that made the flames. I didn't comprehend this gas business at all but I learned later to use it and value its existence in time.

The procedure didn't end there. I watched as they placed shiny metal buckets in a line and then together they poured the liquid into these buckets. Anna left me to help them and I watched as she covered each bucket with a white cloth.

She joined me after finishing her task and told me we were going back upstairs. I was eager not to miss anything but as she pushed me up the stairs she said, "the mixture is left to cool overnight Caty, the Lads are just clearing up and then they'll join us."

We went to the kitchen where we saw that Mama Monteverdi and the children had all cleared everything away from the table but were enjoying the left-over bits of ice cream from the big cans that had been on the carts. Mama Monteverdi had scraped it out into cups for them.

"They are always glad when there is a bit left at the bottom. It's their treat for helping Mama to clear away. Come on Caty we can wash the cans together – the work never stops around here. Help me carry them outside, it's easier with the hosepipe."

I didn't mind helping at all. This family was being so kind to me it was the least I could do. Together we lifted the large cans, but as we passed the cellar door the delicious cooling milk mixture wafted up to fill my nostrils with a tempting odor. Accompanying this smell were singing voices from the basement. Their songs seemed to be a culmination to a job well done and indications that work was over for the day. It wasn't long; in fact, it was just as the sun went down when everyone took to their beds. Another work day was fast approaching these early risers.

I also woke up early not sure of my bearings, but the light through the small window enabled me to appreciate I was in a secure place; a place of opportunity, a place; with good friends to help me. I smiled at the thought.

I waited for Anna to take me downstairs and together we went into the kitchen. We had some fresh bread and cheese for breakfast, but there were only us two and the children around the table. I was curious about the noise coming from the cellar so I asked if the men were working down there again.

"I suggest you stay here and finish your hot tea Caty," said Anna. I'll just give you the details of what is happening because they don't like us women to be around for this strenuous job."

She explained that last night was only the preparation and that they were now commencing the main task of 'freezing' the ice cream. For this they needed to fill large tubs with ice and salt and then the milk was poured in. Mama Monteverdi sat down at the table and occasionally interrupted Anna's explanations but spoke to her in Italian. Yet, after nodding to Mama, she went on with this fascinating account making sure that I capture how hard the men worked and did it as a team; a family business.

This part of the job, she said, was very strenuous and they had to take turns in churning the mixture which required a lot of strong arms and young bodies. Later they would have to turn and turn the tubs until the inside mixture was frozen and this took time, but the result was well worth the labour.

"Amen to the men." She ended with her typical hilarity.

Mama gave her a round of applause and added, "Now we havva to sell it which isa no problem in tha warm weather, but notta so good in the winter. Thena we havva to sella tha wood or the chestnuts."

Anna patted her mother's hands which lay on the table to explain to her, "Caty has heard enough about our business, she has her own problems. She needs a job, am I right? Do you want to go to the shop and see if you could help around there?"

I was saved from answering this self-conscious question by the entrance of the men of the family entering the kitchen looking for their well earned breakfast. Mama Monteverdi looked embarrassed for a moment but then she put her hands on her ample hips and began to sermonize to them in a very loud Italian voice which I didn't understand, although her message was clear in its tone.

I looked up and tried to get the attention of Angelo, indicating to him that I wished to see him outside. I whispered to Anna that I had to use the privy and went outside where Angelo was waiting. He was smoking a cigarette in a comfortable stance against the wall so I went up to him, not knowing where to start. He was watching my face too closely, I felt a knot in my stomach and for some reason I felt guilty for what I had to tell him.

"What is it?" he said stubbing his cigarette out on the ground.

He took my arm in his recognizable way and we walked outside of his family yard. On mutual ground I felt a little stronger to explain my dilemma.

"Angelo, you and your family have been so good to me but I can't work in the shop. I hardly speak and understand this English language. Angelo, I can't read or write and adding up this money and giving the customers the right change is just something I'm afraid of. I would make a mess of iy, I know. I don't want to be ungrateful but it's just not me. You do understand Angelo I have to find something else to do and somewhere else to live. Am I making sense to you? Do you understand what I am trying to say?"

He brushed the tears from my cheeks, holding my face in his outsized hands; he was tall and agile, strong in stature and in character. I knew he would understand my situation.

We walked in silence and then he spoke. Too quickly at first for me to grasp, but then he stopped walking to look at me.

"I've just had an idea Caty. I heard from my aunt that they are always looking for women to work in the cotton mill down Queen Street; the women come into our shop on a daily basis, before and after work so she knows them well. She tells me they have plenty of money to spend on the little extras she sells, so they must be well paid. How does that idea sound Caty? Do we find out more?"

I looked up into the eyes of this man who was trying so hard to make my life better and I wanted to thank him so much but didn't know how. He held me in his arms and then he kissed me with a very passionate but gentle kiss and I waited for my loins to arouse me but there was no swelling emotion. Why was I not feeling the butterflies in my stomach; the yearnings that I had with my seaman. I wanted to love Angelo, he was a good man and would take care of me like I always wished would happen. Perhaps I had rushed myself to finish the embrace before he or I was ready. I held on to him and spoke softly, "do that again Angelo, please."

He pushed me to a nearby wall and with my back firmly against it he pressed his lips to mine. I waited again for the magic to happen but all the sensation I got was an uncomfortable feeling that my generous bust was an obstruction and my secret pocket holding my winnings was definitely in the way. I moved gently under his arm. He had placed his hand flat against the wall, but his arm was long and thin so I was able to maneuver away from his embrace.

"What's wrong Caty, I thought you wanted me to kiss you?"

"I'm sorry Angelo but it's not the place or time for me. Not in the open like this." I added trying to sound sincere. "I'm sorry Angelo, but I must first get settled with a job and a place to live then we can spend time together, do you agree?"

I was hoping to appease him with my common sense approach. I squeezed his hand tightly to pacify him and kissed him lightly on the cheek, all the time knowing that Angelo could never be my lover, but always a friend.
"Do you have time now to take me to the shop to talk to your aunt?" I wanted to do something positive and I did need his help.

"Of course, I always have time for you Caty Luby," he said with affection that only made my position worse. Why was he not a pushy, loud mouth rogue that I could bash in the face for his philandering? Men were just too difficult to understand.

The shop was just round the corner so we were there in no time at all. Although the shop was very small it was packed with goods. Perishable and non-perishable goods these were available for the local folks to purchase for cash or on a weekly 'tally.'   Angelo told me that many of the mill workers would pay at the end of the week and his aunt had seldom had a problem with getting her money. If there were troubles, sometimes through ill health or pregnancy, then one of the Monteverdi family would visit the defaulter to check and in this close community 'keeping face' was important.

Angelo's aunt was a very cheerful woman who looked very much like his mother. Her English, however, was much better, probably because she had more chance to practice with her customers. Angelo introduced me to Aunt Maria who greeted me with the usual Italian clinch and I responded to her, as now I knew how to react.

Luckily, there was no-one in the shop so she was eager to show me around and explain her business to me. This only confirmed the fact that I was over-whelmed with the idea of working alongside this very competent woman. Angelo, nevertheless, sensed my uncomfortable situation and quickly changed her attention to the information we had come to find out.

"Aunt Maria," he began, "Caty is interested in working in the cotton mill in Queen Street. I told her you know a lot of young Lassies who work there and maybe you could, sort of, guide her in the right direction and introduce her to some of them so she can find out the present situation there."

"Now, at this present time, my dear Angelo, I think I can do better than that," she said with a big smile. "I happen to know a man called Mr. Hargreaves who is a big boss there and one of my best customers here at the shop, that's the chap she should be talking to. He comes in here most days after work to get his special cigar. So, leave it with me and come back tomorrow and hopefully I will have some good news for this Lass."

It was more than I could have hoped for and I couldn't resist hugging her and thanking her at the same time.

"Well Lass that's what family is all about round here, am I right or am I right young Angelo?"

"You are the shrewd one in the family Aunt Maria and I trust your smart judgment with this. I know it will be just fine left with you."

"So be off with you then and let an old woman get back to work."

"Old woman be done, you will never be old Aunt Maria just mature and wise with it. Is it not true that all the family comes to you to solve their problems?"

She laughed as she pushed us out of the shop in a friendly gesture, adding before she shut the door, "see you both tomorrow."

I was so happy I felt like skipping along the street, yet my flourishing bust would not look right jigging about. After all, I was to be a working Lass and I am not sure if that would be the correct behavior for a budding cotton mill employee. I also had a problem with my increasing foot size. These boots, I had traveled from Ireland in, were really feeling tight and prevented me from jumping around. My toes were compressed together so taut that when I took them off at night my toes fairly shot out of the boots.

We walked back to the family home where Angelo pecked me on the cheek and told me he had to get back to work. He led me into the kitchen to see Mama Monteverdi and the girls all doing the household chores. I asked if I could help but Anna said they were just about finished so we could go up to her room to talk and she could learn about my morning absence.

We sat together on the bed in a girl like way and I told her about the morning. Leaving out the dreamy romantic stuff with Angelo and emphasizing the positive suggestions of her Aunt Maria. She acknowledge the practical side of her Aunt whom she obviously loved a lot and said that she always 'came up trumps' in every situation.

"It's because she knows so many people Caty. The customers who come into her shop, the people at the church and the older Italians who come to her to translate their official papers. She's the true matriarch of our family."

As we continued talking I was fidgeting around with my blouse pulling the buttons together. I twisted my ankles around in circles to keep the blood flowing to my aching feet and Anna noticed my uncomfortable outfit.

"Do you have a change of clothes Caty, I noticed your small parcel, but I haven't seen you change yet?" she added with her hand over her mouth, "Oh! Caty my big mouth again, I'm sorry I didn't want to offend you, but I want to help."

I told her I had lost my clothes in a burglary along with some money I had with me from Ireland. I didn't expand on this story but added that I did have some money left to buy clothes and shoes if she would tell me where I could buy them.

"Yes Caty I will show you, we will go to the market stalls on Saturday, but first we will visit a special place. We will go to Victoria Public Baths, that's its real name but people round here call it the 'Water Palace.' It looks like a palace; Caty the stonework outside is very ornate and there is a separate entrance for men and women.. There are stained glass windows and mosaic floors, done by us Italians of course. We can bathe in clean water that comes from its own well water pumped into the baths; I don't know how they do that but it is fresh and clean. You do want to go Caty, please say you will."

I of course consented and that night I felt like a Queen who had been to her palace and bathed in luxury. M'Ma and Grandma back home would never believe such wonders exist. Yes, my new found country had a lot to offer.

Chapter 43
Finding Harmony

I didn't have to visit the shop the next day the message came to me by way of Angelo's Uncle. The message was from Aunt Maria. I was to go this very day, at noon, to the mill to see Mr. Hargreaves. He would be in his office on the ground floor near the entrance to the mill.

Mama made sure I had a full stomach before I left on the walk to the mill.

"Nothing can be got on an empty stomach," she had told me in her usual singing voice. Go and get the job Caty, you have the strength, energy, and resolve to make a success of it. I know that for sure."

With her words in my heart I felt confident to meet this challenge. I would try to use my best English and listen closely to everything that was said to me. With this resolution I entered the offices of the mill and asked for Mr. Hargreaves.

A young bossy girl asked me my name and then told me to sit on the bench and wait while she checked if, in fact, Mr. Hargreaves would see me. She went through a door, but then to my surprise she came out quickly saying nothing but glaring at me with distaste. She was followed by a man who looked very similar to Mr. Jones, the boss at the pit. He even had his bright smile and wore the same eye glasses.
"Come along into my office Lass, I've heard all about you."

I could feel the young girl's knife-like eyes piercing my back as I walked into the office. However, I soon dismissed the feeling to pay attention to my future prospects.

"You come with a good recommendation my dear and what I see I like. You look strong and healthy."

Once more I felt as if I was being looked at like a racehorse. Was I worth betting on, would I be a winner, did I have the stamina to finish the course? Then he shocked me out of my preoccupation by saying,

"When can you start?"

"Excuse me Sir," I began in my Ladies Circle voice, "are you offering me a job? Are you saying I can start working here?"

"Yes, I am Lass, if you are up to hard work and long hours?"

"I am ready to start, when you want me to, Sir," I responded politely, thinking all the while that I was now going to join the workers I would be in the race at last. I was over the first hurdle.

"I think you should start Monday, the beginning of our work week. Can you do that Lass?"

I nodded profusely and waited for him to continue. I had to listen intently to his instructions so I didn't interrupt.
"You will start at 7 o'clock prompt, report to me here first and I will take you to a supervisor to be 'trained up'. The supervisor will teach you how to use the looms; these are the machines we use to weave the cotton. You will watch and learn how to tie knots and put threads in and most importantly how to find the right place when the weft breaks."

I must have looked stunned because he came round from his seat behind his desk to put his hand on my shoulder and continued, "all new words to you I know, but in a few weeks you'll be handling one loom and

247

later, one or two more and then a 'set' where there is good money to be made."

The last few words I understood completely so I told him I would work hard, train hard and manage a 'set' in no time. He laughed at my eagerness and led me to the door saying:
"Tell Maria I will see her tonight and I approve her choice of Lass. Are you staying with the Monteverdi family, she said you were?"

He didn't wait for my answer but instead, shuffled me out to the bossy girl's office and told her to get my name that I was starting Monday next.

I gave her my name and told her, again using my posh voice, that I would bring my current address to her on Monday. I knew Aunt Maria or Angelo would write it down for me. I wasn't as confident when I reached the street outside. I had no idea what I was letting myself in for? I hadn't even seen inside the factory to look at a 'loom' nor did I ask how much I would be paid? I chastised myself in my silent thoughts - Caty Luby must be more organized for sure. I decided to go to Maria's shop and talk to her, I needed my confidence bolstering and for someone to advise me about this occupation.

When I reached the shop it was early afternoon and so I was lucky that it was empty of customers. Maria was organizing her shelves but turned around immediately to welcome me.

"Caty, Lass, did you go to the factory? Did you get the job? Let me close up the shop for a bit so we can have some tea together and talk."

She turned the notice around on the door and locked it, then pushed me through to the back where there was a small kitchen and an equally small table. In no time at all there was a hot drink and muffins laid out for us both to enjoy.

"Take your time Lass, you must be hungry, I have plenty more where they came from."

I was rapidly acknowledging the fact that Italians always wanted to feed you and I wasn't unfavourable to that piece of information. I was a big lass, after all, and I had plenty of space to fill with good food.

During bites of food and drink I told Maria my hopes and fears about the job and how I had forgotten to ask the important question about pay. I also told her the truth that I had wanted to get the job only for the money as I was on my own in this country and needed to earn a living. To my surprise this disclosure didn't shock her at all.

"Well Lass, isn't that the case for all us immigrants? Man or woman alike. Nobody gives it to you on a plate we all have to work to exist. Now I'm not saying that a bit of help here and there is not welcome and the good Lord teaches 'that what you sow you will reap, so I keep Mr. Hargreaves happy with his special cigars and he returns the favour by interviewing you for a job. I'm sure the time will come for you to return a good deed to me. For now I am sure you can eat more muffins."

She continued to tell me that the job could not be too difficult if the Lasses she knew could manage to work all day and keep their husbands and kids happy as well.

"They live in clean cozy houses and clean their front step every week and take time to finish off the edges of the step with a 'donkey' stone so they must have some energy left after work. Talking about houses makes me remember, Caty that you were going to come here to live. Am I right?"

"Well, Angelo thought I could help you in the shop in exchange for a room here but now this has changed. I will be working at the factory during the day," then I added quickly, "but I can help you when I finish work. I can lift and carry your sacks and boxes around and do any other heavy task you have, I'm as strong as any man."

After this last remark Maria burst out laughing and had to wipe her tears on her apron before replying,

 "Caty Luby you are a case! If you lift my boxes like you lift my spirits then we will have a rollicking good time, I know it and I need to have some young company around me, it can get lonely here in the evenings."

She went on planning my future as if I was her long lost daughter she had suddenly found. She didn't give me time to refuse or consent to her preparations but assured me that by Monday, after I had finished work I was to come to the shop by which time my accommodation would be sorted.

Chapter 44
Ending the journey.

I started work at the factory and eventually got used to the good and the bad it enclosed. The surroundings were stuffy. Cotton mills kept their windows closed to stop the thread from drying out and breaking. However, by 1910 the old Lancashire looms were being replaced with automatic shuttle changing and the job got a lot easier. I got my 'set' and so my earnings improved. The noise was deafening and I soon learnt how to lip read, often finding out some spicy bit of gossip in the bargain.

Aunt Maria, as she insisted I call her, helped me manage my money. We had two tin boxes hidden in a wall, one was hers, and one was mine. My beginning money from my secret pocket was soon spent on clothes and shoes for work. I also offered to pay for my first week's rent, but she said it was better spent on a comfortable second hand bed and some drawers. Of course, she knew where I could obtain these at a good price.

At work I met some cheerful lassies who taught me to sing their funny songs and I would render a few samples of them to Aunt Maria in the evenings. She encouraged me to mix with them and not stay every evening with her. Our special group would go to the Church Hall on Fridays to the dances and this was my highlight of the week.

Sometimes I would see Angelo there with his friends, but it was hard for me to escape his protection when a young lad would ask to walk me home. I had to resort to my cunning sneaky tactics to escape. One of my friends, Maureen, really liked Angelo so I introduced them and for weeks encouraged them to date, and as their friendship blossomed my freedom followed. Looking back on those times I maybe should have stayed with Angelo and his Catholic morals, but I had always wanted more. Danger and pleasure went together in my mind and I had no restrictions stopping me to enjoy 'the pleasures of life'.

It was inevitable that I was to follow my mother's plight and get 'caught'. It was amazing to me how I didn't anticipate the outcome. I knew first-hand the consequences but Caty Luby's heart ruled her head. The strange part was that I felt happy at the prospect as the months went by. My size hid my secret but this time it wasn't money I was hiding.

I would survive, I always had. The lad in question disappeared as fast as he had come into my life, but this fact didn't deter me; my optimism, my love of life, my affection for my new found country filled me with hope.
I had one important task to do before it was too late. I asked Aunt Maria to write a letter to Uncle John to tell him where I was. I knew if the vicar got my letter and John wasn't there, he would know where to forward it. Tuam wasn't a big place after all.

Maybe when I have saved enough I can send for my family in Tuam? No, hold on, I have a family of my own to look after now, Caty Luby, a mother. Who would have thought it possible? Perhaps that is my role in life; I always loved the babbies you know.

To be continued – follow how Caty gets on in my next novel – "Caty, the woman".

BACKGROUND OF WRITER

Judy Serventi was born in a cotton mill town in the North of England called Farnworth. She was the middle child of Edward, a fireman and Edith, a cotton weaver.

She grew up in the war years when milk and eggs were the powdered kind but her extended family life was rich with fun and laughter. In 1960 she married Bruno, the son of an Italian immigrant whose family had an ice cream company.

On reaching her mid-forties, teaching and bringing up two wonderful sons she wanted more self-achievement and obtained a Fulbright Scholarship to America.

The family moved there and a few years later, with the help of her husband, they developed an International Language school that catered for young executives from all over the world. They bought a Hotel on Miami Beach which housed the school, students, and tourists and had two Summer schools at M.I.T. Boston and another in Tampa Florida, however after 9/11 their large school population dwindled to 2 because of the difficulties obtaining student' visas.

Undeterred, she made the necessary changes and built the school back up to over 100 students. Eventually the business was sold and Judy went into semi-retirement – teaching executives to make presentations and doing local consultation work.

She had always loved to tell stories, it was a family pastime and the urge to write them down was now her passion.

Her first attempt comes from the memories of her Grandmother on her Father's side. She knew her Grandmother traveled to England at the age of 16 alone to seek a better life and this was a desire the writer could relate to and of course, she repeated the aspiration. "Caty" is her first book but there is a sequel waiting if the readers do need to know more about this spirited young woman.

Made in the USA
Charleston, SC
19 February 2011